KNIFE & DEATH

A DCI JAMES HARDY THRILLER

JAY GILL

BOOKS BY JAY GILL

Knife & Death

Walk in the Park
(A Short Thriller)

Angels

Hard Truth

Inferno

A free bonus chapter is available for each book. For more
information visit, www.jaygill.net

CHAPTER ONE

Strictly speaking, this wasn't my case, and I was only there because Detective Inspector Rayner had called in a favour. He needed backup, and I owed him.

We had arrived at the home of Simon Baker just after 7 p.m. It was a warm summer's evening and I was meant to be home. I definitely wasn't in the mood for the bluster coming out of Baker's mouth. Another team was meant to be handling this search, but it had been dropped in my lap at the last minute.

Baker stood in his doorway, his hands pressed deep in his pockets and his face like thunder.

"What the hell is this all about? I'm just off for a dinner engagement, an awards ceremony. Whatever it is it'll have to wait, so if you'll excuse me, officers," he boomed.

"Could we speak with your wife, please, Mr Baker?" asked Rayner.

"She's not well; she's sleeping. I really am in a hurry, officers. I'm already running late, so if you can call back at a more convenient time, and perhaps phone ahead next time—"

"It's Detective Inspector Rayner and Detective Chief Inspector Hardy. And this won't wait," barked Rayner.

"You could be the King of England for all I care," Baker shot back. "Turning up out of the blue is very inconvenient. We can't all work to a police timetable; most of us plan our days. So, as I have already said, I'm afraid whatever it is will simply have to wait. I have to be at this ceremony, and you're making me late."

"We have a warrant to search the premises," said Rayner, passing him a sheet of paper.

"What are you talking about?" said Baker. "Why would you need a warrant?"

Rayner had now had enough of standing on the doorstep trying to ask politely. I suspected he wouldn't be applying for a position as hostage negotiator anytime soon, and he definitely didn't have the temperament today. He was through with Baker's waffling and so pushed the front door open. He breezed past Baker, who was now incandescent. And to my mind, Baker was showing signs of a man who was more than just furious at being made late for a party.

"How about you take a seat, Mr Baker?" I insisted. "Detective Inspector Rayner is going to take a look around. If you have any questions about the warrant, feel free to ask. Otherwise, we'll be out of your way quicker than you can say 'Vincent van Gogh.'"

Baker looked unimpressed. He was watching and listening for Rayner as he began moving from room to room.

"Which room is your wife in?" I asked. Baker looked at me but didn't answer; his attention was still on Rayner.

"Your wife," I repeated. "Which room?" Baker sat in dumb silence.

Rayner moved upstairs. I could hear drawers and doors opening and closing. After a while Rayner came back down and stood at the foot of the stairs. He peered around as though looking for something or trying to find his bearings. He glanced at me and then turned and hurried along the hall to the kitchen. A few moments later he came back and stood in the doorway.

"The door in the kitchen," he said to Baker. "The one on the right. It's padlocked. Where do you keep the key?"

Baker looked at Rayner, then at me, then back at Rayner.

"The key?" repeated Rayner. "Either that or I crowbar it off. It makes no difference to me. In fact, I'd enjoy using a crowbar."

Baker got to his feet as he patted himself down and, without a word, passed me the key from his shirt pocket. I handed it to Rayner, who then disappeared back into the kitchen. Baker was leaning forward in his chair as though he was just as interested as I was to learn what Rayner might find. For several moments it was quiet, and then I heard voices followed by sobbing.

"Hardy, I've found Mrs Baker," called Rayner. "You ought to take a look at this. Cuff him first. We're going to want to take him with us for questioning."

Baker jumped to his feet and ran for the front door. I moved quickly and, with a forceful push, redirected him so he hit the door frame face first. He fell backwards and landed on his backside. I turned him over onto his stomach and, with my knee pressed firmly into his back, cuffed his hands behind him.

"I don't think you'll be making it to your party tonight, Mr Baker. Still, I'm sure back at Scotland Yard they'll rustle up some canapés for you, if you ask nicely. Though I think we're all out of champagne." As much as I dislike sarcasm, I couldn't help myself. I hauled Baker to his feet, dragged him to the kitchen and sat him in a chair.

"Through here," called Rayner.

I went through the unlocked door and found Rayner comforting a woman who I guessed to be Mrs Baker. I looked around the room, which was full of art; there were canvasses everywhere. There was also a bed and a small table. An area had been partitioned off, and this contained a sink, shower and toilet. Mrs Baker looked pale, and though she was trembling, she'd stopped crying. Instead, she was sitting upright and was trying to be strong.

"I won't let that man see me crying. You know it was my art that kept me going. My art, not his. Mine. I prayed every day and had faith that eventually the truth would come out," said Mrs Baker.

"What are you telling us?" asked Rayner.

"I'm telling you my husband has kept me here," she gestured around the room. "He kept me a prisoner in my own home. If I didn't produce art for him, he would stop feeding me. He sometimes turned off the water for days so I couldn't drink. He beat me and threatened me. Said he would kill me and no one would ever know."

"You're safe now," I said. "When you're ready we're going to get you out of here. You need never worry about your husband again, I assure you."

"Where is he?" said Mrs Baker.

"He's just outside in the kitchen. He's handcuffed. But don't worry – I'll take him away and you won't need to see him. Just give me a few—"

Mrs Baker interrupted me. "No. I want him to see me as I walk out of here. I want that talentless coward to see me. I want to look him in the eye."

Rayner and I looked at each other. Rayner nodded in agreement. I went ahead and stood next to Baker. Rayner brought Mrs Baker out through the door and into the kitchen. Baker kept his head down and said nothing. Mrs Baker glared at him as she walked past. At the kitchen doorway, she turned and spat at him.

"You're finished. The world is going to know the truth – that you took my art and passed it off as your own. You talentless, worthless nobody. I hope you rot in hell."

Baker said nothing. He sat a little straighter in his seat, lifting his eyes only slightly to watch his wife attempting to leave the house with pride and dignity.

"You know none of this is what it seems, Chief Inspector," he said once his wife had left.

"Really?" I said in disbelief. I was curious, almost despite myself, about what he could say that would change what was clear for all to see.

"She asked to be locked in there. So she could work. So she wouldn't be distracted. It was her idea. The sad thing is, I think she has been in there too long and become delusional. You see, she lived for the art. I begged her to come out and to enjoy life, to take some time off. But she's obsessed. It breaks my heart to see her like this. The woman I married is still in there somewhere, I know it, but she's buried deep inside a woman who has become obsessed with creating another and another and another piece of art."

"While you profited?"

"I suppose that is how it could be perceived by the casual observer."

"To the casual observer it appears that you as good as locked your wife in a room for years. That you told the world your wife was dead. That you passed off her work as your own. That her talent made you rich. That her talent made you a celebrated artist the world over. To the casual observer I would say you look a fraud."

"What do you know of the art world?" Baker demanded huffily.

"Not a lot, I suppose. But I do know that if what you say is true and your wife is ill, most husbands would have sought treatment – not a padlock." I'd heard enough from Mr Baker for the time being. I lifted him out of the chair and led him to a waiting squad car.

CHAPTER TWO

Three Years Later

* * *

River Thames, London, England

From their manner you'd never guess the two men were driving to the river with the Albanian's dead girl in the back of their Mercedes C-Class.

"I told her that's how I've always made tea. Milk and tea bag in a mug, then pour on the bloody boiling water," said Jimmy Kane. "You know what Aggie said?"

Chris Perkins shook his head. He couldn't speak; he was laughing too hard. "Nah, go on, tell me."

"She said I was 'uncouth.' So I asked her, 'What does *uncouth* have to do with making a cup of bloody tea? Do you want a cup or not?'" The two men were laughing so hard they had tears in their eyes, and Jimmy had to concentrate to drive in a straight line.

"You know what?" said Jimmy. "She then got all upset with me – yeah, with *me*. You know how she gets all huffy and puffs out her lips. Saying I was spoiling her *Downton Abbey* time."

"You better watch it, Jimmy. I reckon she'll have you dressed as one those *Downton* butlers the way she's going. Sounds like your Aggie is getting herself sophisticated. I hear they call it Downtonitis." The two men cracked up again.

Jimmy flicked on the indicator and parked up alongside the river. The two men put on their caps, lifted their collars and got out. Chris looked over the side of the bridge to the cold, black water of the Thames below.

"High tide. Just like I told you," he said proudly.

Jimmy opened the boot of the car and the two men grabbed either end of the plastic sheeting the girl was wrapped in, then carried her to the wall, where they rested for a moment.

Chris checked the time on his phone: 3.25 a.m. "It's my birthday today."

"Really? Well, in that case you're buying breakfast, mate," said Jimmy.

The two men rolled the body back and forth and started to sing. "Happy birthday to you. Happy birthday to you. Happy birthday, dear whoever you are . . ."

They rolled the body off the bridge and waited for the splash. ". . . Happy birthday to you!"

That done, they jumped back in the Mercedes and headed off through the early-morning streets.

"So did your Aggie want a cup of tea in the end?"

"No. In the end she decides she wants coffee. And get this – I got that wrong as well. I made regular coffee but she now drinks decaf. I tell you, things are getting very complicated in my house. I love her to bits; don't get me wrong. But things are complicated."

"Sounds it," said Chris sympathetically.

"Just you wait. Your girl will have you running 'round in circles soon enough. You mark my words."

CHAPTER THREE

I was feeling proud and at the same time there were butterflies in my stomach. Like the rest of her orchestra group, my little Alice was on stage clutching her violin. Her music teacher was at the piano and the performances were about to commence.

Faith was sitting on my lap, her eyes wide open, taking it all in. She adored her big sister and couldn't wait to see what was going to happen. Faith's little arm was up behind my neck and her fingers were making circles in my hair. In her other hand she was clutching Mr Puppy, her comfort toy, who smelled ready for another trip to the land of soap and water. Mr Puppy went with her everywhere and was looking pretty battered these days, but Faith didn't care. She was probably a little too old to still have him, but Mr Puppy had comforted her through a lot of tough times and wasn't going anywhere for the foreseeable future; he was a part of the family. Faith squeezed Mr Puppy and made sure he could see Alice up on the stage.

Alice caught my eye from the stage and we exchanged excited smiles. I gave her a wink, and she sat a little taller in her seat. She was a confident and pretty girl, looking more like her mother every day. I looked up and prayed their mother was with us tonight and could see her two little angels. *I miss you, honey.* I looked at Monica, and she put her hand on mine. We both had tears in our eyes, and she knew what I was thinking: I missed my beautiful wife Helena, who had been Monica's best friend.

"Thank you," I mouthed. Before I could continue, Faith began bouncing up and down excitedly and tugging at my hair with her little fingers. "Daddy, it's starting. Daddy, look at Alice."

The three rows of children got to their feet and, tentatively, the first piece of music began. Alice was in the back row and one of the tallest. I remembered when she was one of the little ones in the front row; even then she seemed to have a confidence beyond her years. The courage of all the children always surprised me; they showed no nerves and took in their stride the fact they were playing to a hall full of parents, grandparents, siblings, friends and teachers.

Throughout the performance the children took it in turns to play a solo or duet. Faith watched in wonderment as her big sister Alice's turn came and she walked to the front to play her solo. She played the grade two piece that she'd been practising for weeks. It sounded perfect to me, and I was ready to burst with pride and admiration. I felt like shouting out to the room, *Do you truly appreciate what she just did? Do you know what she's been through? Can you comprehend at all what she just did?* Instead, I filled up and gave Faith an extra big squeeze and perhaps clapped a little louder than I should have. I didn't care.

Performance over and after a few announcements from the deputy head teacher, we said our goodbyes. Later than usual, we arrived home and sat down to Monica's homemade lasagne.

"To Alice," I said, raising my glass of water, "whose performance tonight was perfect, and who looked beautiful. Yes, I noticed the new dress," I said, and nodded to Monica.

"Speck-tack-leeyer," added Faith.

"Spectacular," we all agreed.

"I kind of messed it up a little in the middle, but it was okay," added Alice modestly.

"Well, if that's true, then none of us noticed. We all loved it. I'm so proud of my girls. Well done, baby."

Glasses of water raised, we toasted the evening and being together. The girls loved to hear the chink of glasses as we toasted around the table, and we used any excuse to do it.

Later, I read stories to the girls and cuddled them. We talked for a while about school and friends and Mummy. I cuddled them some more and tickled them a little.

Usually the girls shared a room. As a treat tonight, they were sleeping in my double bed. As usual when that happens, I'd sleep on the pullout sofa bed or, more often than not, on my big old recliner chair – although, if I do that and the girls catch me, I'm lovingly scolded.

Monica slept in Faith's box room, which still had Winnie the Pooh curtains and wallpaper. My daughters had been pressing me for a while to change the rooms around and organise a more permanent room for her. In their childish imaginings, unaware of the bigger picture, it seemed only logical. After all, Monica effortlessly filled the role of surrogate mum.

Monica slipped in to say goodnight to the girls as I poured myself a single malt and listened to the girls chatter. Life felt complicated, but I knew she was good for them. They needed a woman around, and at the moment Monica needed us. It sometimes felt that since Helena's death I was getting more wrong than right. I often felt guilt for not being there for my girls, but they knew I had a job to do and that job meant keeping people safe, and they were okay with that.

A few months back it felt like I was only just keeping my head above water. If it hadn't been for my girls, who knows – I might have been ready to give in and drown. Right now, though, things felt good. I might still be struggling with the balance of life and all the emotions, needs and wants of a family, but life was returning. Occasionally, I still felt like I was being stretched in too many directions and sometimes didn't know all the answers, but that was normal. I knew I couldn't give the girls *everything* they needed, but I knew I'd do all I could for them, unconditionally and without hesitation.

Life hadn't been fair. Their precious mother had been snatched away from them, and God knows I wanted my wife back. But we were feeling strong again. We were close and all together and filled with love. Yes, I'd got things wrong, and yes, I'd made all kinds of mistakes during the darkest days, but nothing major. So, on days like this, when the house was filled with so much happiness, so much love and so much laughter, *the way it used to be*, I knew I must be getting it mostly right. Days like this were now far outweighing the bad days. So, each day I counted my blessings, worried a little less and felt more confident we were going to be all right.

CHAPTER FOUR

Ice skating was not a favourite activity of mine, but Alice and Faith loved it. Helena used to bring the girls and go out on the ice with them. Today it was me on the ice, and I wished I had done it when the girls were small; that way I'd be pretty competent by now.

The girls didn't care about my skating ability, however; all they cared about was that they had me all to themselves for a few hours. They whizzed around the ice and held me up as I slipped and staggered from one wall to another. I looked over at Monica, who laughed and videoed me on her phone from the safety of the benches.

"Looking good, Detective Inspector," she called, laughing.

"Your turn to put on the skates," I called back.

"Sorry, I can't hear you!" She grinned at me.

"Look, Monica! See what we can do," called Alice and Faith in unison. The girls took it in turns to do jumps and skate backwards and do all sorts of fancy stuff. I watched in exhausted admiration. I, on the other hand, concentrated all my energies on the not-so-simple task of hanging onto the wall and not landing on my backside.

I watched how the girls adored Monica. Monica had been staying with us since before we lost Helena. Monica was Helena's best friend; they had been like sisters from the day they met as toddlers in nursery school. So when Monica's new husband, Scott, had turned to drink and become violent, she had moved in with us.

I still fondly remember how there hadn't been any real discussion between Helena and me. Helena had simply told me Monica needed our help and that she'd prepared a room for her.

"Monica will be staying for a while. That's okay, isn't it?" she'd said, more telling me than asking.

That was nearly two years ago. A few months later Helena was dead. In the wrong place at the wrong time, she had been the victim of an addict's need to feed his heroin habit. As she'd fought to keep him from snatching her handbag, he'd stabbed her. My beloved Helena had bled to death in the street, surrounded by good Samaritans, strangers and onlookers.

Monica was always a good friend; she was there for Alice and Faith when they needed her most. She adored them, and they adored her, welcoming her as a motherly figure. And the arrangement seemed to work for Monica while her divorce was being finalised. She didn't want to go back to her parents' home, which I understood. She wanted to stay in London but couldn't have possibly afforded to rent on her own.

The arrangement worked for me as well; she was a good listener, and we both enjoyed talking about our memories of Helena. Having Monica around kept Helena alive for me.

After the skating, we all headed to a family restaurant

that served high-quality burgers and milkshakes. All sorts of Americana adorned the walls. I couldn't help (once again) boring the girls by explaining who was in some of the photos: Elvis, James Dean, Clint Eastwood, Marlon Brando.

They got me back by asking me questions about pop stars in their favourite groups.

"Which pop group did Zayn Malik belong to, then, Daddy?" Alice asked.

Then Faith asked, "Name three songs from *Frozen*, Daddy. That's an easy one."

Both girls giggled as I contorted my face, trying to think of the most famous one that everyone knows.

"Hang on, hang on – I've nearly got it. 'Let it snow'?" I said finally. The girls booed and teased me. I held up my hands and admitted defeat.

My phone rang. I instinctively knew who it was without looking. I took the call outside, where I paced up and down as Rayner went over the situation he was responding to. A woman had been found murdered, and there was a strong possibility that I was going to be back on another slow, painful investigation. We agreed he'd go to the scene; if it turned out to be something of the nature he anticipated, then he'd call me back. This call, he told me, was just a heads-up.

I finished the call and watched through the large glass windows as Monica distracted the girls. She looked over and smiled knowingly. Her expression said it all. *I've got this. If you need to go, then don't worry. The girls and I will be fine.*

As I watched my daughters drawing and laughing, I felt the feeling I often got before an investigation started. My limbs would grow heavy and the energy would drain from my body. Yet I knew that when the investigation began and the pieces started coming together, my energy would return. I once imagined it as a tide of emotion coming down on me, weighing heavily on my mind as fear and apprehension descended. Then, when the time was right and the tide began to turn, my need to win would take over and propel me forward.

CHAPTER FIVE

I walked to the river's edge, which had been cordoned off by Forensics. It was a beautiful summer morning and, as the sun came up, I took a moment to look down and across the Thames to where I could see the Palace of Westminster and Elizabeth Tower, more commonly known by the name of its main bell, Big Ben.

In front of me tents and screens were in place. I felt the anxious knot in my stomach grow. Detective Inspector Rayner was talking to the forensics pathologist, Heidi Hamilton.

"Look who it is," Rayner joked as he spotted me. "I know you're supposed to be resting, but I thought you'd want to see this. How are you feeling?"

I was still recovering from a few injuries sustained while apprehending a lowlife who preyed on the elderly. "Bit bruised and sore, but I'll live," I said. "Next time I'll call for backup sooner. I promise."

"You'd better," said Hamilton.

"So what have we got?" I asked.

Hamilton looked at her notes and began to unzip the

body bag as she spoke. "Young woman. Early twenties. Bruising around the neck indicates strangulation. Also, multiple stab wounds to the abdomen. I counted at least fifteen."

I looked at the young woman's face. It seemed familiar but difficult to place under the circumstances. My mind began racing, trying to place the face. Hamilton was still talking, but it was only background noise. I *knew* this young woman, I was sure of it. She was a sweet girl, foreign – Eastern European, perhaps Polish. I'd spoken to her only a couple of days ago. It finally fell into place. It was after Monica's evening class. Monica taught English, and the girl was a student of hers, and an enthusiastic one. She and Monica had formed a sort of friendship; they'd chatted a lot. Monica had introduced her to me after a class. We had spoken on and off since then, usually when I was picking Monica up after a class, but only briefly.

"Delina," I said finally.

Rayner and Hamilton looked at me. "Are you okay?" said Hamilton.

I put a hand out to steady myself. "Delina Berisha is her name. I know her. She's become a sort of friend to Monica. She's Eastern European. She attends one of Monica's evening classes."

This case was suddenly close to home. How had she ended up like this? Was this a random attack? Had she been in the wrong place at the wrong time? Or had she known the killer? Could this have been done by a boyfriend? Was this related to her past, her life back in her country of origin? My mind began to race.

Rayner and Hamilton looked at each other. There was something they hadn't told me. Something important.

"What is it?" I asked, even though I wasn't sure I really wanted more bad news.

"The thing is," began Rayner, "she had a silver case in her purse with a few of these cards in it." Rayner handed me a business card that had the usual lines about offering "discreet and professional" services.

Hamilton took over. "The thing is, your friend was very likely offering escort services. Maybe one of her clients turned out to be a psychopath."

I was stunned. My mind ran through the brief conversations we'd had. I was searching for clues. How had I missed something like that? Then again, being a prostitute isn't necessarily one of the things she'd want coming up in conversation with a police inspector.

I turned to Rayner. "Well, I guess we'd better get started."

CHAPTER SIX

Rayner and I were met at the door to the flats by Delina's landlord.

Leonard Kingsbury was a sprightly, elderly man who looked as though he was dressed for a day at the office. Even though the heat outside was in the mid-seventies, he wore a navy tie and jacket. His shoes had a high gloss, and I guessed he had at one time or other served in the military. He held himself very upright and had an air of confidence about him. He scrutinised our badges before leading us up the two flights of stairs to the room on the top floor.

"My flat is on the bottom floor, and I rent out the top floor. Here we are, detectives. And please call me Leonard," he said as he opened the door. "If I get my hands on the coward who did that to her, I'll gut him. The things I learned how to do to a man I'll never forget. I was a paratrooper, you know. Served all around the world.

"Pretty little thing she was," he said sadly. "Always happy, always smiling and very polite and friendly. Foreign, of course, but I don't mind that. I've met all sorts, all around the world. Anyway, nowadays the foreigners are more polite than those born and bred around here; lazy, foul-mouthed little sods most of them."

I put on my gloves and began looking in each room. I wasn't sure what exactly I was looking for; often I don't know until it jumps out at me. Looking around, I realised I knew precious little about Delina's private life, her background and her day-to-day challenges since her arrival in the UK. I'd only known a young woman who missed her family and had talked of being excited about having moved to London. A young woman who was full of dreams and the possibilities for her new life here.

At the back of a bottom drawer I found more cards. I looked through her wardrobe, checking pockets of coats and jackets. I noticed the shoes. Half had been placed on one side of the wardrobe and half on the other. I looked back at the clothes hanging there, and then I looked back at the shoes. I looked around the room. Two single beds. I grabbed a photo off a chest of drawers and showed it to Leonard, who was still chatting to Rayner.

"Back in my day we used to call them 'Ladies of the night,'" he was saying. "I don't know if it's true, of course. I heard it from—"

"Who is the other girl?" I asked, pointing to the photo.

"Anya. Her name is Anya Tanush," said Leonard with surprise.

"Why didn't you tell us two girls lived here?"

"I assumed you knew. I assumed that was why you were here. To ask her questions and to ask me questions," said Leonard. "Mind you, I haven't seen her for a few days. Not since Delina disappeared. I try to not come across as a nosey landlord, so I don't ask too many questions."

The gravity of the situation suddenly dawned on Leonard. He straightened his perfect tie nervously. His hands were trembling as he slumped into one of the armchairs. He began mumbling and scolding himself. "Useless, silly old sod. Should have been looking out for those young women. One dead, one missing, and where were you? You let them get taken from right under your nose. There was a time nobody would have dared cross you. Now you're nothing, just a frail old man."

Rayner, who was now at my side, called it in. He photographed the picture of Anya with his phone and sent it over to Scotland Yard's missing persons department. He then opened the back of the frame and took out the photo, which he slid into a pocket. We would put it up on our evidence board.

As we walked back out to the car, my mind began to tick over. Where was Anya? Did she know who had murdered Delina? Was she dead, too, and resting at the bottom of the Thames? Or was she hiding from the killer, or from the police – or both?

CHAPTER SEVEN

Finding Anya was now my top priority. A description and photo were already in circulation. If she was alive and in the Greater London area, then there was still a good chance we'd find her.

If she was in fact in danger, our best chance of protecting her was if she came forward. Failing that, our next best hope was to find someone who had recently seen her.

I decided to head home and break the news to Monica. There was a slim chance she would know where Anya might go. Perhaps she knew some of Anya and Delina's friends or hangouts. In any event, I wanted to speak to Monica before Alice and Faith got home from school. I knew it wouldn't be long before Delina's name hit the news channels, and I didn't want her finding out that way. We were holding the name back for now, but eventually it would come out. I wasn't looking forward to the conversation but felt Monica deserved to hear the news from me first.

Monica was marking test papers for her class, and she

could see from my face I was the bearer of bad news. I told her what I could, then we talked and she cried and I comforted her. It was a rough few hours.

Monica told me she and Delina had talked a lot, and that on occasion she had mentioned a friend named Anya.

"She talked about the usual things; nothing out of the ordinary. I never got the feeling she was scared of anyone. We talked about food, family, friends, men, money and her homesickness," said Monica.

"Delina was a bright young woman, quietly confident with a positive attitude. She came alone to the UK. She knew no one to begin with. She left her family and everything she knew to start a new life. That takes such courage. Then some monster does this to her and she's gone. Just like that – gone."

Monica and I drove to Spring Castle School together to pick up Alice and Faith. We watched as they came running across the playground, and I felt my heart lighten as they came crashing into me for a hug. It's incredible how children can instantly change your mood with their love, energy and excitement. I picked them up from school as often as I could. It was as much a treat for me as it was for them when I was at the school gates when they came out.

"Who wants to go and get an ice cream sundae?" I suggested.

"Really?" Alice and Faith began jumping up and down excitedly and calling out the flavours and toppings they'd like. Monica hugged and kissed the girls and smiled for the first time in hours.

CHAPTER EIGHT

I was the only one still up when Rayner arrived just after
eleven. He put his files on the desk while I grabbed us both
a cold beer from the fridge.

We were in my home office, which was a converted
garage adjoined to the house. Rayner and I needed to talk.
There had been a development in Delina's case, the worst
kind of development. A second body had been found. This
time a Thames River Police patrol boat had pulled the
body out of the river. It was another young woman,
wrapped in plastic sheeting, the same way Delina had been
found. Rayner knew what I was waiting to hear.

"It's not her," he said. "It's not Anya."

I'm not sure "relieved" is the right word, but I felt
something similar. Anya might be our only link to the killer,
and we needed her alive. Just the same, though, the body
was still that of a young woman, still a daughter, still a
sister, still somebody's loved one. A young woman whose
life had been cut brutally short. She most likely had family
who were worried about her. A mother and father who
were desperate to hear her voice and hear she was okay.

Instead, the next news of their sweet daughter would be contact from one of my police officers, and it would be the worst kind of news a parent could receive.

Rayner opened a case file and spread out a series of photos. They were hard to look at. Another young woman, too young to end this way. I could see the same bruise marks around the throat and the same abdominal stab wounds, this time many more stab wounds. Rayner sat back in his armchair and stared at his notes. He looked exhausted. He took a sip of his beer.

"Forensics will know more tomorrow, but what they can tell us right now is she's been dead a while, certainly a while longer than Delina. It seems she may have been dead a few days and then her body was moved and put in the Thames."

"Do we have a name?"

"No name. We have nothing. Unlike Delina, this young woman has nothing to indicate who she is. We've got to hope fingerprints or missing persons turn up something. Or maybe her family will come forward."

I could see from the photos in front of me that this young woman had a tattoo on her shoulder, a simple wolf design. We both looked at each other. The same thought process had gone through our heads at the same time: identifying marks.

I grabbed my phone and called Hamilton. "Pick up, pick up," I muttered.

"Delina definitely had a tattoo," said Rayner.

I nodded in agreement.

Hamilton answered. "It's a good job I'm a workaholic with no social life who enjoys being called late at night by tall, dark, single men. How can I help you, James?"

"Sorry to call so late. Delina, the young woman—"

"Yes. I know the one."

"Did she have a tattoo? I mean, I remember she had a tattoo – what did it look like?"

The line went quiet. Presumably Hamilton was referring to her files.

"Yes. She had a tattoo. Black and white. About five centimetres by eight centimetres. On the back of her upper left shoulder. A tattoo of a wolf."

This was either a hell of a coincidence or Delina and this young woman knew each other. At the very least they were connected, but exactly how was unclear at the moment. We had our first development, and that felt good.

"I assume Rayner is with you," said Hamilton.

I put my mobile on loudspeaker so Rayner could hear.

"As you're both there, I will tell you now. The murder weapon used on the victim pulled from the Thames today is the same as the one used on your friend Delina. She had multiple stab wounds that were made with the same weapon, and she was also strangled in the same way. In fact, her throat was virtually crushed. In my opinion, whoever did this held the victim by the throat and at the same time stabbed her. He was over his victim; he was up close and personal when he did this. Whoever this man is, he is strong, and I'm sure I don't need to explain to you the sort of person you're dealing with here."

I rang off and sat back in my chair feeling drained. Reading between the lines, it was clear these two murders were related. Already we had a lot of evidence, but as yet I couldn't see the big picture. I felt sure that unless this killer was caught, he would do it again and again. Anyone capable of this kind of brutality enjoyed it, or at the very least felt compelled to do it. This man needed to feel power over his victims, and that kind of power is considered to be addictive.

Rayner drained his bottle of beer and headed for the

door. "We'll start again in the morning. Stay where you are. I can show myself out. And get some sleep. You'll think more clearly in the morning if you do."

I looked at the clock. It was after 1 a.m. I made some coffee and began to read through the files again.

CHAPTER NINE

Papa sat at the back of his restaurant. Six a.m. was his favourite time of day. Caesar's would open in a few hours, but right now it was closed and quiet. He could read his paper, smoke his cigar and think. The opportunity to think and reflect was something he cherished.

Papa remembered that when he was a boy, he would often sit with his father at their kitchen table and talk. Papa knew only that his father had many visitors and was said to be a man of his word. He was also aware that his father was respected by other townsfolk, and that his family was wealthier than anyone he knew. This made the immature boy both proud and at times boastful. He later learned his father was also feared and respected in equal measure not only by his townsfolk but also by many in neighbouring towns.

Papa often got into fights with other boys, some his own age and some older and bigger. Tired of using his belt on his son for fighting, his father one day sat him down to talk.

"I hear you've been fighting again," he said. Without

waiting to hear his son's side of the story, he continued. "Your strength as a man comes from respect. Without respect you are nothing. True respect can never come from a fist, a knife or a gun – only fear."

With surprising speed and strength his father grabbed his hand and looked his son in the eye. He then pressed a finger hard into the boy's chest.

"Listen to me. True respect comes from power. True power comes from respect. Stop thinking with your heart and think with your head. Your heart makes you act from passion: fear, anger, lust – all come from your heart. These feelings will make you act on an emotional level and your decisions will be irrational. Irrational decisions will land you in trouble."

His father then pressed the same finger to the boy's forehead. "Better to use your head; learn to think first. Give yourself time before reacting or making a decision. Just think for a moment of all the truly powerful men in history. First and foremost, they were thinkers, strategists. If you can think for others and can deliver for them the result they desire, you will be a respected and powerful man. But first you must learn to think for yourself."

His father took out his knife and stabbed it into the table in front of the boy. "I am not saying you will never need to fight. On the contrary, there are times when it is unavoidable. You will learn when those times are, and then when you do fight you will be sure it is the right and only course of action and that it is the last resort. Be sure also that, at all costs, you win that fight. Strike hard, strike fast, and strike with ruthlessness and finality."

His father then removed his belt and punished the young Papa that way for the last time.

CHAPTER TEN

Orel placed a strong black coffee on Papa's table and went back behind the bar, where he continued cleaning glasses. He held up each glass to the light, polished it, inspected it and placed it neatly on the shelf.

A loud *rat-a-tat-tat, rat-a-tat-tat* cut through the silence in the restaurant. Orel walked over to the glass door, took a deep breath and opened it.

Vlad erupted into the room, looking out of place in the traditional surroundings. With his shoulder-length hair, dark glasses and expensive suit he looked like a rich city banker who'd gotten lost and stumbled into the wrong bar.

Vlad patted Orel on the shoulder and pressed a wad of cash into his top pocket. He headed to the back of the restaurant and sat down opposite Papa.

Orel nodded politely to the driver outside, closed the door and locked it.

"What?" asked Vlad.

Papa said nothing. He continued to read his newspaper.

"What?" Vlad repeated. He raised his hand, winked at

Orel, nodded and pointed to Papa's coffee. Lighting a cigarette, he sucked hard and blew a large cloud of smoke into the air. Orel put a coffee down in front of Vlad and returned to polishing his glasses.

Papa put down his newspaper and sipped his coffee. "Why would you do that?" he asked Vlad in a low voice.

Vlad shrugged and shook his head. "Why would I do what?"

"Every week you come in here and every week you give Orel money. Why would you disrespect him like that?"

"I don't mean any disrespect. I'm sure you don't pay him enough, and, anyway, I see it as insurance."

"Insurance?" said Papa. "Really? Explain that to me."

"You know what? Let's not do this again. Let's enjoy our coffee. Orel's coffee is the finest in London." Vlad raised his cup, saluted Orel and drank the strong, rich coffee.

Papa ran his hand over his balding head and stared at Vlad. The two men sat in silence for a while.

"You know this isn't the way I had intended to run things after we returned to London. I thought that after a few years I would retire and you could sit where I am sitting. I see now that you enjoy getting your hands dirty," said the old man.

"I am ready to sit where you are. I just need a little more time putting the right people in the right seats. To do that, I need to be out there. I need to be seen."

Papa looked dissatisfied. "The longer you are out there the more exposed you are. In here, you distance yourself. With distance you gain perspective."

Orel returned to top up the coffees then respectfully returned to the bar.

The old man's face turned hard; his eyes darkened and

narrowed. He laid both his hands flat on the table. "I want the truth. The young woman. Was that you?"

How did the old man know about that? Vlad turned and looked at Orel behind the bar and then back at the old man. Of course he knew. The old man knew everything.

Papa asked again. "Who was she?"

"She was no one, a whore. I had information she was talking to the police. I felt sure the information was good, and so I acted in the interest of the business. Sad, yes, but necessary. These girls like to talk when they think they can get citizenship in return."

Papa knew he was being lied to again. *My God, his arrogance. He doesn't even try to hide his lies any more.* "Did you know she was Albanian?"

"No. I didn't know she was from home."

Another lie. "It's your job to know those things," said the old man angrily. "The girl was from your uncle's town." Papa put up his hand to stop Vlad speaking. "She was not just some whore. Her name was Delina. Her family are asking me to find her. We are the very people expected to protect our country's sons and daughters when they come to London. Tell me, what should I tell them?"

Orel sat down at the next table and said nothing. He looked straight ahead and sipped his coffee. Vlad watched Orel's muscular, tattooed arm as he placed his coffee cup back in the saucer.

"Vlad, this is very important," said Papa. "You will speak to the girl's family. Offer our condolences. Send them a gift, a generous gift. Let them know the man who did this to their daughter will be brought to justice. They'll know what you mean."

Vlad showed no emotion as he listened to Papa.

Papa continued. "I am not *asking* you to do this. Tell them what they need to hear and do it soon."

Vlad lit another cigarette. He turned in his seat to lean against the wall. "I'll do as you ask, Papa."

Orel got up and walked to the restaurant door, unlocked it and opened it. Vlad looked at Papa and then at Orel.

"Guess it's time to go," said Vlad with a smile. "So good to catch up again. I do love our morning strategy meetings."

Nobody replied, and Vlad strutted out of the restaurant, pausing only to knock over some chairs on his way out.

CHAPTER ELEVEN

Around midnight I heard a knock at the front door and the doorbell being rung repeatedly. I checked my phone. It wasn't Rayner; he always texts me before coming over late. It wasn't my parents; they would call first.

"Okay, okay," I called to the late-night visitor. I looked out the window and my heart sank. "Scott. It's late. How can I help?" I said as I opened the door. I didn't need to hear him speak; I could see he was drunk. I watched as he swayed and tried to gather his thoughts.

"I want to speak to my wife. She's still *my* wife." Scott looked past me and into the house. Then he started calling her. "Monica! Monica! I want to talk." I saw a light go on across the street. I stepped forward to quieten him and calm him down.

"Scott – look at me, Scott," I said soothingly. "Monica is asleep. It's after midnight. My daughters are in the house and they're fast asleep too. I don't want them disturbed. What I suggest is you go home, sleep it off and call Monica to arrange a good time for you both to talk, preferably with your solicitor present. Take my word for it – that will be better in the long run. You don't want her seeing you like this. How about I call you a cab?"

"Who the hell do you think you are? I know what you're up to. You're screwing my wife, aren't you? Think you're above the rest of us, don't you? Get out of my way. I want to talk to Monny now." Scott staggered forward and tried to push me aside. I stood firm on the front step. With fury in his eyes, and one foot on the doorstep, he looked up at me. From behind me I heard Monica come to the door.

"Scott? What are you doing here? Do you have any idea what time it is? Christ, you're drunk."

"I love you, Monny. I do. I'm so sorry. Sorry for everything. Sorry for what I said. Ashamed of what I did. I never should have hurt you, I know that. I will get help, I promise. I'm getting help. I'm going to be different. I want you back. I want to start again. Can we start again? I just want to hear that we can try again and I'll leave. I promise I'll leave. Just say it." Breathing heavily and swaying, he took a few steps back from us and held his arms outstretched.

"Scott, you're drunk. There are children asleep in the house. You're waking the whole street," said Monica.

"I don't care. I love you. Say you'll give me a chance."

I could see this conversation going in circles. I came off the front step and put out a consoling hand. "Scott, now is not the time. Let's do this later. Could you call a cab please, Monica?"

"Who the hell do you think you are?" Scott lunged forward, gave me a shove and then took a wild swing at me, which I sidestepped with ease. He lost his balance and fell onto his side. He got back up and looked around for Monica, who stood with her hands over her mouth, looking dismayed.

"Monny, I just want to talk." Scott turned his sights on

me again. "Why don't you sod off, Hardy? Just leave us to talk. You're always around, aren't you? No wonder we can't put our marriage back together, what with you moping around her all the time, hovering like some pathetic injured child."

"Okay, that's enough. Monica, please call a cab now or call the police. I really don't mind which," I said.

Monica stepped towards Scott, and I immediately stepped between them. I hadn't seen Monica like this before. She was furious. And so was I. How dare Scott come here and bring his aggression and foul mouth to the place she felt safe?

"Scott, just go home," she said, struggling to keep her voice level. "I don't want to talk to you. You're a weak man. You're a bully. You're not a man. A real man doesn't hit women. A real man doesn't blame his wife for his problems. You're nothing. You abused me, and that is unforgivable. I never want to see you again. You hear me? Never again. Now – *fuck off!*"

That had the textbook effect I'd been hoping to avoid. Scott completely lost it. He began pacing around in circles on the small front lawn, ranting and raging. He turned his focus to me again and charged at me. I grabbed him and held him while he spat more abuse in my face.

"She's my wife," he roared. He looked at me with loathing in his eyes. "You had your wife. She's dead. Bled to death in the street like some whore. Some copper you are. You're not a man. Can't protect your own wife. How are you going to protect your kids when you can't protect your wife? I bet you were screwing my wife while yours was dying in the gutter."

Without hesitation I punched him. His legs buckled and he fell to the ground; he was out cold. I dragged him by his coat and lay him on his side, then tilted his head to clear his airway in case he vomited. I looked up at Monica. Without a word she walked into the house and returned with my mobile phone and two coats. We sat huddled together on the front step with Scott snoring on the lawn beside us. I looked at my phone, then at Monica.

"Shall I call the police or an ambulance?" I asked.

Monica shrugged. "Ambulance, I suppose."

I made the call, then looked over at Scott and spoke to him as if he were able to hear me. "You know, Scott, I had a really bad day and you were able to make that bad day worse. That really is some talent. Now look at the three of us. You with your face in the dirt. Me effectively talking to an unconscious drunk. And Monica – well, Monica has dropped the F-bomb. Who knew she could swear like a sailor?"

Monica laughed and shoved me with her shoulder. "I know lots of swear words. Shall I tell you some of my favourites?"

"Perhaps we should save them." I gently nudged her back. "That would be too much excitement for one day."

CHAPTER TWELVE

Papa and Orel were drinking Rakia and playing chess. Over the last few days Orel had noticed a change in the old man. He looked troubled.

"We've been friends a long time, Papa. Together we've been through a lot. Ups and downs. You've never questioned my loyalty. I've never asked for anything, and yet you've always been good to me."

Orel was a quiet man. When he did speak, Papa had learned it was always for good reason. So he watched out of the corner of his eye and listened as he pretended to study the chessboard.

Orel topped up each glass, drank his down in one gulp and topped it up again. "Growing up I had a dog. I loved the dog. I think the dog loved me. But the dog was unpredictable. I felt the dog couldn't be trusted. But I loved the dog, so I did nothing. One day my beautiful baby sister was playing with her dolls by the fire when the dog attacked her. Unprovoked. It nearly killed her. It grabbed her by the shoulder and thrashed her like she was nothing.

She screamed and cried and there was blood, lots of blood. This only increased the dog's blood lust.

"My father heard her cries and ran into the room and without hesitation grabbed a fire poker and drove it straight into the dog's skull. My sister survived, though she was scarred down her face, neck and shoulder for the rest of her life. She was scarred because I avoided doing what I knew had needed to be done. If I could have my time over again, I would not hesitate. I would cut that dog's throat the first time it looked at me the wrong way."

Papa sat back in his chair, amazed. The two men had known each other for over fifty years, and that was possibly the longest he'd ever heard Orel speak.

"What a load of nonsense," said Papa. "You must be the worst storyteller I have ever heard. You never had a dog. You never even had a sister."

Orel looked at the old man with shock on his face. Then the two men laughed, the sort of laughter that brings tears to the eyes. When they had regained their composure, the two men lit cigars.

"Thank you," said Papa. "Watch him. I need to be one hundred percent sure it's him. I want to know everything. If it is him, then I have protected him long enough. If he does anything to put the business at risk, then I can no longer protect him. If Vlad behaves like an animal, then like an animal he must be put down."

Orel knew this was hard for the old man. "I'm sorry," he said.

"I know. Now pour me some Rakia. That bloody story of yours – 'I think the dog loved me.' Christ Almighty, you should have been a comedian."

CHAPTER THIRTEEN

Anya stood smoking her third consecutive cigarette outside in the car park of the school. She had cut her hair short and was wearing sunglasses, but she doubted her new look would fool anyone who knew her. She felt exhausted and hadn't slept properly for days. Every sudden noise or voice caused her to jump.

She watched as students began leaving the building. It was late evening. The students were adults of all ages, attending the school for a wide range of courses, some looking to learn computer skills, some wanting additional qualifications and some learning a new hobby like pottery, art or photography.

She crushed out her cigarette with her foot and walked over to the building. As she wove amongst the crowd, her eyes scanned the faces, looking for the teacher. She had met her once or twice; her name was Miss Reilly. Monica Reilly. Delina had talked about her a lot, the way she always did when she learned something new or had a new idea. She would talk and talk and talk, excited and full of enthusiasm like a child.

Anya continued to scan the faces of the crowd. She was worried now that she wouldn't recognise her. Then it crossed her mind that Miss Reilly might still be in the classroom. She started up the steps of the school, and then, in the sea of faces, she recognised the one she was looking for. Miss Reilly was walking towards her, talking to a student. Anya had to speak to her: perhaps her husband the detective would help her.

Miss Reilly looked up and recognised Anya straight away. She immediately ended her conversation and walked quickly towards her.

CHAPTER FOURTEEN

The two women sat in Monica's little Ford Fiesta and talked.

"You must go to the police," said Monica. "They're looking for you. Police officers all over London are looking for you. We thought you might have been, you know, killed."

Anya began to cry; it was the first time she'd been able to. "Your husband is a detective? Will he help me?" she asked.

Monica put her arms around Anya. "James is a good friend," she said. "He's not my husband. We're friends. It's complicated, but none of that matters." She handed Anya a tissue. "Yes, of course he'll help you. You should come with me back to the house. You'll be safe. He'll be at home putting his children to bed right now. We can meet him there. You can shower, get a change of clothes and have something to eat."

Monica hugged Anya again. "You're going to be okay. James is a good man."

Anya nodded and looked at her lap.

The car park was empty of cars now; there was not a soul in sight. The night air was hot and full of the smell of cut grass. Monica started her car, turned on her headlights and headed down the drive towards the road. She stopped at the entrance to check for oncoming traffic. Out of nowhere a black Mercedes 4x4 appeared and pulled up in front of her little Fiesta. The two women watched in alarm as the doors of the Mercedes opened and two men jumped out and ran towards them.

One of them wrenched Anya's door open, and she screamed as a large, muscular man grabbed her hair and arm and tried to drag her out. Without thinking, Monica threw the car into reverse, and the Fiesta began lurching back up the driveway.

Anya's attacker lost his footing. She grabbed his arm and bit down on it as hard as she could. The man cursed loudly, pulled back his arm and fell backwards onto the freshly cut lawn.

His partner looked at him and laughed. "These two have got some fight," he said. "This should be fun."

They both walked back to the Mercedes and, with little haste, followed the reversing Ford Fiesta up the driveway into the car park. They had no reason to rush; they knew there was nowhere for the little car to go and no escape for the two women.

CHAPTER FIFTEEN

Sometimes police work comes down to a little bit of luck. My father, once a detective himself, always told me we make our own luck. He also liked to tell me the luckiest detectives he'd worked with were usually those with the greatest levels of perseverance – and so it was today.

I'd spent the day calling every detective and investigator I knew, and some I didn't, and eventually I got a lead. A vice detective I knew called Bartholomew Bellamy – everyone calls him Barty-B – told me of a case he'd worked on a few years back.

He'd been on a raid trying to bust a fast-growing prostitution racket in West London. Girls were being brought in from Eastern Europe and forced into sex work to pay off their debt to the traffickers. On this particular day the plan was to raid three flats at the same time in different parts of London. The idea was that none of the flats would get tipped off about the raid because they'd be all raided simultaneously.

"If I remember rightly the flats were all above tanning and beauty shops. Anyway, we got the call, and my team entered our target from the front of the shop and headed up the stairs," said Barty-B.

"When we reached the top of the stairs, we met no one, which was really odd. Initially, I thought we had the wrong place. Usually there are women running around and clients trying to get out of windows with their trousers around their ankles. I'm exaggerating, but you know what I mean. It usually gets chaotic for a while, but not that day. That day there was no one in the shop, no girls on the stairs hurling abuse; the place was quiet. It wasn't until the team started checking and clearing the rooms that we understood why."

Barty-B cleared his throat and continued. "On a bed in one of the rooms, the bodies of four young women were piled one on top of another. It's hard for your mind to comprehend when you see something like that. All those young women had been stabbed over and over again. I don't mean stabbed just to kill them; I mean some of those young women had pieces of themselves hanging off, and some of the pieces were on the bed and some on the floor. I'd never seen anything like it before and nothing like it since. There was blood everywhere. I mean a lot of blood. One of the guys said it was like a bomb had gone off in a butcher's shop, and I understood what he meant."

At first I was unsure how this horrific story related to me and my enquiry. Then he told me each girl had been strangled and stabbed multiple times in the abdomen. He told me it was as though their necks had been put in a vice. Someone with a tremendously powerful grip had held each girl and crushed her throat while at the same time cutting and stabbing her.

"All three raids reported the same thing," said Barty-B. "In total, eleven girls were found murdered in the three flats. Why? Well, at the time we assumed someone had become aware a raid was imminent and was covering his tracks in case any of the women decided to talk. Dead women don't talk."

He then told me that, unsurprisingly, no witnesses had come forward. A wall of silence went up, and they never got the guy they suspected of doing it.

I was hooked. I sat with the phone pressed to my ear and my pen poised, waiting for the name. This had to be my guy. There were too many similarities.

"If I were you," said Barty-B. "I would look at a man called Vladimir Kastrati. Known to his friends as Vlad the Wolf."

"What else do you know about him?" I asked.

"Not much, really. Your man Vlad is Albanian mafia and, as you'd expect from any mafia boss type, he's a real nasty piece of work with a ruthless reputation. I won't go into details right now, but as far as we can make out, he's into everything: people trafficking, prostitution, drugs, money laundering – you know the kind of stuff. He's also right at the top of the food chain, so he's always got someone willing to provide an alibi. Failing that, witnesses simply vanish or, like these girls, wind up dead."

"So how do I get near him?" I asked.

To my surprise, Barty-B laughed. "You won't have too much trouble with that."

"I won't have too much trouble getting near him? What do you mean?"

"Vlad is a real wannabe playboy. He loves an audience. I think he's a little confused about whether he's a gangster or a playboy. But whatever you do, don't for a second forget what he is. From what I've heard, he'll flip in a second from name-dropping to dropping you off a building."

I could hear someone calling Barty-B's name, so I knew he'd want to wind up the call.

"Listen, Hardy," he said, "if you get anything on this animal, let me know. I can also tell you there are detectives in vice, serious crimes, fraud, Flying Squad, you name it – they all have their own reasons for wanting to see Vlad the Wolf taken down. So, anything you need, just ask. Right – gotta go. Good luck, mate."

With that, he hung up. I sat in my chair and drew a line under the name "Vladimir (the Wolf) Kastrati." Was he Delina's killer?

I spent several more hours calling detectives back, pulling files and learning as much as I could about Vlad the Wolf.

CHAPTER SIXTEEN

The gallery had been closed an hour now. Simon Baker watched from across the street as Toby Fielding stood at the front door of the gallery and gazed out of the window, looking up and down Old Potter Street and checking his watch.

"Twenty minutes late," Baker said to himself. "I'll give it ten minutes more to really piss him off, then I'll pay him his visit."

Nine minutes and fifty seconds later, Baker crossed the road and appeared at the front door of the gallery just as Fielding began to pull down the blinds and close up. He opened the door and scowled at Baker.

"I'm so sorry I'm late. Why do our trains never run on time? It's me, Richard Money," said Baker. "We have an appointment?"

Fielding smiled politely. "No bother," he lied. "I was just catching up on paperwork. Very pleased to meet you, Mr Money. Please come in."

"Thank goodness for paperwork," said Baker. "I really thought I might have missed my opportunity. Since I heard the canvas had become available, I have been unable to think of little else. If I had lost it to another buyer, I would have been more distraught than you can ever imagine. You know how it is? Well, of course you do – a man of your extensive experience."

Baker was enjoying this already, more than he had anticipated he would. *This fool has no idea who I am,* he thought. *I'm standing inches away from him and he doesn't have a clue.*

"Can I get you a tea, coffee, glass of wine perhaps?" said Fielding.

"A white wine, if you have it, would be perfect. Thank you. I really must apologise again for being late. It really is so very good of you to have waited."

Baker took off his coat and placed his briefcase on Fielding's desk. He watched as Fielding disappeared into the back office to fetch the drinks. He was a little concerned that in his excitement he was overdoing his performance. He took a deep breath, then unclipped his briefcase in preparation.

"So, what do you do? I mean, what's your line of business, Mr Money?" called Fielding from the small office. "That is, if you don't mind my asking?"

"I'm semi-retired. For many years I had a successful business exporting British luxury goods around the world. I had very little in the way of overheads and was able to build quite a nest egg. Then three years ago I was forced to reassess my life and change direction. Due to unforeseen circumstances, I had to – well, let's just say I came to a crossroads and had to rethink my priorities. Fortunately, as I said, I had a little tucked away for a rainy day. Which was just as well because boy, oh boy, did it rain. But you know how it is. We brush ourselves off, pick ourselves up and move on. One door closes, another opens, and all that. I now look at those experiences as being little more than chapters in my life story."

"Yes, life can throw us all sorts of unexpected challenges, can't it? But we move on." Fielding eyed Money's gold watch and expensive shoes. "You certainly seem to have bounced back from whatever your challenges were." He handed Baker a cold glass of white wine. "To challenges," he said, lifting his drink. "And to new chapters."

"To new chapters," agreed Baker. Laughing inside, he watched Fielding sip his wine.

"So, Mr Money, shall we take a look at what you came all this way to see? I have it prepared in a private viewing room, which is just through here." Fielding led the way. He opened a door to a small private room off the main gallery. The limited-edition canvas was on the wall of the warm and brightly lit room. There were two double sofas and a small glass table upon which sat a bottle of champagne on ice and a silver plate of canapés.

"Here we are," said Fielding with pride. "The latest piece from Meredith Churcher. In my opinion, her finest work to date. It certainly reinforces her position as one of Britain's finest contemporary artists."

Baker stood admiring the canvas for a long while. He put on a pair of glasses and stepped closer. He then took the glasses off and stepped back. He stood to the left of the canvas, then moved to the right. He said nothing for as long as he could stand it, savouring every blessed moment. He was having so much fun.

"Is it genuine?" Baker said, deliberately mumbling.

"I'm sorry, Mr Money? I didn't quite catch that."

"Is it genuine?" said Baker. "It's a simple enough question."

"How do you mean, genuine?"

"How can I tell this canvas is genuine? I don't mean to be rude, but for all I know you may have knocked this up in your garage." Baker could feel the excitement rising within him.

Fielding was unsure how to respond; he wasn't entirely sure he was hearing what he thought he was hearing. Instead, he opened and closed his mouth a few times like a fish.

Baker pressed on with his taunting. "You tell me Meredith Churcher splashed the paint on this canvas in this child-like fashion, but for all I know one of her spoiled grandchildren did it and she is passing it off as her own. I'm looking at the price tag and I want to be sure it's authentic."

"I have all the paperwork to verify its authenticity, if that's what you mean, Mr Money."

"I'm a very cautious man, Fielding. I once read of this man, I believe it may have even been in an article you wrote, who had his life destroyed by accusations of fraud. Now I come to think of it, it *was* you who wrote it. What a coincidence. It seems this artist was accused by you of passing off his wife's art as his own. I believe you said, and I paraphrase, 'It is talentless fraudsters like Simon Baker who bring disrepute and uncertainty to an otherwise proud art community. Men like Baker should be imprisoned and given very long sentences as a deterrent.' Did I get it about right, Fielding?"

"I think you had better leave, Mr Money," said Fielding. "I am not sure what is going on here or what you are all about, but I think you had better leave right now."

Baker moved quickly to lock the door and remove the key, which he held up for show and then put into his pocket. Fielding stood paralysed with fear and could only stare at Baker while his mind raced with possibilities. After some time processing the situation, he now found his eyes beginning to fill with tears.

"Who are you? What do you want?"

Baker moved to his briefcase and opened it. "Have a think. Have a guess. Take a wild shot. Who do you think I really am? Have you been looking over your shoulder? You should have been."

"You're not Richard Money?"

"Nope."

"So, you're not here to buy the painting?"

"Nope."

"Do I know you?"

"Yep."

Fielding looked hard at the face of the man in front of him. The answer was there somewhere. Did he want the answer? If he worked out the name, then what? Eventually, from a lost vault somewhere deep inside his brain, and after a lot of frantic processing, a name was served up.

"Simon Baker?"

"Bingo! Right first time. That was fun."

Fielding changed his approach now and became chummy. "It's you, Simon Baker. So how have you been? Ha – the beard fooled me. You're looking good, considering – well, considering all that nonsense that went on. It's good to see you. So, what's this all about? Some sort of prank, I suppose. Just you wait until I tell everyone I bumped into you. They won't believe me. It's so good to see you again. You had me really going there for a while. You know, I thought I recognised you, but you know how it is; people change. And that beard – yes, definitely the beard."

"Save it," Baker said coldly. "We weren't friends. We only ever met twice. That didn't stop you joining the pack when everyone was out for my blood, though, did it? Well, now I'm here for yours."

"Look, I can explain," said Fielding hastily. "It was my editor, Guy Lyons. You know Guy. He asked me to write that article. Everyone was talking about you at the time, how you – well, you know. With what happened and the arrest, and the court case and how they said you kept your wife prisoner and passed off her work as your own. We were all taken in. Everyone was talking about it, so Guy said he only wanted an article about what was happening with you. I never believed the stories coming out about you, of course. I just had to write an article on what I was told. Anyway, no harm done – look at you now. You're doing all right."

"You should listen to yourself," Baker sneered. "'No harm done! Guy made me do it, blah, blah, blah.' Don't worry. I will visit Guy as well, but all in good time. Today I am visiting you."

Baker opened his briefcase and took out a pair of eye protectors. He then put on some latex gloves. Next, he held up a cordless power drill, whizzed it few times and put it back in the briefcase. Next, he held up a taser, then a hammer, a screwdriver and a pair of pliers.

"First things first, Fielding. Today you and I are going to create a very unique piece of art. It may not be to your taste, but I know I'm going to like it."

Fielding stepped back, putting the two-seater sofa between himself and Baker. He began to beg. Then, as Baker closed in, he screamed, then he cried, and then he bled.

All of which was exactly what Baker had hoped for and imagined for so long.

CHAPTER SEVENTEEN

I called to check everything was okay at home. Mum was babysitting tonight while Monica taught her evening class. When she answered, she sounded concerned.

"I'm sure it's nothing to worry about, James," she said. "But Monica's not back yet."

"Perhaps she went for a drink after class, with colleagues or some of the students," I said.

I was trying not to sound concerned myself and was racking my brain, trying to remember whether she'd told me she was going out after class.

"She always calls if she is going to be late. Always," said Mum. She went quiet for a moment and then said, "I didn't like to try her mobile like some worried old woman, but I wish I had. I think you should. Will you call her for me?"

Monica's mobile went straight to voice mail. I left her a message and called Mum back. She sounded very anxious now, so I made a suggestion that I thought might calm her nerves.

"I didn't get an answer on Monica's mobile, so what I'll

do is head over to the school to see if she's still there. She's probably just talking to friends; you know how she likes to talk. If she's not there, I'll go to the King's Head pub just down the road from the school. That's where they usually go if they are have a drink afterward."

"You'll call me as soon as you have any news, won't you?"

"Of course I will. Now don't get yourself worked up. I'm sure she's fine."

CHAPTER EIGHTEEN

I went to the King's Head pub first and looked around. It was a quiet night and the barman assured me he'd not seen Monica or any of the teachers that evening. I drove the mile or so to the school, half expecting to get a call from Mum telling me Monica had arrived back home.

It was dark now, and my headlights lit the driveway as I approached the school. The car park was empty and I was getting a little more concerned. I sat in the car and decided to call some of Monica's girlfriends. They all told the same story: None of them had seen or heard from Monica, as it was her teaching night.

I was turning the car and starting to head out of the car park when I saw tyre tracks across the playing field, close to one of the teaching blocks. I pulled over close to the grass and grabbed my Maglite torch from the glovebox. I stepped out, clicked the torch on, shone the light on the tracks and followed the tracks.

They ran the length of the school building. As the torch lit the side of it, I noticed the wall was scratched and chipped as though something heavy had run up against it and scraped along it. Further on and at the corner of the building I noticed blue paint and then glass from vehicle lights.

I began to move faster and then I began to run. I quickly passed the end of the school building and came to some tennis courts. Still shining the torch on the tyre tracks, I followed them up and around the tennis courts, and then, through the darkness, I caught sight of Monica's blue Ford Fiesta. I could see the doors were open and the car looked empty.

My heart was beating out of my chest as I ran at full speed over to the abandoned vehicle. I couldn't see Monica. I began to panic, cursing under my breath as I frantically searched the car. What had happened?

I ran around the back of the car, and there on the grass was Monica. She was on her knees, trying to get to her feet. I sat her down and checked her over. I was thankful there seemed to be no serious injuries.

Her face and blouse were bloodied from a cut to the head, and her blouse was torn. She looked pale – so very pale. I was scared of what might have happened to her. So many thoughts ran through my mind. She told me about the two men and Anya.

"They weren't interested in me. They wanted Anya. We both fought, but they were so strong. They took her. There was nothing I could . . . I tried to fight, but one of them hit me." She touched the cut over her eye. "That was the last thing I remember. Then you arrived."

I held her close and then got her to her feet and helped her to her car. I got into the driver's seat and drove her to the car park at the front of the school, where we got into my car and I drove her to the hospital. She didn't want to go; she wanted to go home, but I insisted she get checked over.

I called Mum, and she stayed to look after Alice and Faith that night. I stayed at Monica's side while she got checked, and the following morning, after assurances from doctors she'd sustained no serious injuries, she was allowed to go home.

CHAPTER NINETEEN

The room was white and sterile in appearance. There were two fold-up chairs and a microphone stand with a microphone. The microphone went nowhere, it was simply for appearance, but they both knew that.

Vlad had explained that he was only interested in real talent, and in this room, one to one, he would know instantly whether or not Clara was the real deal. If she was, then not even the sky was the limit. He'd make her a global superstar. He had both the money and the connections.

Vlad had been very attentive while he listened to her sing. She could tell he was impressed. Why wouldn't he be? Her mum, dad, grandparents, friends and the rest of her extended family had told her many times since she was about four years old that she was amazing and that she had a gift.

By the time she was eighteen, they were saying it was shocking she hadn't been snapped up by a record label. By the time she was twenty-one, she'd had a top ten hit as part of a girl band, but the band had folded when the lead singer got caught up in a sex and drugs scandal with a rapper named RIPPEMUP. Back when they were flying high in the music charts, she and the other girls in the group had secretly called him "Flippin' Muppet." That was back when they thought the dream would never end.

The record label had blamed their being dropped on poor sales. They also suggested it was to do with the minor incident in which a small quantity of cocaine was found in one member's hand luggage before a flight out of Canada. That was, of course, complete rubbish; drugs were handed to them freely at the time and considered almost a perk. The truth was, all record labels were struggling, and piracy was to blame. Illegal downloads were killing the music industry and, until a new business model was found, even the most talented artists were being dropped.

She still remembered them saying during the final tearful meeting, "This isn't the end of the road for you girls. You're so talented. This will all blow over and we'll be in touch. Think of it as a time to recharge your batteries. This isn't about you; it's about the changing face of the music industry."

Well, screw them, she'd thought. She was a fighter. What most people didn't know was that every successful singer is first and foremost a successful businessperson, and Clara intended to become just that.

She never heard from them again, and that was fine; she was over it. Eventually they'd be begging to take her back, and when they did, she'd dictate the terms of the contract. She'd be the one with the power. In her heart, she knew one way or another she'd be front-page news again.

Her time was now – she could feel it. Today was just a business transaction, nothing more. And for this type of transaction, she wouldn't need cash. So many artists these days were breaking into the music industry independently, and she knew she had as much talent as any of them. She couldn't remember, though, who had told her this guy Vlad was well connected. He was certainly wealthy, which meant he was successful. All these Russian types were rich. Oligarchs, most of them.

The house was huge. He'd given her a tour, and he'd been a real gentleman. He dressed well and smelled gorgeous. Her priority now was to make sure she was top of his to-do list. And if that meant she had to do *him*, then she was comfortable with that.

Soft music played through speakers in the ceiling, and she swayed seductively to the beat. She knew she was hot. She worked out every day, she hardly ever ate carbs, and she drank more water than a fish.

After a few moments, Clara moved in to close the deal. She ran her fingers through Vlad's hair and began to unbutton his shirt. She wasn't a big a fan of tattoos, but she'd make an exception on this occasion. Just as well; this guy was a walking gallery. She slipped her hand inside his shirt and ran her nails over Vlad's hard chest. *Someone else works out*, she thought.

She unfastened her dress and let it fall to the floor. She gave him her best and most innocent smile, one that said, "Whoops, look what just happened. Now what shall we do?" She'd read somewhere that most famous women had to kiss a few toads to get the top. Fortunately, this guy was hardly a toad, and her mantra these days was "Whatever it takes."

Vlad got to his feet so she could unfasten his belt. She could see he was ready. They kissed, and he lifted her with ease. She wrapped her legs around him as he gently lowered her to the floor. He's strong, she thought. Now he was over her, kissing her neck, caressing her breasts and stomach. She unzipped his trousers and pushed them down. His hand moved from her thighs to her lips, then her face and then to her neck.

Clara tried to lift her head to kiss him again, but he held her down by her throat. *That's okay*, she thought. *He likes to be in charge.*

Then he was squeezing. Gently at first, then gradually harder. At first she smiled; then she was confused, then concerned. She opened her eyes and looked at him. There was no mistaking his intention. His eyes no longer sparkled. Now they reminded her of the cold, black, dead eyes of a shark.

Clara tried to move, but he was a dead weight on her. Tears welled in her eyes. She struggled to breathe. Panic overwhelmed her as the stupidity of her situation dawned on her with crystal clarity. No one knew she was there. He'd deliberately asked her to be discreet and to tell nobody. She was helpless and alone in a house with a psychopath.

She kicked and clawed and scratched, but that had no effect on him; he hardly noticed. She felt herself being lifted like a doll and pushed against the wall. Suddenly it all felt so surreal, as though she were an observer who had no control over the situation happening around her.

Over his shoulder she could see the fake microphone stand.

"It's simply a prop," he'd said. "Some performers prefer to perform with a microphone. I want to make you feel at ease so you perform at your best. This is all about you. I have a feeling you are going to stir something deep inside of me."

He'd flattered her, told her what she wanted to hear.

Suddenly being famous no longer mattered. She spoke to God for the first time since she was a child. She promised him that if he'd help her now, she'd be happy to never sing again. Then, at the moment Vlad showed her the knife, she knew for sure God wouldn't be rescuing her, that in fact it was Satan with his dead black eyes, and not God, who had appeared for her today.

CHAPTER TWENTY

It was 4 a.m. and the streets were deserted, apart from the occasional road-cleaning vehicle and taxi. Jimmy and Chris were under strict instructions to dump the woman's body in the Thames. It seemed a strange thing to do, as the previous bodies had been found really quickly. They knew better ways to dispose of a corpse; after all, that was their speciality and the reason they were in such demand all over the UK and Europe. Still, he'd insisted, and he was paying for their premium-rate service. So they just did as they were told.

"She's staying with her mother at the moment," said Jimmy.

"Your Aggie?" said Chris.

"Yes. Said she had to have a little time to herself," said Jimmy solemnly. "'Time to yourself?' I said to her. 'I'm out all bloody day. And sometimes I'm gone for days on end. Time to yourself? How much more time to yourself do you need, you stupid cow?'"

"Perhaps that was a little strong, mate?"

"Yeah, it was. I was annoyed. You understand?"

"Of course I do," said Chris. "And rightly so, with everything you do for her. You don't think your Aggie is, well, you know . . ."

"No. There's no one else. It crossed my mind, though, so I followed her, and for a bit I watched the mother-in-law's house as well. Plus, I went through all her stuff back home. I found nothing to indicate – you know."

"So what are you thinking?"

"You know, I think she might be menopausal. You know, that thing some people get in middle age. Men go get a sports car or a hot twenty-something, while women become even more emotional but with hot flushes to boot."

"You reckon it could be that?"

"I'm no psychologist, but all the signs are there. More irrational than normal. Snappy. Crying a lot. Comfort eating. Banging on about romance and surprises and holidays and affection. Talking to her mum for hours on end. Not wanting to go out as much. In fact, I can't remember the last time we went to the pub together. And you know, not wanting to . . . well, you know what I mean."

"Blimey. Really? Well, if you don't mind my saying, she has put on a bit of weight recently. Still very attractive, don't get me wrong. But maybe a little softer around the edges."

"There you go, see? You noticed the signs as well," said Jimmy. The two men were silent for a while as they contemplated their considerable body of evidence, neither of them really sure what to say next.

"You'll figure it out, Jimmy. You and Aggie are so good together," said Chris. He hadn't seen his mate like this before and wanted to help. Yet, at the same time, he felt ill-equipped and more than a little awkward. Relationship talk of this nature was usually part of the male "no-fly zone."

"Yeah. It'll come good," said Jimmy almost inaudibly.

In an effort to lift the mood, Chris tried to think of something upbeat to say. In the end he just said, "Right, we must be nearly there. Let's get this body dumped in the river. Then we'll head over to the Butter Fingers cafe and I'll treat you to a nice bacon-and-egg roll with brown sauce. How does that sound?"

"Great idea. I might even have a few fried mushrooms."

"This'll do. It looks as good a spot as any. There's no one around. We'll dump her over the side here."

"Spot on. Let's get this done."

"You know, I decided to put extra sheeting down in the boot. I was worried about leakage."

"That makes sense. Though you always do such a good job wrapping, I don't really see leakage as a problem. Then again, it's always worth taking those little extra precautions. It's what makes the difference between amateurs and professionals."

"Of course it is. The prisons are full of amateurs who cut corners. It must be hell waking every day in a cell and knowing you're there because you got sloppy."

"Talking of which, you know, I think it might be time to move on, make this our last drop for this Russian. I'm not so sure Vlad the Wolf is the full picnic. I mean, why use us when he has his own men and all he wants is a river drop? It just doesn't stack up."

"You know, I was thinking the same thing. This is the sort of thing we left behind years ago. Yeah, the money is good, but any idiot can drop a body in a river, and these days the risks are way too high. We could end up on bloody YouTube."

"That's settled, then. I mean, we've got all the equipment for making bodies vanish – incinerators, liquidisers, acid tanks, chippers and shredders – yet here we are outside freezing our nuts off at an unsociable hour about to do an old-school body drop."

Suddenly, the two men were back to their old selves and everything seemed right with the world. Chris felt relieved to hear Jimmy humming a little of Queen's "Bohemian Rhapsody" as they swung the body high over the railings and into the Thames. It was good to see his mate back to his old self again. "I'll tell you what. After brekky, we'll swing by Covent Garden and pick up some flowers for your Aggie. She'll like that."

"That's not a bad idea. We'll make a fresh start," agreed Jimmy.

"Good man. Right, let's go get a cuppa and a fry-up. And later I'll make some calls, put the word out we're back on the market for some *professional* work. While you, my friend, are making up with your Aggie."

"Now that sounds like a plan."

CHAPTER TWENTY-ONE

Simon Baker sat in a bamboo chair in the corner of the room. He was sweaty and out of breath, and right now he wasn't happy.

"Idiot. That was too close," he mumbled.

He chewed his thumbnail and looked at the bed and the room. In his mind, he went over the events as they should have been. He pictured himself skilfully prizing open the patio door then moving silently through the house. In his planning, he was over her when he grabbed a clump of hair on the back of her head and forced her face down into the pillow. It was simply a case of holding her there until she passed out and finally suffocated.

In reality, she'd bucked and kicked like a rodeo horse, and he'd ended up on his backside on the floor. Then like a lunatic she was in his face screaming at him, hitting him and throwing at him anything she could lay her hands on. The whole thing had been a disaster. Having to improvise wasn't fun at all. He'd ended up having to punch her to the ground, corner her and strangle her with the cable from a bedside lamp.

Baker shuddered. He felt dirty. He felt like a monster. He wasn't supposed to feel this way. This was supposed to be retribution for what she'd done to him, not a scene from a low-budget slasher movie. He kicked the lifeless body lying in front of him.

"Stupid, stupid, woman. Look what you made me do. First you ruin my life, then you ruin your own murder."

Baker began to laugh. He laughed, and then he sobbed like a child. After a few minutes he wiped his nose on his arm, sniffed, and cleared his throat.

"I should have drugged you. That would have made things simpler. I specifically chose not to do that because I was going to tell you who I was while you suffocated. You spoiled that. Now, of course, you're dead and you don't even know why."

Baker got to his feet and started dragging Katharine through the house to the bathroom. He turned on the taps and checked the temperature. *Odd*, he thought. *No need to check the temperature, not like she's going to complain. But it seems the right thing to do. Should have drugged her for sure; it definitely would have made things easier. No distressful fighting. How would I have explained it if I'd ended up with a black eye or scratched face? And look at your neck now, and your face, all bruised and blotchy. It's not how I pictured this scene, not at all how I pictured you.*

Baker stepped over Katharine. "Excuse me a moment. I just need to get a few things."

Baker went to his rucksack in the kitchen and, while he was there, he flicked on the kettle and put a teabag and milk in a cup ready for later. He grabbed a Tupperware box from his rucksack and went to Katharine's wardrobe and then to her chest of drawers.

"Aha." Baker turned off the bath taps and pulled back the shower curtain. He then decided it would be better to remove the shower curtain completely. He grabbed

Katharine's wrists and pulled her completely into the bathroom, then turned her so she was alongside the bath. He was about to lift her when he decided he should take some photographs.

"Won't be a minute – I just need to grab the camera." A few moments later he returned with a tripod, a Nikon camera and his rucksack. After taking a few shots from various angles and feeling disappointed with the lighting, he gave up. Instead, he decided it was time to create his scene.

Worried about hurting his back, Baker decided to do the move in three stages. First, he started by lifting Katharine to a sitting position on the edge of the bath. Second, he lifted her arms and wrapped his own arms around her body in an attempt to lower her into the bath water. But he was unable to hold her there and was pulled into the bath as she slumped backwards into the tub. Bath water spilled over the sides and out across the bathroom floor.

Baker took some towels from the heated towel rail. "Don't want any accidents, do we?"

He got down on his hands and knees and began furiously mopping. "Right. That's that. Now let's top up the bath and then we're almost done. Wasn't so bad, was it?"

Picking up the silk scarf he'd found in Katharine's drawer, he gently tied it around her neck. He stood back to look. Satisfied, he opened the Tupperware box.

"Look at this." He showed the lifeless body the contents of the box. "Rose petals. Just for you."

He sprinkled the rose petals on the water around Katharine and then placed one on each eye and a few in her hair. "For when the police officers arrive. We want you to look amazing."

He stood back and looked at what he'd created.

"Katharine, you look beautiful. Just like Ophelia. It's better than you deserve, if I am being perfectly honest. You were a real bitch. You and the others have got only yourselves to blame. You're the reason I am doing this. I was perfectly happy. But sadly, you decided to be a bitch, and here we find ourselves."

Baker caught his reflection in the mirror and saw his wagging finger. "Anyway, now I'm happy. Just in a new way. And now it's time for a shower and to freshen up a bit. You don't mind if I use the en suite, do you? Okay, thank you. I think also I'll have a nice hot cup of tea."

Baker stood in the hallway for a moment, trying to decide whether to leave the bathroom door open or shut it. He decided on shut.

Back in the kitchen, he flicked on the kettle to re-boil the water to make his tea. While the tea brewed, he walked about the house trying to decide on a suitable memento.

"I am going to take a shower. I just decided I'd have my tea first. And no, I'm not looking for a trophy," he shouted to Katharine. "I'm not some sort of serial killer cliché who needs to collect locks of his victims' hair or pieces of jewellery or underwear or a finger. I'm not sick. I don't have voices in my head telling me what to do, you know. All this is merely transactional. Everything you made me do is payback. You screw up my life, I screw up yours. The difference being, you mess with me, you don't get to mess again. Ever. The memento? It's for a friend."

Baker lifted the teabag out of the cup and dropped it in the bin. He began opening cupboards.

"Have you got any biscuits, Katharine? I've got the nibbles."

In a cupboard over the sink he found a tin tucked away at the back behind gravy granules, stock cubes, herbs and spices. The picture on the front of the tin was of the Virgin Mary holding the Baby Jesus. He lifted it out and looked at it for a moment. "Are you religious, Katharine?"

Inside were family photographs. Little Katharine. Katharine as a baby and as a child. Pictures of her as a little girl holding a baby, probably a sister or brother. He saw a small Katharine sitting on her dad's shoulders by the beach. Toddler Katharine eating ice cream with a little brother and their mum. Another of little Katharine learning to ride her bike – a bike with streamers hanging from the handlebars.

At the bottom of the tin he saw a silver chain. He lifted out a Saint Christopher necklace and held it up in front of him. He watched it swing from side to side. *The patron saint of travellers*, thought Baker. *I suppose we're all on journeys of one sort or another, and none of us knows when or how they'll end.*

Baker closed the lid and sighed. He put the tin in his rucksack. He drank half his tea and poured the rest away; he no longer had the taste for it. He showered in silence. He dressed slowly, then collected his rucksack and looked around the house one last time. He stood for a long while looking at the bathroom door. He chose not to speak to her again or to go back in. Closing the front door behind him, he left the house and didn't look back.

CHAPTER TWENTY-TWO

It was dark out when Baker arrived home. He was exhausted. It had been a long and emotionally draining day. He also ached; he was bruised, and he felt like he'd pulled a muscle in his shoulder. Yet he still had plenty to do and it was likely to be another late night.

A little louder than was necessary, he shut the front door behind him. He hung up his overcoat, took off his outdoor shoes and put on his Wallace and Gromit slippers. *They look like they've been chewed again*, he thought irritably. *Bloody rat dog.*

He shrugged it off. Not even Beckham was going to spoil this day. Baker looked in the hall mirror and smiled. He tightened and straightened his tie, then brushed his hair. The smile lessened. He could hear her. The rasping and wheezing. He waited in silence, motionless. A different sort of smile came across his face. *Just a little fun. No harm done. Come on. Any second now.*

"Simon? That you, my love?"

"Yes, Mother. I'm just putting on those Marks &

Spencer slippers you got me for my birthday. They're lovely and cosy."

"That's good, sweetheart."

Baker stood motionless. Waiting. Holding back the laughter. *Here it comes. Five, four, three, two, one.*

"Simon, sweetheart, did you manage to pick up my cigarettes?"

Suppressed laughter sprayed from Baker's lips. He covered his mouth with his hands. Instead of replying, he rooted around the pockets of his coat and found what he was looking for. Baker looked at his reflection. He waited again, smiling.

"Simon, love? Did you hear me? I wonder, did you manage to pick up a packet of slims?"

Baker paused just a moment longer and then, with a hand behind his back and a big smile on his face, walked casually into the sitting room.

"Good evening, Mother. I got you something better, something you'll enjoy much more than a packet of cigarettes."

"What do you mean?" Disappointment spread across the old woman's creased and powdered face. "Don't play your silly games, Simon. I really am not in the mood. It's been a long day and Beckham is just not himself." She patted Beckham, who was panting heavily. His large pug eyes glared at Baker.

Simon stepped close to his mother. She smelled of lavender soap, stale cigarettes and dog. Beckham growled. Baker leaned over Beckham and kissed his mother's forehead.

"Thank you, sweetheart. Simon, what do you mean, 'something better'? You know I like to enjoy a Friday evening cigarette. It's one of my last remaining luxuries. A small sherry and a slim cigarette. I am sure that bitch ex-wife has messed with your brain. You used to be so on the ball, and now you forget the simplest of things."

Not wanting his mother to start on about his ex-wife, he fast-tracked his surprise. Baker rolled up his sleeves and began waving his arms around like a magician. "Mother. Look. *Ta-dah!* Two packets."

"Oh, Simon. You naughty boy. You had me going again. You are so naughty, teasing me all the time. Thank you, sweetheart."

Beckham rolled his fat body off her lap as the old lady rose to her feet. She walked over to the drinks cabinet and poured herself a large sherry. Beckham stood guard beside her and stared at Baker.

Baker glared back and showed his teeth. Beckham's flat face looked more wrinkled than usual as he growled, panted and growled some more.

"Stop it, Beckham. It's Simon."

The old lady, sherry in hand, walked to her favourite chair, which was close to the window. Baker opened the window as his mother eased herself down into the cushions. She took a quick sip of sherry and then, picking up a lighter from the window ledge, lit her cigarette. Baker watched as his mother closed her eyes, sank back in her chair and slowly exhaled a large cloud.

"Thank you, Simon. You know, when you get to my age, it's the small things that give a lot of pleasure. You're a good boy. I know moving in with me is hard at your time of life. But you'll get back on track. You'll put the lies and betrayal behind you and move on. Isn't that right, Becky-Boo-Boo?" She stroked and patted the dog fondly.

"I know. It's you I worry about, though, Mother. You know you shouldn't be smoking at all. Your chest. Your breathing. It's getting worse. Are you using the oxygen?"

The old lady put out her hand and Baker sat down next to her. He took her frail hand and looked at it.

"I know, sweetheart. You're a good boy. I do use the oxygen, but the mask, it frightens Beckham. He gets upset and doesn't stop barking until I take it off. I don't like to worry him." She looked down adoringly at the pug, who was using his big glossy eyes to encourage more stroking and tickling.

"I know you love the dog, Mother, but for Christ's sake, you need to use the mask. I don't know – perhaps lock the fat hamster in the kitchen while you use the mask." Beckham growled and barked at Baker.

"Please don't raise your voice, sweetheart. Beckham isn't himself today." The old woman gave Beckham a few kisses. "He's very sensitive to change. You know he never used to bark and growl at you." Beckham circled a few times on her lap and then settled, his eyes fastened on Baker. The old lady began stroking him again then lit a second slim.

"Okay, if you're not going to listen to me, then I have things to do. Now, before I start, can I get you anything? Some dinner, perhaps?"

"But you've only just got in. You'll make yourself ill if you don't take some time to relax. I know you're in a hurry to get your life back in order after what happened, but don't hurry on my account. I enjoy having you around. This big old house can get very lonely."

Baker ignored her and repeated his question. "Dinner? Would you like some? I think we have some nice cheese, but if you'd like something hot, we have some ping food in the freezer. I can microwave something for you when I do mine if you want?"

The old woman looked out of the window at the darkness.

"Mother? Some food? I think there is a shepherd's pie, a lasagne and maybe a biryani. I'll do some peas as well."

"Thank you, darling, but Mrs Benson visited earlier with a chicken casserole. We ate together. Poor woman is beside herself with worry. You remember her eldest boy, Gareth? Well, he's been posted to Afghanistan. I always thought he was gay, but it turns out he's doing well in the army. They probably drummed that nonsense out of him. Mind you, in my day plenty of officers were gay. If the army found out, they just sent you off to Africa or some remote post. Out of sight, out of mind. I suppose things just move on.

"Everyone is so very liberal-minded these days. Every time I turn on the television, it's men kissing men and girls kissing girls. If it is a man and woman, well, they're all about safe words and tying each other up all over the place. God help the next generation; they'll end up having to take a degree course before knowing what they want to do in the bedroom."

"Thank you, Mother. Glad to hear you and Mrs Benson had a nice time. I'll grab some dinner and help you to your room around ten. But I want you to start taking better care of yourself. I might not be around forever."

He instantly regretted saying the last part. Baker got up to make a hasty retreat before his mother began worrying or had time to move on to her next favourite subject: illegal immigrants.

"What do you mean? Are you leaving? I hope you haven't gotten yourself mixed up with another tart already. For Christ's sake, Simon, don't you ever learn? Your life is in tatters, your reputation in pieces, every penny you worked so hard for taken by *that* woman or spent on lawyers, and you're gallivanting about. Ready to jump in bed with the next floozy looking to take you for every penny you have. Which, if I might add, is most likely to be your inheritance – the way my health is deteriorating. Six months they give me. Six months. And here I am worrying about the reputation of this family. A family name with a proud history. You should be spending every second of the day restoring our family name. Not running around with your trousers around your ankles. I thought I brought you up to have more sense than that.

"Your father, God rest his soul, and I spent a fortune on your education. We were too soft on you. We should have made you go into law or become a doctor. Instead we indulged you and tried to accept that you were an artistic boy and not so academic. Perhaps your father was right. Perhaps I did spoil you. Perhaps I should have made you follow him into law. That law firm would be yours now. You'd want for nothing. Where do you go all day, anyway? Not that we need it, but I don't see any money coming in. So, you're not working."

Mother began gasping for air. Beckham jumped from her lap and looked on with a mixture of curiosity and concern. Baker collected the oxygen from beside the drinks cabinet and gently slid the mask over his mother's face. She looked at him wide-eyed.

"Breathe. Slowly. Calmly. Breathe," said Baker reassuringly.

A tear rolled down the old woman's face, and Baker stroked her back and kissed her.

"Mother, listen. We've been over this. I am not going anywhere. I am here for you. And same as before when you've questioned me: I am not about to run off with a tart. Nor have I suddenly become gay like Gareth. I haven't become a religious nut, or a terrorist, or a paedophile. I also haven't joined the Labour Party. And I did vote Yes to Brexit, just like you asked."

His mother smiled and laughed through the mask. Baker continued while the old woman couldn't talk back.

"I will restore the family reputation. As it happens, I am working on ensuring my name is remembered for a very long time; you must trust me on that. And just as you and Father taught me, I will also ensure those who betrayed me pay a heavy price, and that they are made aware that we Bakers have long memories and an even longer reach. I have been too trusting in the past and too forgiving. Now I am looking out for me and for you and for family. And even for Beckham here." Baker reached out and stroked Beckham. Mother lifted the mask.

"Good boy. Remember, you have Baker blood in your veins. I know you're tired of me telling you and it sounds far too overdramatic, but our particular Baker bloodline can be traced back beyond the Crusades. We didn't survive all those centuries by being weak. You understand me? I know you're a sensitive soul, but you can no longer afford to be sentimental. You'll be on your own soon. There will be time enough to continue the bloodline. Right now, you need to restore and repair. So go continue your work. Go and do whatever it is you need to do. As for me, I am going to finish my sherry and watch *Newsnight*. Hopefully I'll see some liberal politician squirm a little. That always cheers me up."

Baker closed the window a little, replenished his mother's sherry glass and retreated upstairs.

CHAPTER TWENTY-THREE

Alberto and Vlad had known each other since boyhood. They had grown up in the same village. Their fathers regularly did business together and, like his father, Alberto was a man of integrity and unquestioning loyalty.

As boys, Alberto and Vlad had worked out that in some distant way they were cousins, and that had sealed their brotherhood. They had become blood brothers and dreamed together of becoming rich in America, powerful and fearless like Al Capone. They had childishly vowed that together they would take on the world and probably die side by side in a blaze of glory.

Alberto's wasn't the sort of loyalty driven into men by military service. His was the family loyalty that you cannot explain, the ancient, instinctive kind that binds us unquestioningly to those we love. It ran through his veins and was DNA deep. He truly would protect and, if necessary, die for those he considered family.

Today his loyalty to Vlad meant he was presenting him with an innocent young woman. A young woman who had done nothing more than suspect her friend's murder was linked to rumours about a man called the Wolf, an Albanian mafia millionaire who was said to be killing young women for kicks. So, when she had suspected her friend had been murdered by him, she'd decided she didn't want to stick around and made a run for it. Unfortunately for her, in Vlad's eyes that made her a problem; it made her look like she knew something. *Why run if you know nothing?*

Alberto watched the girl as he sipped his Pepsi. She had spoken only to tell him her name, Anya. He liked her spirit; she was a real fighter. In a very traditional way she was also incredibly beautiful. Looking at her made him remember home and his first girlfriend, a local girl whom he'd promised he'd return for after a few months when he'd first left for London with Vlad. That was nearly twenty-five years ago. He'd changed a lot in that time; he'd gone from a teenager full of excitement and ambition to a man hardened through tough choices and blood-soaked hands.

Alberto looked at his watch and drained the last of his Pepsi. He got to his feet and put out a hand to show Anya the way. It was time to take her to Vlad. Another tough choice and very likely more blood on his hands.

CHAPTER TWENTY-FOUR

Vlad picked up the remote control and turned off the latest episode of *Narcos*. He felt an affinity with the Columbian drug lord Pablo Escobar as he was portrayed in the series and was watching the first season for a third time. Escobar had been a smart man, and a lot could be learned from his successes as well as his failures.

Vlad was in a good mood and smiled graciously as Alberto brought in the girl, Anya. He studied her as she stepped hesitantly into the room.

"Come in, come in. I won't bite, I promise," he said. "Thank you, Alberto. Anya and I will be fine now. I will call you if we need anything."

He smiled and gestured for Alberto to leave. Alberto gave Anya a firm prod to encourage her into the room and then departed, closing the large carved oak doors behind him.

"Please sit down," said Vlad, gesturing to a chair. "I am sorry about Alberto. He can be a little rude in his manner and a little rough. He forgets that you are a young woman and so should be treated with tenderness and with care."

He smiled warmly and poured Anya and himself each a glass of red wine. As he poured, he watched as her eyes darted around the room. Her vulnerability sent a charge of adrenaline through him. He passed her a glass and sat down in his favourite leather armchair. He drank and watched her. *She really is as beautiful as I was told*, he thought. *Her rich brown eyes. Those lips. Those long, slim legs.*

"Anya, I understand you come from a small village not far from my own hometown," said Vlad. "Do you have family there?"

He saw her hesitate for a moment, no doubt wondering how he might know that about her, and tremble as she struggled to get herself back under control.

"Yes," she said. "My parents are still there."

"A little brother too, I understand." Vlad smiled reassuringly.

"Yes, I have a brother."

"I am sure he misses you a great deal. I should imagine they are reliant on your sending them a little money from time to time? Things are tough in the world at the moment; financially, I mean. I am sure they appreciate and perhaps even rely on your support. A little money goes a long way back home."

She was watching him closely. *Good*, he thought. Now he had her attention, he wanted her to focus and understand what he was implying – and also what he was offering.

"I'll be straight with you. I feel responsible for what happened to your friend Delina. I feel an obligation to look after, or at least look in on, those who arrive here in London from Albania. I feel I let you both down. Especially Delina. I want you to know I have taken steps to reach out to her family.

"When you arrive here you are vulnerable. Back home,

you are sheltered and protected by family. I recall how things were when I first arrived here. I would not have survived long and would very likely have ended up in jail had I not been taken under the wing of a successful businessman. This was a man my father had arranged for me to work for. Since then, I have made my fortune and send what I can back home to help the poor and sick."

Anya was still watching him uneasily. Concerned he might have overdone his performance, he decided to rein it in a little and get back to the point.

"I know things can be hard at first. I too worked my way up. You're a smart, strong and intelligent woman, which means there are opportunities. Because of what happened to your friend I feel it is important I keep you close. I would not want you to meet a similar fate. Do you understand?"

Anya nodded uncertainly; Vlad was sure she understood the meaning behind his words. She picked up her wine with a shaking hand and drank it down in one.

Vlad took the glass from her and filled it again. Before handing it back he spoke softly.

"I am sorry my men were heavy-handed with you when they picked you up. Your friend Monica is fine. I have checked, and even though she was in hospital she was there only as a precaution and was quickly back home. I was shocked when I heard what happened. I have reprimanded the men who picked you up. They were under strict instructions only to find you and ensure your safety by bringing you to me so we could talk."

Anya took a cigarette from her purse, lit it and exhaled heavily before she began to speak, choosing her words carefully.

"I know who you are and I know what you are, so save it for someone else. As I see it you have already decided

86

whether or not you should kill me. I assume because I am sitting here and not dead already you don't consider me a risk and so are not going to kill me. You also know if I was going to talk to the police I would have already. You also know that, as an Albanian in London, I would not talk to the police because of our distrust of them. I assume, then, when you say you want to keep me close you mean you want me to work for you. I also assume you're not planning on paying me for my typing skills."

Vlad laughed and passed her the glass of wine. "You're right. I don't have much need for typists. I will get straight to the point. I can put you in touch with some very wealthy friends of mine who would love to meet you. Instead of being an escort to average businessmen, come work for me. I will protect you, watch over you and introduce you to the wealthy associates I know. I assure you, you will very quickly become a very rich woman."

Anya finished her cigarette and slowly drank her wine. She then stood and walked over to Vlad.

"I guess if you're going to be recommending me, then you had better make sure your friends will be satisfied." She ran her fingers through his hair.

"Perhaps you are right," said Vlad. "Though the longer I am around you, the less I want to share you with anyone else."

Anya wasn't sure whether Vlad had bought her sudden change of heart but she thought if she could keep him satisfied for now, he would be less likely to want her dead. Men were so weak that way. She had to do this, she told herself, if for no other reason than to give herself time to consider her options.

CHAPTER TWENTY-FIVE

I was in Harrow, at the first-floor apartment of Toby Fielding. A constable was stationed outside the door. She assured me someone was home and that she had spoken to no one. She was sure no one had been in or out of the upstairs apartment since she'd arrived, which had been around forty-five minutes earlier.

After knocking and waiting a few seconds I was met at the door by Stuart Walsh. He looked on edge and his lean figure immediately became tense when I introduced myself. He motioned me inside. The apartment was expensively furnished, and large art pieces were tastefully displayed. Dotted around I noted pictures of Toby and Stuart.

"What's your relationship with Toby Fielding?" I asked. I was pretty sure I knew the answer.

"We're married. We've been married just over two years; we kept our own names. Why are you are asking me that? Tell me what's happened. Has something happened to him? Is he hurt? Where is he?" Stuart began pacing.

"Please take a seat, Mr. Walsh. I have some bad news."

"I'm fine. Is he hurt? He's dead, isn't he? I knew something was wrong when he didn't come home last night. I went to the gallery but it was locked up. I called our friends. Nothing. It was just so unlike him not to call me if he was going to be late."

"We discovered his body at his gallery. We're treating his death as suspicious," I said, not wanting to go into detail. "I know this is difficult, but can you think of any reason anyone would want to harm him?"

This was part of the job no police officer liked. I'd visited loved ones with bad news more times than I ought to have, and I could recall every single one of the families and all the reactions. People responded in different ways and at different times, but they all experienced similar emotions: shock and denial, incomprehension, distress, despair, anger, helplessness, acceptance.

Walsh dabbed away the tears rolling down his face. "Toby was a gentle man," he said hoarsely. "Kind. Loving. Compassionate."

"It's possible he knew his killer," I said. "There was no forced entry into the gallery, so perhaps his killer was a client or a friend."

"All his appointments go in his work diary at the gallery. As for our friends, I can give you a list. Someone might know something."

"I checked his diary. His last appointment was with a Mr Richard Money. Do you recognise that name?"

"No." Walsh looked as if he wanted to say something but was holding back. "This is going to sound stupid. But he did say he thought he was being followed. He told me he thought a man was following him. We just laughed about it. 'You should be so lucky,' I said at the time."

"When was this?"

"A few weeks ago, I suppose."

"What did this man look like?"

"He didn't say. I don't know for sure whether he actually saw anyone. I think it was more of a feeling, really. We never took it seriously. Now I wish we had." Walsh got up and went to his bedroom. "I just remembered something," he called over his shoulder.

A few moments later he returned and handed me a card. "We got this through the letterbox a few months ago. Toby said we should destroy it but I decided to keep it. It's nothing, I'm sure. I've had hate mail before. Growing up it was obvious I was gay, so I've had to deal with all kinds of abuse. For Toby it was different, though. This was the first time he'd received anything of this kind. You know, he left his wife and children for me. He sees his children again now, but..." Walsh broke off mid-sentence and broke down again. "Toby's children," he said.

"There's a detective with them right now. They're being looked after." I opened the card and read it to myself.

So glad to see you're happy. You don't deserve to be. I'll make sure you suffer. Keep looking over your shoulder. One day I'll be there and it'll be the last thing you see.

"When did you get this?"

"Six months ago, maybe."

"Did you report it?"

"Really? And what exactly would you lot have done?" said Walsh bitterly.

In reality, Walsh was probably right, and now wasn't the time. Walsh curled up on his armchair while he waited for his family to arrive. I looked around the apartment for anything that might give me an insight into what had driven someone to so brutally murder Toby Fielding. Could his murder have been random? Was it a hate crime? Or, as with most murders, was it someone he knew, a family member perhaps?

And why was the murderer so filled with hate?

CHAPTER TWENTY-SIX

Baker shut his study door with his foot and placed a selection of crackers and cheeses, a bottle of red wine and a glass down on his desk. His mother could no longer manage the stairs and the whole floor was his.

Baker powered up his laptop and began flicking through pictures and video. He was pleased; the colours looked vivid, and most of the pictures were sharp. His phone had picked up the sound well, better than he had hoped. Phone and laptop synced, he began uploading the images. While they uploaded, he signed into the members' site; this was going to be good. By now other members must have thought he was either all talk or dead or arrested. They were going to be surprised when he not only signed in again after so long but also had something to contribute.

With the images loaded onto his laptop, he opened Photoshop and began editing the pictures, brightening, sharpening and tweaking the contrast and saturation until he was satisfied.

Baker talked to himself as he worked. "Katharine, you

look so beautiful. I think I'll soften you a little. There. Perfect. Of all my work you are by far the best. Toby was just a bloody mess; no finesse. You, on the other hand, are exquisite. They are going to love you."

He got up and ran a finger over his books. He pulled out a copy of *The Great Gatsby*. He turned it over, lifted the back cover and, with a scalpel, cut around a USB stick into the pages. He pushed the USB stick into the little divot; it fitted perfectly. He removed the USB, then transferred the images and video onto it and set it back in the space he'd cut at the back of the book. He put the book into a jiffy bag and addressed it with a marker pen. He checked twice he had the address correct. Next, he took the tin from his rucksack and took out the Saint Christopher necklace, which he slipped inside the envelope. Finally, he wrote two quick notes. The first read:

A gift as promised.

I call this "Ophelia." All went pretty much to plan.

Thank you, once again, for your help and advice.

Kind regards, S.B.

P.S. Next already scheduled.

Baker slipped the notes in with the book and placed the jiffy bag next to the door, ready for posting.

For the next few hours he chatted online with fellow members. It was good to catch up. He waited as long as he could before posting a few images and then finally a short video. He ate crackers and cheese and sipped wine while he waited for feedback.

He didn't need to wait long. Within just a few minutes,

the comments began pouring in. He felt a real sense of pride and accomplishment as he began receiving praise.

@dracs: Congrats.

@singlewhitefemale: Well done, buddy

@thegentleman: You one stone killer now

@hannibal: Nu u hd it in u. Smkn

@thementor: Congratulations and Welcome. I will upgrade your account once I verify.

@crucified: Awesome. Bet you're feeling better now. Congrats my friend.

@cody666: Nice. She's hot.

@hannibal: @cody666 u thnk nythng tht mvs is hot

@cody666: FU @hannibal. Least I've got a pair

@hannibal: Wht?

@saucyhorse: Well done. Bet you have a real taste for it now.

@thinkhappythoughts: top work. See you in hell, ha ha

@hannibal: Scrw u @cody666

@admin: @hannibal, @cody666, please remain courteous and professional or you will be asked to leave and blocked from membership.

@hannibal: I aplgs

@cody666: Sorry.

@cody666: That dick @hannibal started it

@miamimurders: Well done you. Go get em.

@thecrow: very well done

@priest: Welcome to the elite

The praise kept coming, and certain members, the usual suspects, scrapped it out like wild dogs. Baker finished off the wine and yawned and stretched. He was still aching, but all in all it had been a pretty perfect day. Tonight he would sleep like a baby.

Before going to bed, Baker went to his rucksack and took out the tin of photographs. He looked around the room and then placed the tin on his bookshelf. Finally, he opened a desk drawer and pulled out his list. He crossed through Katharine's name and put a tick next to the name beneath hers.

CHAPTER TWENTY-SEVEN

When the phone rang in the early hours there was a better than average chance someone was dead. I sat up in bed and fumbled the phone to my ear. It was the station sergeant. Seemed there had been a tip-off. Someone was keen to show off their work. It was rare, but it happened. I wrote down the details before I was even fully awake. I felt dazed; the body count had just jumped again.

I threw on some clothes, brushed my teeth and headed out to the car. I was on my way to a bungalow an hour or so outside London. A little off my usual patch, but the gallery murder and bungalow murder must be linked in some way if the tip-off call was delivered in the same way.

When I arrived, I was introduced to the Thames Valley Serious Crime officers, who had taken control of the murder crime scene; their investigation was already well under way. Press were just setting up and were looking to find out whether this was newsworthy. I spotted some familiar faces. A cameraman from ITV was there; as soon as he spotted me, I knew word would spread this was a murder investigation and a big deal.

I entered the house and was introduced to Detective Inspector Stowell. Our paths had crossed a few times and we'd discussed cases and suspects over the phone on several occasions but never really got to know each other. Considering the circumstances, he seemed in a buoyant mood and was keen to share what he knew so far.

"Housekeeper's name is Mrs Anne Partridge. Around six a.m. she found the body of her employer's daughter. She had come to prepare the house for the return of Mr and Mrs Wells, who are returning from a week in Portugal. Has worked for the family for about nine years. She was pretty hysterical when we got here.

"Dead woman's name is Katharine Wells. She's thirty-three. Lives here with her parents. This is the home of the parents. Parents are Diane and Terry Wells. Mr Wells is a builder who made a fortune renovating and selling properties.

"Mrs Wells was a science teacher for thirty years. Both are retired now. Lucky them. Mr and Mrs Wells have a place in Portugal. They go there regularly, usually at least once a month."

Nice, I thought.

"Katharine stayed behind," Stowell went on, "which she often does, according to the housekeeper. That gives them all some space once in a while. We're waiting to speak to Mr and Mrs Wells to find out whether Katharine couldn't afford to move out of the family home or whether she lives here for another reason, like a relationship break-up.

"Mrs Partridge always topped up the fridge and generally made sure they had a few essentials before they arrived back. She let herself into the house as usual and did her thing. She presumed Katharine was still in bed, so she carried on with a quick tidy-up and check of the rooms, and that's when she found her dead in the bath. At first, she thought Katharine had fallen asleep, but then when she couldn't wake her, she called an ambulance. Paramedics could see straight away death was suspicious from the neck marks. They called us."

He closed his notebook. "Now you know as much as I do."

"When are the parents due back?"

"I had them picked up. They're on their way from the airport right now. Should be here within the hour."

"So, do you mind?"

"Not at all. I'd be interested to see what you think. Go right ahead; she's through there."

We walked through to the bathroom, where Forensics were examining the woman and taking samples.

"Bit crowded in here, detectives," said a voice I recognised. "Thought I heard your voice, Hardy." Hamilton got to her feet and held out her hand. "Guess you're here for the same reason as me. Possibly the same killer as the victim at the gallery?"

"Guess so, Heidi. It's good to see you."

"You two know each other?" said Stowell. "I was wondering why we needed Scotland Yard Forensics here. And this is part of a bigger investigation? Your investigation? Well, that's just great. Don't I feel like the tea boy?" He scowled.

"Listen, it's early," I told him. "We don't know all the facts yet. This incident could be linked or it could be isolated; it's too early to say. All we know right now is that we received an anonymous tip-off similar to one we received about a body found in a London gallery."

"We know this was not suicide, nor was it an accident. We know she was strangled with some sort of cord," said Hamilton, trying to shift the subject back to the here and now. "We also know she's been dead around twenty-four hours. We know she was killed in the bedroom and dragged through to here and put in the bath. We know she fought back. We also know the killer staged the scene."

Stowell handed me a rose petal. "These were scattered in the bath with her."

I stepped carefully into the bathroom to take a closer look. *Such a brutal way to go; she must have been so scared.* "Was that over there when you got here?" I pointed to the shower curtain, which had been folded and placed on the wash basket.

"Yes. We haven't moved anything yet," said Hamilton.

"Scarf?"

"The scarf was added post mortem. Most likely added once she was in the bath."

I looked at Stowell. "Any sign of a break-in?"

"Still working on it," said Stowell.

Hamilton shook her head and shrugged. "I've been in here. Not heard anything about the break-in. I do forensic pathology; I leave broken windows and jimmied doors to you and your friends – no offence."

Stowell looked offended.

"You'll get used to her," I said. "She thinks because she has a microscope at home, she's the only one who does any real detective work around here." I smiled, trying to ease the tension.

"Well, it's true, isn't it? You boys just drink tea and chat all day." Hamilton looked at my face, which was still a little bruised. She winked at me. "Some of you also like to pick fights with bullies."

"Let's leave the Death Detective to her work," I said to Stowell, turning away. "We'll check out the rest of the house."

She wouldn't have admitted it, but I knew Hamilton,

like many of us in the business, used black humour when she was upset; she liked to pretend she was invincible. I'd worked that out a long time ago, and I sensed she was feeling it today. I made a mental note to call her later to see how she was doing. I'd see if she needed some company; perhaps we could finally go for that drink I'd been promising her, be a supportive ear for her. She'd been there enough times for me in the past; it was the least I could do.

I worked my way through the house slowly and methodically. About twenty minutes later, I heard the parents arrive. I stayed away from them for the time being. Left it to Stowell. I would speak to them later. I didn't need to be there when they heard the news no parent ever wants to hear. Right now, I was more use to them doing what I was doing, looking for evidence that would lead to their daughter's killer.

CHAPTER TWENTY-EIGHT

Katharine's parents had given DI Stowell the name of Katharine's best friend. Tara Bishop and Katharine had been friends in school and were still close. Tara's flat was on my way back to London, so I suggested to Stowell I pay her a visit.

The road was full of parked cars, so I parked a few streets away and walked the short distance to 17 Dereham Mews. I rang the doorbell and waited. A face appeared at the window on the second floor. I showed my warrant card. A few moments later a young woman in a dressing gown appeared at the door.

"Hello?"

"I'm Chief Inspector Hardy. Tara Bishop?"

Tara nodded. "What's wrong?"

"Do you mind if we go inside? I need to talk to you, ask a few questions, that sort of thing. Not the sort of thing to be done on a doorstep."

"Let me see your police badge again."

"My warrant card? Of course."

Tara carefully inspected the warrant card, presumably

in her mind satisfying herself it was genuine. I followed her to her one-bedroom apartment, which was warm, if a bit of a mess, with clothes scattered on chairs and some on the floor. She gathered an armful together to reveal an armchair for me.

"Sorry," she said. "No maid service; you know how it is. Tea? I was just making some."

I noted the pile of unclean dishes piled up in the sink and over the worktop. "That's very kind but, no, thank you. I have some bad news."

"My dad, I suppose." Tara began looking at the cups amongst the dirty dishes, checking them to see if she could find one clean enough to use.

"No, not your dad. As far as I am aware, your dad is fine. I'm here about your friend Katharine."

"Katharine. What has she done now? Whatever it is, I can't help. I haven't seen her in a couple of months. Is she all right?" Tara stopped trying to find a clean cup and looked at me. "What is it?"

"I'm afraid not. She was murdered. Possibly yesterday, possibly the day before. We'll know for sure tomorrow morning. Her body was discovered early this morning at her parents' home."

Tara stood and stared at me. For a while she couldn't speak, or at least didn't know what to say. I sat her in the chair she had cleared for me and made her some tea while the news sank in. For some reason, I was tempted to do the washing up but thought better of it. I sat with her and drank tea. A biscuit would have been nice; I was feeling hungry.

I watched her for a while. She looked pale, red around the eyes, but there was no crying. I was keen to get on with the questions but held back. No point pushing her straight away; better to let it sink in, and then the brain can process questions easier. I looked at the clock on the front of the oven; it was nearly six.

"You knew her well – Katharine, I mean? I understand you were school friends."

"Yeah. Best friends since primary school. She used to look after me. I used to get bullied a lot. I was quiet and very shy," Tara explained. "Made me a perfect target."

"I'm sorry."

"I haven't seen her in a while. I moved in here with my boyfriend." She looked around her apartment. "Her work means she sort of vanishes into her world, and for a while she sort of falls off the radar for a bit. Then after a few months she sort of pops back up again and we catch up. Then a few months later it starts all over again."

"What work did she do?"

"Journalist. She was always clever. I lost count of the number of times I wished I could be like her."

"For who? Who did she work for?"

"Nobody and everybody. She does her own investigative journalism; said she was freelance. Just like school, she likes to report on bullies and help the little guy. She's always been a fighter. She exposes all sorts of stuff. Corrupt politicians, dodgy coppers – sorry. Perverts, drug dealers. She's done stuff on how much the armed forces spend on renewing missiles. NHS wastefulness. Charity scams. She's fearless. If she hears about someone who's corrupt or has got away with something, something that Katharine feels she can report on, then she does a video and posts it online. She's got so many followers, millions of followers, all around the world. Look."

Tara called up one of Katharine's videos on her phone and showed me. Right there in front of me was the girl I'd seen lifeless in the bath. Now alive, vibrant and full of indignation.

"Do you know what she was working on recently?"

"No. Like I said I haven't seen her for a few months. Since before the summer, I think. Last I heard she was hanging out with some club owner. She was trying to find out about how freely drugs were available in clubs. She did whatever it took to get the information, if you know what I mean."

"What did she do for money?"

"Parents looked after her. They're loaded. She also made money from her videos somehow. I'm not really sure how. She sold her stories to national papers occasionally. You know, I don't know. I'm just guessing. She told me she'd use whatever it took to, like, get in with the right people. Her dad's money. Herself. Blackmail if she had to.

"I once went to a party with her when we were fifteen. Professional footballers, one of the big clubs. I remember her, like, telling one of them she was only fifteen. This guy was all over her. It was like she couldn't see what he wanted. There were drugs as well, pills of some sort. Some guy was videoing the party. I remember he wanted to get close-ups of us girls. It was creepy.

"I was really uncomfortable, scared. I wanted to leave, and so me and Katharine, we, like, ended up having a screaming match outside. She got me a cab and I left. I was afraid for her. I just wanted my friend with me, safe. I wanted to help her but she kept pushing me away. It was like she was deliberately putting herself in harm's way."

"So, what happened?"

"I went home and told my mum and dad, and I was grounded for months. Of course, I later realised Katharine had sent me home on purpose. She'd got her first story. That's how she started doing what she does – what she did. She told me later she'd done it for a girl at our school who said she'd been raped by two footballers. The footballers said it was consensual. They said they also had no idea she was underage. The girl was too scared to go to the police. She didn't think anyone would believe her story.

"Katharine decided she would do something about it. She put herself in harm's way to get the evidence. She recorded it all. She planned the whole thing. They went to prison but got ridiculously short sentences. But their football careers were over. She also made sure anyone who offered them a job got press clippings in the post. She was a hero, and my best friend."

I left Tara's feeling depressed and exhausted. It seemed to me someone like Katharine would have an endless list of enemies. What would drive someone so young to put herself in harm's way like that? There are plenty of ways to expose corruption and miscarriages of justice. Doing what she did, she must have known it was only a matter of time before someone caught up with her.

CHAPTER TWENTY-NINE

It was late and I was driving home. I was trying to spend as much time as I could at home, but my workload right now was taking big chunks out of each day.

I was thinking how every investigation so quickly becomes personal when my phone rang for what felt like the hundredth time that day. I recognised the number; it was the mayor's office. I was tempted to ignore it but decided to brave it out, so I reluctantly pressed the answer button on the steering wheel.

"Caroline Kemp from the mayor's office. I have the mayor on the line for you."

We had a new mayor, and Caroline Kemp wasn't a name I recognised. I presumed she was his P.A. Broadly speaking, I got on well with the mayor's office. Though I stayed as far away from politics as possible, I recognised things worked best when there was an amicable relationship. The mayor of London was an elected politician, and as each politician came and went, they wanted to leave their mark. As long as that mark wasn't me being left out to dry, I was pretty easy-going.

"I'm driving at the moment, Caroline," I said. "But I'm happy to speak to the mayor. Thank you."

"Inspector Hardy," said a man's voice. "This is Nick Glover. It's good to finally speak to you, though if I'm honest I was hoping it would be under different circumstances. I've heard so many great things about you. You're something of a legend."

I could already sense the political overtones. "Likewise. How can I help, Mayor?" I wasn't in the mood for dancing around. I wouldn't be getting this call unless Mayor Glover had an agenda, and I had a feeling my interests weren't of paramount importance to him at this particular moment.

"Look, the thing is this," started the mayor. "Tourism, as you know, is vital to the economy of London, and to the whole of the UK for that matter. Well, I've just been informed another dead body directly associated with the investigation you're on has been found. So, I suppose what I am saying is that national and international lead stories about London serial killers on the loose do not benefit the capital. I also have it on good authority that a Hollywood film crew has suddenly pulled out of filming in the capital and moved their location to Amsterdam.

"Do you have any idea how much work it has taken our ministers to make London desirable for filming? This crew pulled out, apparently, because the director's new wife was nervous about bringing their new baby into the country while we have a killer on the loose. A bigger concern is how much damage will be done once that story circulates around Hollywood. There's a growing sense of paranoia surrounding these murders."

I interrupted without thinking. "Perhaps you should mention the inconvenience to all the families of the victims."

"I don't need a smart mouth, Inspector. I need results. I

107

need to know you're on top of this. I know you've been successful in the past. Maybe you had a lucky streak, or maybe you have other priorities now. I don't know and I don't care. What I need is someone who can deliver results, and right now I'm not seeing any. So, first, I want to know that you are the right man for the job and second, I want assurance that you are on top of this thing. I need this – *London* needs this resolved, and resolved quickly."

I tried to stay calm but with little success. Our new mayor wasn't out to make friends today; he was on a damage-control mission.

"I thought it impossible," I said, before I could stop myself, "but you're perhaps more of a bloody idiot than our previous mayor. I'm sorry our serial killer hasn't considered the implications for the UK economy before embarking on his killing spree. I'll be sure to take it up with him when the time comes – I'll include it on his list of crimes, shall I?

"Now, Mr. Glover, unless you can convince the killer to hand himself in during your next TV sound-bite, then I'll continue to investigate how I see fit. That means doing my duty for the benefit of the victims and the victims' families.

"I will bring this killer in, and I will ensure the families see this man behind bars for a very long time. I will do all I can to keep citizens safe. What I can't do is second-guess what the killer will do next, and what I won't do is take shortcuts that put more lives at risk.

"So, unless you have valuable information that might lead to an arrest, I suggest you leave me alone to do my job. If you have a problem with me or with any of that, I suggest you speak to my boss. Do you have the number for the chief?"

I was getting increasingly angry, so I pulled the car over and parked. There was silence for a moment. I could hear a slight cough, whispering and a clearing of a throat on an otherwise quiet line. It then dawned on me that, over the noise of driving, I hadn't been able to tell I was on a conference call with any number of people. I had little doubt that Chief Superintendent Webster was part of the meeting. Not that it made any difference. At that moment I didn't care. What I'd said was the truth and how I felt. The prime minister could have been part of the conference call and I wouldn't have changed a word. I'd put myself under enough pressure thanks to the facts, evidence and possibilities floating inside my head every minute of the day without this moron's political agenda thrown into the mix.

Finally, the mayor spoke again. "That won't be necessary. I'll expect an update from Chief Superintendent Webster as soon as there are any more developments. In the meantime, do get this situation under control, and I mean sooner rather than later. Thank you for your time this evening, Inspector."

I wasn't sure what else was said in that room after we rang off, and I didn't care. I was just glad I was being left alone to get on with it.

CHAPTER THIRTY

There was no denying Katharine had made him question whether what he was doing was right. For the first time, he'd felt shaken and disturbed by his course of action. She had gotten to him.

Emotions had crept up on him like a dark shadow, and it had undeniably shocked him. Remorse was something he had not expected to feel. After all, he was the victim in all this, even if he was the only one to see it. Distance and time had helped; it had given him back his perspective and he could once more see his justification in continuing.

He'd also considered the loneliness of other great men who had stood by their convictions when all around them lesser men trembled with uncertainty.

Baker sat in his car and looked up at the house. "I see your children, Detective Chief Inspector Hardy. I see your girlfriend. I don't see you. Where are you this evening?"

He was sketching. He'd drawn a superhero complete with cape, utility belt and a huge "H" on the chest. The superhero was holding a woman in his muscular arms, his cape blowing in the wind. The woman was lifeless; water dripped and rose petals fell from her to be caught and scattered in the same breeze that lifted the hero's cape. Across the top of the page in comic book–style lettering he'd printed,

---

HARDYMAN
 Scotland Yard's Crime Crusader
 Man or Myth?

Then across the bottom he'd written,

Coming to a Cinema Near You Soon

In the background, Baker drew a shadowy, masked villain with bulging muscles and grimacing face. The villain brandished a blood-soaked blade and held aloft a severed head. He stood atop a mountain of skulls. Baker looked up as a car pulled up; it was Hardy arriving home. Baker began speaking to himself in an old-fashioned police constable voice, like he'd seen in black-and-white movies. "Evening, all," he intoned. "What's all this, then? Where do you live? Nine-nine-nine Lets-be Avenue."

Baker watched as Hardy was met at the front door by his excited daughters. The detective chief inspector scooped the girls up in his arms, kissed them and carried them into the house.

Sleep tight, Hardyman. You're going to need your superior Scotland Yard sleuthing senses.

Baker tore the drawing from the pad, signed it, folded it and slipped it into a clear plastic bag. He sealed the bag and got out of the car. Pulling a cap down to disguise his face, he walked over and lifted the windscreen wiper of Hardy's car. He placed the bagged drawing underneath.

There we go, my friend. I'm applying a little extra pressure. Now you know for sure I'm more than one step ahead, and that I also have my eye on you and yours.

CHAPTER THIRTY-ONE

Things had just got very personal. Rayner saw where I was heading and could see from my face something wasn't right. He jumped up from behind his desk and followed close behind me. I knocked once and opened Webster's door without waiting.

"He came to my home last night and tucked this under the windscreen wiper of my car." I placed the clear plastic evidence bag containing the drawing on his desk. "He knows where I live, where my children live."

"Slow down. Who did?" asked Webster. He looked up from his pile of paperwork and motioned for Rayner to come in.

"The Gallery Killer," I said.

"You're sure it's him?" Webster picked up the drawing and began examining it.

"He must be watching you. He must have followed you home," added Rayner from behind me. He shut the door and stood beside me. "I'll run surveillance twenty-four-seven and if he turns up again—'

"We'll do this properly," interrupted Webster. "Where are your family now?"

"They're with my parents. Dad's there and he understands. He's had similar situations in the past, as you know."

"Okay, good," said Webster. "What does this even mean?"

"The drawing itself most likely has very little meaning. The significance comes from the fact the killer is sending us a message. He wants us to know he can reach out and touch us whenever and wherever he wants. I've seen this before. Sometimes for the killer, the focus shifts from killing to communicating, showing whomever he deems worthy that he is smarter than them. It becomes about proving they are inferior beings. Sometimes it can be taunting; sometimes it's cryptic messages. That said, we're jumping ahead of ourselves here. This is a single incident, but it feels as though this is a message along those lines."

Webster looked uncomfortable. "What do you suggest we do about it?"

"Nothing. We let Forensics examine it, but we keep this to ourselves. It may encourage him to send another or communicate in some other way, and if he does then he may make a mistake or create a break in the case in some other way."

Rayner brought our attention back to the present. "I want to be involved in overseeing the safety of Monica, Alice and Faith."

"You're right. That needs to be the priority here," agreed Webster.

I was happy to hear that, and the three of us spent the next hour working out a plan and organising resources to ensure there was a police presence at both houses. It was decided Monica and the girls would remain at my parents' home while I stayed at the family home. We'd run a surveillance team headed by Rayner in case the Gallery Killer came back, which in reality we all felt was unlikely. My instincts told me this was nothing more than the Gallery Killer showing me his superiority and that he could reach at me and my loved ones whenever he chose to.

Eventually we turned our attention back to the drawing. "Can we learn anything from it? Apart from the fact he likes drawing caricatures, of course. He's actually pretty good at it," said Webster.

"He's either mocking me, taunting me or challenging me. At the moment it's too early to say. To have spent time tracking me down shows an interest in the investigation. Otherwise why bother? If he wanted to hurt me or my family, he would have done it. If that was his intention, why warn me like this? Though I'm concerned, I don't think harming us was his true intention. At the moment, my instincts tell me he's challenging me, trying to show me how smart he is. If he wanted to taunt me or mock me, he could simply have done that at the murder scene, so everyone could see. No, I think that, in his mind, he's starting a game of cat and mouse."

The room was awkwardly silent for a moment while we all considered the facts. "I'll get this down to the prints lab and forensic team to see if anything turns up," I said finally.

"Is there anything else you need, Hardy?" said Webster.

"I need space and time, that's all."

"Sorry about the mayor. I'll keep him off your back as long as I can. He's new in the job and has found himself under pressure from Downing Street. He'll calm down, or something else big will come along and he'll find himself wrapped up in that. You know how it goes."

I nodded appreciatively. Rayner looked my way and wondered what he'd missed, but he knew better than to ask and find himself unnecessarily drawn into police politics.

Webster didn't waste any time. He dispatched officers to my house and my parents' place. I requested more be posted at my parents' home since all I needed was surveillance; I saw no point in using the limited manpower guarding my home, which would mostly be empty while I worked. It was Alice, Faith, Monica and my parents I wanted to protect.

As soon as I was out of the office I got on the phone and called in a favour from a buddy of my brother. Frank Brown was ex–British army, intelligence corps. He and my brother had been at school together and had joined the Royal Marines at the same time. My brother was still serving. When Frank had decided to leave after a bad fall during a night-time training exercise, he set up a company in the private sector. He was now in demand installing state-of-the-art security systems and supplying highly trained and disciplined security guards and bodyguards to the rich and famous.

By the end of the day, Frank had personally surveyed both homes and his team had installed security systems, run penetration tests and supplied location-tracking devices. Frank even offered manpower in the form of an ex–SAS service team, which for the time being I declined.

Once the team had gone, I went over to Mum and Dad's. Mum was in her kitchen baking with Alice and Faith, trying to portray a sense of life going on as normal. Rayner was in the kitchen too, and, much to the delight of the girls, had become their "royal taster." After one last cookie and another theatrical poisoning to amuse the girls, he winked at me and prepared to make his escape. He turned to Alice and Faith.

"Time to go see my Jenny. She'll be wondering where I am, and I don't want her forgetting my name, now, do I?" Rayner hugged the girls and gave Mum a kiss, and I walked him out.

"It's going to be fine," said Rayner.

"I've got a bad feeling about this one," I said once we were out of earshot. "I just don't understand it. I must be missing something. Why bother coming at me? Why take that chance? It's like poking a hornet's nest. You don't do it unless you're crazy."

CHAPTER THIRTY-TWO

I found Monica in the upstairs bathroom. I could see she was upset, although she was pretending she wasn't. We talked for a while, and I explained everything was under control and that we were probably now the safest family, after the Royal Family, in London.

"Will you teach me to shoot a gun?" she said out of the blue. I knew where she was coming from, but all the same her request took me by surprise. She was perched on the edge of the bathtub and I took her hand.

"You don't need a gun," I assured her. "We have officers outside and a state-of-the-art security system. You have all that so that you don't need a gun. I or Rayner or a fellow officer will be around to do the school run."

I was concerned Monica's life was becoming overly complicated, so I took the opportunity to say a few things that had been on my mind for a while. "To a certain degree, Helena knew what she was getting when she married me. She knew the type of work I do. I was very clear about that."

"What are you saying, James? I don't understand."

"You've found yourself mixed up in my life, in part because you needed a refuge from Scott, which was fine; just like Helena was, I'm here to support you one hundred percent. But now it seems that refuge might not look so safe.

"You're mixed up in all my problems, and it wasn't what you bargained for. We love having you with us. The children adore you and love you, and I honestly wonder how I would have coped without you. You've been so generous and kind. You've done more than you ever needed to or should have. Since losing Helena, it has worked well for us both. It's just . . . I don't want you feeling you *have* to stay. I also don't want you to feel that I'm taking advantage of your kindness."

Monica sat looking at me, an inscrutable expression on her face, but said nothing. I pressed on.

"What I am saying is I'd understand if you wanted to get as far away from all this as you can. I'd figure something out. I know my parents would help out with the girls. Maybe you'd feel happier staying with one of your girlfriends or even back with your parents? Somewhere less complicated."

My voice trailed off, and I waited to see what she would say.

"Are you asking me to leave?" Monica looked heartbroken and her eyes filled with tears.

"No, no, no!" I said, putting a hand on her arm. "Stop – don't cry. Oh please, I'm sorry. I just wonder whether you'll ever be able to move on with your life when you're mixed up in all the dramas of mine. I'm not asking you to leave – you must understand that. I'm just saying you don't need to be mixed up in all this. You're free to leave anytime you feel less than safe. Please don't feel you have a responsibility to us; we'll cope without you somehow." I paused, searching for words and feeling a complete idiot. "I mean, all the time you're here I feel responsible for you as well as Alice and Faith."

I knew immediately I'd said it all wrong. This was one of those moments I wanted to rewind and start over, but in real life that just didn't happen.

Monica pushed past me and went to her room. The slammed door sent a clear message. I buried my face in my hands, cursing my idiocy. *Damn it.* As I came out of the bathroom, I met Mum, Alice and Faith at the top of the stairs.

"I suppose you heard all that?" I said. From their expressions I had little doubt they had.

My daughters looked at me stony-faced, and Mum looked ready to strangle me.

"Sometimes, James Hardy, you're a bloody fool, a bloody fool who cannot see a good thing even when it's right under his nose. Get yourself downstairs. I'll speak to Monica."

Alice crossed her arms and little Faith rolled her eyes at me and tutted.

CHAPTER THIRTY-THREE

"He's not in any sort of trouble, is he? He's a good boy. Very bright. Extremely bright. Always has been. He's always on his computer. He tells me he's being good, but I don't know. I mean, I trust him. We both do. But you know how fifteen-year-old boys can be. All that . . . you know, testosterone," said Mrs Rose, looking at her husband for reassurance.

"Oh, yes," said Mr Rose. "I'm pretty sure we'd know if he was up to no good. Not that I know one end of a computer from another. Never used that Facebook or the other one, Twitter. Obviously, I've heard about them but I haven't used them myself. Don't see the point. But Joshy, well, he's an expert at all that stuff. Isn't he, love?"

Before Mrs Rose could continue, I interjected. "He contacted us. I gather he has some information, and so, as far as I am aware, he isn't in any trouble. I shouldn't worry too much, for now."

Mr and Mrs Rose shifted uneasily.

"I see," said Mr Rose. "Well, best you just ignore us. Bit out of touch."

"Joshy, love," called out Mrs Rose. "Joshy, love, are you there? There's an Inspector Hardy here to see you."

"He's a detective chief inspector, love," corrected Mr Rose.

Mrs Rose looked at me apologetically. "Detective Chief Inspector Hardy," called Mrs Rose again, this time with anger and frustration in her voice.

"Okay, okay, keep your hair on. Just give me two minutes, all right?" Josh called back. Mr and Mrs Rose looked awkwardly at each other and then at me.

"Tea, Inspector? I've got some fruitcake as well, if you'd like some?"

"That would be lovely, thank you. Tea, milk, no sugar," I said, more to ease the awkwardness than anything.

Josh appeared at the top of the stairs in black socks, grey jogging trousers and a 'Muse' t-shirt. "Come up, then," he said, disappearing back into his room as quickly as he had appeared.

Mr Rose smiled apologetically. "First on right."

"Perhaps you'd accompany me? Josh is a minor, so it would be best if one of his parents is with him."

I was expecting Josh Rose's bedroom to be a complete mess, but I was pleasantly surprised. The room was neat and tidy, and I didn't get the feeling his mother had just tidied it. Instead, it seemed Josh liked order. Mr Rose sat on the bed behind us. A chair was waiting for me, so I introduced myself and sat beside Josh in front of his computer and three display monitors. On the desk were other devices, all of which were neatly arranged.

"I got your message, Josh," I said. "I am assuming you have something you want to share with me."

Josh stopped typing. Closed all the windows on his screens and leaned back in his chair. He was appraising me. Satisfied, he looked at his father and then back at me.

"So, like, I know what I'm doing isn't strictly legal. I'm, like, also aware that Scotland Yard can't trace what I'm doing or where I've been," he started.

"For the love of God," said Mr Rose. "You told your mother and me that you weren't doing anything illegal. You haven't hacked into the Pentagon or the FBI, have you? You haven't joined that Nigel Farage at WikiLeaks, have you?"

"Shut up, Dad. You sound like an idiot. Farage is nothing to do with WikiLeaks."

Mr Rose grumbled, folded his arms and crossed his legs, then uncrossed his legs and sat there with a worried expression on his face, probably fretting about what was going to come out of his son's mouth next.

"Ignore him," Josh told me. "He's just worried how Mum will take the news if their son is wanted by the US government. I mean," he added sarcastically, "who would feed the cat if they had to spend time visiting their son in a high-security prison in the United States? And imagine the pointing and behind-the-hand whispering at church."

Mr Rose bit his tongue and shifted uneasily.

Josh turned to me and continued. "Before I tell you anything, I want you to listen and understand."

"Okay, that sounds fair. The least I can do is listen," I said. Josh appraised me again, perhaps feeling that was a little too easy. "I'm under the impression you can help me," I offered with a friendly smile. "I'm all ears."

"Right. So, like, I belong to a small, elite community that specialises in policing the internet. We go after serious crime. There is too much regular crime, so we pinpoint the top one percent of potential cyber criminals or other criminal activity we can access online. We visit places that are supposed to be impenetrable and take a look. We're like the online equivalent of the SAS. We go in, gather intel and get out fast. Sometimes there's a bit of a firefight while we cover our tracks. Usually, though, it's boring and nobody knows we were ever there. When we find something of significance, we pass it on. You following so far?" asked Josh.

Mr Rose mumbled something inaudible about privacy laws. I nodded and made a mental note to ask Josh later who he passed his information on to.

"Anyway, I'm checking out this one guy in New Zealand. No reason to go into why exactly. I'm running some data through this software I've written that saves me, like, hours. So, I'm waiting for it to do its thing and I'm, like, looking at a few large cash deposits, and that leads me to this dude's browsing habits. And I come across this secure site this guy's a member of. Right? Got it?"

"Yes," I said. Though in reality I was not sure why Josh had asked for me or where this was going. "Please carry on."

Josh turned to his monitors and began typing. In a few seconds he had a website up and continued talking, some of which I actually understood. "Look, Inspector Hardy, I see all sorts of crazy stuff online. Most of it I'm not interested in, even though those involved definitely need locking up. Online, right now, it's like the Wild West. The Wild West but without any lawmen to stand up and fight. Mainly because governments don't know what's going on, or don't have the skill set or resources to fight back, and also because just like the Wild West, the internet is one vast, untamed wilderness. Instead they fight fires and make noise about doing something. In my opinion, they need a tactical approach and need to grasp the magnitude of what is going on and do something before cybercrime is too unwieldy to tackle.

"Anyway, my team and I are just getting on with doing what we can ourselves. We usually expose mega stuff, nothing on a personal level. By that I mean we're not interested in low-level scams. We're exposing high-profile stuff; best I don't go into detail. Anyway, this time I wanted to tell someone about a low-level thing I saw. When I show you, you'll understand. I know you will."

Josh was now trying to get into a secure page. He began tutting and sucking his teeth. "Updated the security a little. Pathetic. That all you got? Okay, so I'll just . . . Here we go." I watched as Josh's fingers flew across the keys. On the screen, windows opened and closed. At last, he allowed himself a small smile and turned to me. "Right, so, check this out. Boom! Here we go, Inspector."

I looked at one of the three screens in front of me and began reading. Josh was all smiles and really animated, rocking back and forth in his chair while sipping from a can of Dr Pepper.

"What you have here, Inspector Hardy, is what I believe is an online community of stone-cold killers. Look here." Josh pointed to a line of text on the screen. "This dude is bragging. All looks genuine to me. Well, I wouldn't be wasting your time if it didn't."

There were pictures, videos, posts, comments and even reviews all apparently related to murders. Whether these were old cases or even genuine I couldn't tell. Then Josh opened up a window that changed everything. He slid the window over to the screen nearest me.

"And this is why I asked for you," he said.

In front of me was a series of pictures of Toby Fielding, a montage showing him first tied to a chair and then a sequence of images showing the gradual progress of his being tortured, until finally his lifeless body lay contorted and bloodied. Josh pointed to a final image and looked at me with a huge grin.

I groaned audibly as I realised the very last picture was of me talking to Rayner right before he and I entered the gallery on Old Potter Street.

CHAPTER THIRTY-FOUR

Vlad eyed the fat man. He'd always disliked him but tolerated him because it was good for business. Now, despite the benefits, he could no longer do even that.

His demands, his negotiations, the way he filled a chair, the way he stuffed his fat face, his constant sweating, his stupid German accent. Most of all he despised the way the fat man demanded Albanian women.

Vlad realised this was nothing to do with the fat man's taste in women. He doubted he really had a preference at all. No, Vlad had come to realise it was purely the fat man's way of disrespecting him. Demanding and using girls from Vlad's own birthplace was purely symbolic. It was the fat man's way of saying, "I'll take what I like and there is nothing you can do about it."

Vlad felt himself blaze with fury, but he kept it in check. He'd often imagined gutting the fat man. The way he'd seen his father gut a pig when he was boy. Hung from the ceiling by his ankles, throat and belly sliced open with the intestines removed. Blood gushing and then draining into a bucket. That day couldn't come soon enough.

With an effort, Vlad pulled his mind back to the room. Behind the glass wall, the doors opened and the women filed in one by one and began to line up in front of them. With today's more serious business out of the way, it was now time for the final part of the transaction. The metaphorical cherry on the fat man's enormous cake.

Vlad watched the fat man ease his huge bulk forward to get a closer look. He watched him moisten his thin red lips and narrow his piggy eyes. Each girl carried a number. The fat man read some stapled pages, which contained a brief description of each girl. Height, weight, age, colouring, nationality, fictitious history and sexual preferences. One of Vlad's managers had filled out the descriptions, which were full of creative writing to make the women seem a little more exotic.

The fat man compared each woman with the notes. His breathing became louder, and Vlad watched him as he dabbed his bloated face with an embroidered handkerchief.

After some consideration, the fat man circled the numbers of the girls he wanted and passed the sheet to Vlad. He thanked Vlad for his hospitality and repeated how much he enjoyed their working together.

Without another word, the fat man heaved himself out of his chair and, leaning heavily on a cane, left the room. Once outside the room the fat man was greeted by his aide and bodyguard, Hans Vogt.

Vlad tossed the papers across the room and poured himself a large whiskey. Alberto entered the room and stood beside his boss.

"Everything okay with the German?" he asked.

"I never want to do business with that—" Vlad stopped speaking, walked over to the glass and began watching girl number eight. He picked up the papers he'd thrown across the room and looked at the numbers the fat man had circled.

"We're not sending the German any more girls. It's over," instructed Vlad.

"Are you sure?" asked Alberto. "You know what it will mean."

Vlad walked over to Alberto and stood directly in front of him. Alberto didn't flinch but looked his boss squarely in the eye. "I am sure, my friend. It's time to make the fat German pig squeal for the last time."

"Okay. When do you want me to do it?" asked Alberto

Vlad walked back to the glass and looked at girl number eight. She had removed the heavy earrings and dropped her number on the floor and was now unfastening her uncomfortable high heels. The girls either side of her had stepped away to distance themselves. Vlad smiled as he watched. "I'm going to do it. You can sit this one out."

They stood together in silence for a few moments watching girl number eight.

"Alberto, my friend," said Vlad at length, "I am going to shake things up. Make sure the men – you know. Just keep them on their toes."

"What about Papa?" said Alberto.

"I will talk to Papa. It's time we found a new route through Europe. He'll understand."

Alberto wasn't so sure. "The German's demands are eating into our profits, and, on top of that, German border security is so high these days it's almost impossible to move anything of any size, so now would definitely be a good time to make alternative arrangements."

"My thoughts exactly, brother," said Vlad. He squeezed Alberto's shoulder. "My thoughts exactly."

"That's Anya?" said Alberto, turning his attention back to girl number eight. "I'm not sure how she ended up in the room." The two men laughed as they watched her. She was now sitting on the floor rubbing her feet.

"Have you found out anything more about her?"

"Not really. Nothing more than we already knew. I'll keep digging." Alberto went to leave the room. As he opened the door Vlad spoke to him over his shoulder.

"Leave Anya in the room. Ask all the other girls to come out and just leave Anya in there. I want to watch her for a while. She makes me laugh."

Vlad poured himself a drink and pulled his chair closer to the glass. He smiled as the girls were pulled out of the room and Anya was forced to remain behind. She began protesting, swearing and hitting and kicking the door, and then she turned her attention to the one-way mirror wall and whacked it over and over with the heel of her shoe.

"Let me out," she yelled at the mirror. "I know you're there. Let me out of here – now!"

Fearless when she wants to be, thought Vlad. He sipped his whiskey and wondered what to do with her.

CHAPTER THIRTY-FIVE

Orel watched Papa sitting on his favourite bench near the small patch of green opposite the restaurant. The old man was doing nothing more than people watching and enjoying a warm summer day. In a month or two, a bitter north wind would arrive and the warmth of summer would be gone.

Papa threw a few pieces of bread for the squirrel he'd named Boris. Somehow Boris seemed a fitting name for the little chap.

Orel sat down next to the old man and watched as he talked to the squirrel and threw bread.

"He recognises you. I think you have a friend," said Orel.

"No. He only recognises that I offer free food. He's an opportunist."

Papa threw the last of the bread and the squirrel took it. Then, as quickly as he had arrived, he was gone.

"What news?" asked Papa.

Orel looked around the park before speaking. "I heard

the meeting went well. Our German friend is happy. A shipment will arrive as usual in a few weeks."

"Good. That's good."

"Klaus said he hopes that you and he will catch up the next time he is in London. He says it has been far too long. He would like to thank you in person. He suggests dinner."

"I hope you politely made my excuses?"

"Yes. I thanked him and explained you have handed all business affairs to Vlad. That you are retired and that I would pass on his kind offer."

"Good. Thank you," said Papa. He sat silently for a few minutes enjoying the warmth of the sun on his face. Finally, his eyes still closed, he asked, "What else?"

Orel sighed and paused before finally answering. "Another girl." He watched the old man's hands flinch imperceptibly. "I'm sorry," he said.

"Are you positive it was him?" asked Papa.

"Yes. It happened the same way as the others." Orel squeezed the old man's arm fondly. "I'm sorry, Papa, truly."

He gave Papa's arm a final squeeze, then got to his feet and left the old man alone.

Only Papa could instigate what had to be done, and so he could now only wait for Papa's word. In reality, there was no decision left to be made. It was now just a matter of when and how it should be done.

CHAPTER THIRTY-SIX

Vlad parked a few streets away and walked the short distance to the Carrington Grande Hotel. He sang softly to himself as he smoked and walked. He felt good. Anya made him happy, and finally he was going to do something about Klaus the fat German. He'd heard some music on the radio in the car on the way to the hotel and he hummed the tune that was still swimming in his head. He wasn't sure what the words were, but he liked the melody.

He went around the back of the Carrington Grande, where he'd arranged to be let in by a waiter who knew who Vlad was and knew not to refuse. As he rounded the corner, the waiter was standing by the door smoking. He was talking to a big man who was also smoking.

Vlad instantly recognised the big man as Hans Vogt, Klaus's bodyguard. Vogt turned as he approached, and at first he looked confused, as though he was seeing a face that was out of context.

By the time Vogt registered whose face it was, then answered the question of why Vlad might be at the rear of the Carrington Grande Hotel at such an hour, it was too late. Vogt hadn't even the time to reach into his jacket for his weapon before a bullet struck his chest, followed by another to his head. *Boom. Boom. Down you go.*

Vlad winked at the young waiter, put a finger to his lips and then ran it across his throat. The young, wide-eyed waiter nodded emphatically and held out a key card.

Vlad breezed past him and moved quickly through the hotel. He was excited; he was buzzing now. He took the stairs two at a time and hurried along the corridor looking for the room. Seeing the room number on the door, he paused to savour the moment before slipping in the key card. *Click, click* – Vlad was in, and what he saw was better than he'd hoped for.

To his left a woman sat at a table bent over a line of cocaine. She laughed excitedly, clearly off her head and thinking this was part of the evening's entertainment. Vlad closed the door behind him and shot the woman once in the back and then once in the head. She slumped forward onto the table.

A skinny young black man and Klaus were on the bed. The skinny black man was straddling Klaus with his back to the door. He turned his head to look over his shoulder. Vlad put two bullets in the young man and watched as he collapsed face first onto Klaus's chest.

Vlad walked over to the bed with a wide smile on his face. The fat man's arrogance had evaporated. He struggled to a sitting position, shoving the black man's body off him with difficulty.

"Guten Abend, Klaus," said Vlad in a low voice. "I'm here to formally end our business association."

Klaus gave him a look of utter contempt. "Are you crazy? Who do you think you are? My agreement is with Papa. Only Papa can do that. Now get out of here." Klaus grunted and swung his feet over the side of the bed. "Our arrangement is extremely profitable for all of us. So what is your problem?"

Vlad fired once at the fat man's huge stomach. "Whoops," said Vlad.

Klaus looked at Vlad in total disbelief.

"Are you mad? You shot me," he screamed. He clamped a meaty paw over the hole. "Do you know what my people will do to you? To all of you? Let's be reasonable before this gets out of hand. Call me an ambulance immediately and perhaps we can consider this a misunderstanding. Then at some point we can all sit around a table and renegotiate our business arrangements, if that's your problem."

Vlad fired two more shots. Once in the chest and once in the head. He walked over to a lifeless Klaus and put his ear to the dead man's mouth.

"Oops, sorry. Were you saying something? I may have missed the last part; would you like to repeat it? I'm all ears, so when you're ready . . . What? You can't? Oh, I see – because you're dead. Well, that's rather rude of you. Now I'll never know what you were mumbling about and I'll be left wondering for at least a nanosecond, you grotesque piece of filth."

Vlad felt a little disappointed it was all over so quickly. He would have liked to spend some time on Klaus, but he was consoled by the fact he had important plans that needed his focus. By the time he was back in his car heading home through the late-night traffic, he was singing again and thinking about Anya and how life hadn't felt this good for a very long time.

CHAPTER THIRTY-SEVEN

Baker stroked his beard; he was proud of his beard. Mother hated it, of course. Despite the beard and his fake press badge, he was still reluctant to get too close. These days he hardly recognised himself when he looked in the mirror, so it was unlikely the dear inspector would remember him – that was, if he had any recollection of him at all.

He hoped Hardy *would* remember him, though, and that in time it would all mean something significant. He'd hate to think his was just another case that had now been locked away in a dusty filing cabinet. That could not be allowed to happen.

How their lives were interconnected was important. The chief inspector had been busy during the preceding years, undoubtedly dealing with a lot of cases, so, if need be, Baker would generously remind him of their first encounter. A lot of time had passed, and a lot had changed for the both of them.

Back when they'd first met, Baker had been unprepared and unaware the police were observing him; in retrospect that had been sloppy and foolish. Today, though, he would reacquaint himself with the man trying to catch him. "Know Thine Enemy," he thought to himself.

Observing his adversary was something he should have done at the outset. After all, this was all new territory. All of this was constantly evolving. He'd decided that understanding Hardy would be a big part of his own success.

And if he ever came to write a book explaining his side of the story and why he had embarked on his reign of vengeance, then knowing as much as he could about the lead detective in the investigation would definitely offer his audience a more rounded and satisfying account.

Of course, understanding how Hardy's mind worked would make it easier to impress him – and hopefully even surprise him. That would be fun.

He stroked his beard again and turned his attention back to the activity unfolding in front of him. Watching the inspector in the dark on a busy street or with a telephoto lens from a safe distance was one thing, but watching him just metres away and in broad daylight was very much another. Thus, Baker had decided that today it was safer to follow Hardy to a crime scene not of his own making.

A man standing next to him told him that the victim was a young woman, probably a prostitute. Probably one of those Eastern European girls, he'd murmured, tutting.

The man went on to say, in some detail, how he'd heard the girl had been left semi-naked and dumped behind the supermarket. Apparently stabbed repeatedly by a maniac. More than likely abused sexually – the man lowered his voice conspiratorially at the word – for hours as well.

Baker was intrigued by how well informed the man was and was tempted to ask how he knew all he did. He thought better of it, however. Instead, he nodded, thanked the man for his insights and slowly moved away. Interesting as it all was, Baker's priority was to learn about Inspector Hardy and not the dead girl. He took up a post on the other side of the crime scene, at a discreet distance, and turned his attention back to Hardy. He found it fascinating to see how Hardy behaved – his mannerisms, the way he held himself with such an easy air of authority.

He's tall and athletic, Baker noted. He looks young, possibly early forties. Certainly well respected – I can see that by the way he interacts with fellow officers and the forensic team.

He mentally noted how Hardy approached the victim and familiarised himself with the crime scene. How the inspector pointed, made notes, and exchanged observations with the other scene-of-crime officers.

Fascinating, Baker thought, nearly hugging himself.

Baker laughed out loud as he watched Hardy take a photo of the victim on his phone. *This is so beautiful*, he thought. *If he's taking so much care over some dead nobody, just imagine how relieved he must feel to work on something extraordinary like my case. What a privilege it must be for him to work on an investigation that is so far from mundane.*

As he watched Hardy working, Baker felt almost part of the scene, a member of the team, as it were. Certainly, he was justified in his research here, in the care he was taking to observe Hardy closely: this would ensure the inspector was portrayed as accurately as possible when he began to write. Seeing the inspector at work today, he knew that Hardy's investigation would give his case some real gravitas when the truth finally came out. They would both certainly be remembered, both Hardy and himself. Baker knew what he was doing would be considered historic. He himself might divide public opinion, of course – that was inevitable in the case of any historic figure – but a large number would understand and know what he had done was understandable under the circumstances.

Perhaps in time Hardy, too, would realise that the investigation into the Gallery Killer was a gift, and that both he and Baker were forever bound by it, not unlike Inspector Reid and Jack the Ripper, Ted Bundy and Detective Keppel. Those killers were different from him, of course; their murders had served no obvious purpose and had clearly been the products of diseased minds. He, Baker, on the other hand, had clear motivation. Wrongly convicted men deserved justice.

He was startled out of his reverie when a shiny black 4x4 pulled up in front of him, completely blocking his view. *Some rich bitch, probably*. Annoyed, Baker tapped on the window and waved his arms angrily to indicate the driver should move along.

A tinted window slowly lowered to reveal the driver. Baker immediately regretted his decision. This wasn't some rich bitch; instead, a nasty-looking man stared unblinkingly at him. Tattoos on his hands and up his neck. The man smiled and revealed his bad teeth.

A second window lowered at the back of the vehicle. This man had similar tattoos and his eyes looked black, black like a shark's eyes. Baker could see the man was going to say something. *Please don't speak, please don't speak*, he thought uneasily. *Just move along*.

"Hey, little man, what are you looking at?" said Shark Eyes.

Baker hesitated. He sounded and looked like Russian mafia. *Trust me to tap on the wrong window.* "Nothing," said Baker apologetically. "I think someone has been killed. A woman."

"That is so sad." Shark Eyes rubbed his cheek with a

gun. "Perhaps that dead person tapped on the wrong window. When you don't know who's inside, it is a very dangerous thing to do. Inside, it could be a lamb, or it could be a wolf who will gobble you up. You just never know until it is too late. Run along, little man, or you might get eaten alive."

Baker turned and started walking. Behind him he could hear the men laughing as the vehicle accelerated away. He felt sick. Now his day was spoiled. He could feel anger rising up inside him. His chest felt like it might explode. It needed release. *Damn it*, he fumed, *and damn them*. His anger had been simmering, and now this confrontation had caused it to boil over.

He thrust his hands into his pockets and clenched his fists. Someone needed to pay. Now, immediately. He ran down the list in his mind. He picked a name at random and at once felt the anger simmer down, only slightly, as though someone had adjusted a flame. He looked back across the street at the inspector and saw he was on his phone.

Baker pressed on through the busy London streets. There was work to be done.

CHAPTER THIRTY-EIGHT

I arrived at the autopsy of Toby Fielding more than a little late; Heidi Hamilton had finished with the body, and to some degree I was relieved. She was engrossed in writing her final reports for the day.

I liked Hamilton and had worked with her for years. I remembered her as a student, and now she was one of Scotland Yard's finest forensic pathologists. She'd been given the nickname Death Detective, which I know annoyed her; it struck her as being ghoulish. She was all about the science, the care for the deceased and uncovering the truth of why they had ended up in front of her. In that way, we had something in common.

As I approached, I apologised for missing the appointment. If she was bothered, she didn't say anything. We were all under pressure and priorities could change in an instant, so we knew when to give one another some slack.

"I ran the toxicology first thing to get a head start," said Hamilton without looking up. "It came back clean.

Toby Fielding wasn't drugged. If he had been, it might have been a blessing in some ways. Poor boy."

I knew Hamilton well enough to know that was a starter and she was about to deliver the main course. She turned my way. "You look like hell," she said. "When did you last sleep?"

I shrugged and for some reason felt the need to straighten my tie.

"Toby Fielding was tortured at length and died from blood loss. Whoever did this to him wanted to inflict maximum suffering." Hamilton opened some pictures on her monitor. She pointed to areas of his body on the screen as she spoke. Marks on the wrists and ankles and multiple marks on the torso.

"Toby Fielding was tasered. He had his feet bound with a cable tie and his hands bound behind his back, again with cable ties. Then your murderer used a varied selection of instruments to inflict suffering and pain by burning, cutting, puncturing, stabbing and drilling. So far, I've counted at least thirteen different instruments used, which include different-sized screwdrivers, a scalpel, three different knives, including a kitchen knife and a serrated-edged knife, and an electrical drill.

"He also has multiple rib fractures and broken bones, which were most likely sustained from repeated hammer blows. You get the idea. I'll list them in the report when I finish analysing them. In short, it looks like you've found yourself another hardcore stone-cold killer. I really don't know how you manage it."

"I'm just lucky that way, I guess." Neither of us smiled. "Cause of death?"

"At this point I would say traumatic pneumothorax – his lung collapsed – from one of the puncture wounds. But there was so much trauma and blood loss that any number of factors contributed."

This guy really went to town, I thought. *He must feel a lot of anger to have done all this.* Perhaps the murderer was after answers? Or simply enjoyed torturing for kicks. Or maybe this was staged to look like a maniac had gone to town on the victim; perhaps it was a red herring.

Working back-to-back murder cases now, I had my work cut out. I had already had more than my share of moments where I felt at breaking point, and I knew there were more to come. No matter how much I tried to distance myself from a given case, I eventually came back to doubting my ability to deliver answers. When investigations were so high-profile and under such scrutiny, there was intense pressure to give everyone answers, or to at least make it look like an investigation has progressed.

I thanked Hamilton for her time and went to my own office.

CHAPTER THIRTY-NINE

Matt Swift woke with a jolt. His head was swimming. He looked around, trying to piece together where he was and what was going on.

Adrenaline flooded his body as an intense fear came over him, which quickly cleared his head. He was in his bedroom. He had been stripped of his clothes and tied to the bed. He could hear someone moving in one of the other rooms.

Maybe it's Patsy, he thought desperately.

He looked at the clock on the side table. Sunday. *No, she's still away.* He could hear humming. *It's a man?*

The kettle clicked on and Swift heard the tinkle as a spoon went into a cup. He pulled at the ropes. The bed creaked. The humming stopped. He heard footsteps. A bearded man in glasses appeared at the door.

"What's going on? Who are you?" yelled Swift.

"Hello, sleeping beauty. We'll get to why I am here in good time, Matthew. Now, I'm making tea. I would offer you a cup, but I see you're a bit tied up at the moment." The bearded man laughed at his little joke. Then, unable to hide his unease, he said, "Oh, dear, let me cover that." He took a shirt from the wardrobe and threw it over Swift's private parts. "There, that's better. I don't want to see all that right before I drink my tea. Now, you were saying?"

"What is this? Who are you?"

"Me? Oh, I'm one of your sensational tabloid stories come back to haunt you. I'm here to tell you that you do have a responsibility to get your facts right. A front-page scoop destroyed my life. No amount of apologising can alter that.

"I've been visiting some of those responsible. You may have read about some of them in your newspapers. Now, I don't want to go over the details of what happened during my encounters, but between you and me let's just say by the end they were pretty cut up about it all."

He smiled again. "Gosh, another pun. Sorry, one moment – it sounds like the kettle has finished boiling. Excuse me while I see to it; I always like to use boiling water on the tea bag."

The bearded man left and went back to the kitchen. A few seconds later he reappeared and grabbed a briefcase from a chair just inside the bedroom door. It made a clanking sound, and Matthew's eyes widened as he stared at it.

"This?" said the bearded man, raising the case slightly. "Just a few tools for our little adventure together. Don't worry; I cleaned off the blood and muscle tissue from last time. We don't want germs, do we? Right. Won't be long. Just going to drink my tea. Then we can get on with organising the horror show for when your darling Patsy returns from her conference on Monday night."

The bearded man left and shut the bedroom door behind him.

Swift closed his eyes. He focused on staying calm. *Don't*

panic. He tensed his muscles and began to pull on the ropes. He pulled on all of them together and then each one in turn and then finally focused on just one. He wrapped his hand around the rope tied to his right wrist and pulled with everything he had. The post began to move. He pulled again and again in short bursts.

Beside the bed the phone rang and startled him. He froze and listened to the message being left on the answerphone.

"Matty, where are you, man? We're all at the bar. Footy is starting. You'd better not be hung over. The Jackster is coming over. He'll pick you up in about ten minutes. You really are a muppet. See you in a bit, mate."

Swift stared at the door, which he expected to burst open at any second. He frantically began pulling at the rope with renewed energy. The bedpost creaked some more and then cracked. The bed jolted as the leg slid out. Matt began to scream and shout for help. He could hear movement outside the door. A chair fell over. A cupboard closed. Then the front door opened and slammed shut. Silence.

Matt stopped pulling for a moment and held his breath. *Has he gone?* he thought. *Is it over?*

CHAPTER FORTY

Matt Swift was treated for shock then quickly given the all-clear. He was a lucky man, if luck was the right word to use after his ordeal.

His brush with death, because he was a journalist, didn't appear to dampen his enthusiasm to dish up his own story now to his fellow journalists. He relished the limelight and knew the score; there was only going to be a small window of opportunity for him to cash in.

So he was happy to talk to us, and even happier to be part of his own media circus. Not that I wished it on him, of course, but I wondered whether his revelations might in the end come back to bite him.

My other concern was that the forthcoming front-page stories would give his attempted killer yet more attention.

"He had glasses and a beard, but it was him," insisted Swift as he slid the photo back across the table to me.

"The man in your apartment was this man, Simon Baker?" I repeated.

"Yes, definitely. I recognised him. And he told me as much himself. And it makes sense. I wrote front-page stories on him when he was arrested for keeping his wife as a slave in an underground dungeon." I raised my eyebrows at that, but said nothing. "He now wants payback; he told me that, too. You need to arrest him now." Suddenly the gravity of the situation seemed to dawn on him, and his voice rose. "Why isn't he already locked up? I need to speak to Patsy again – I need to make sure she's safe."

"Officers are with her. She's fine. It's unfortunate you can't remember how you came to be tied to the bed by Simon Baker – if indeed it was Simon Baker."

"I told you, I went to sleep around midnight – alone. There was no outrageous party, no drugs, no alcohol bingeing, Inspector Hardy. I woke up tied to the bed. He must have drugged me somehow. Otherwise, I would have woken up, right?"

Traces of a sedative had been found in Swift's blood, but I didn't need to mention that to him at this point; best to keep some information back. I sensed he was holding back some facts of his own for journalistic and financial gain, so this interview had become more like a game of chess. Difficult to help someone who doesn't want to help themselves. Swift looked restless.

"We're nearly done for now, Mr Swift. So how do you suppose he got into your apartment?"

"Look, I know where you're going with this, and for the last time, I don't know. Maybe he came through a window? It's kind of your job to figure that stuff out, not mine. This sicko would have cut me into tiny pieces if I hadn't escaped, and you're sitting here quizzing me! Question him, not me."

"I'm having a hard time figuring out fact from fiction. You see, your story of the events keeps changing. Originally your friend Jackson Jamil arrived and, with the help of a neighbour, released you. Now you say you 'escaped.'"

"When I say I escaped, what I mean is I got away or was saved. What does it matter?"

"To me it makes a great deal of difference."

Swift looked at me scornfully. "All I am saying is that I was nearly another Scotland Yard statistic. Most likely another unsolved crime. And right now, I've had enough. I want to leave. I want to see my wife."

"Just a few more questions. Trust me, it's best we do this now. And believe me, Mr Swift, all I want is to understand the truth. The better I understand what happened, the easier it will be to make an arrest. If you can stick to the unvarnished truth, that would be helpful."

"Well, perhaps you'll wish you had arrested him when he comes after you," Swift said, narrowing his eyes. "From what I remember, you were the arresting officer. It was you and Inspector Rayner who rescued Mrs Baker from the rat-infested dungeon."

I ignored the dungeon remark again, but the rest of Swift's remark had hit home. The fact I had been the arresting officer had crossed my mind. It was likely part of the reason Baker was taunting us and playing his games.

In his mind, he was reaching out to me and sending me a message.

CHAPTER FORTY-ONE

Not long after my interview with Matthew Swift, I got one of those calls that change the course of your day.

I called Hamilton in Forensics and told her I needed to reschedule our meeting, then headed to the Carrington Grande Hotel just off Bayswater Road, where multiple murders had taken place sometime in the early hours of the morning. I was met in the corridor by a young detective sergeant called Sarah Dark.

"What can you tell me?" I asked.

"There are three in the room and one outside," she said. "All shot. Each one has at least one body and one head shot. So, it looks professional, at least . . ."

"I know what you mean. The deaths don't look to be spontaneous or a random act."

She smiled.

"You're doing great," I said. I could remember being in her shoes, and I could remember how it felt when, in an effort to not say the wrong thing, you could end up not finding the right thing to say.

"I was just on my way to begin questioning

guests," said Dark. "I've had the hotel manager giving me hell, but I think we see eye to eye now. I explained this was a murder investigation and that I would be discreet, but if he didn't allow me to do my job, I'd have no choice but to close the hotel indefinitely."

That brought a smile to my face. I guessed she'd let him have it. "Good. Also make sure he gives you all CCTV footage, both inside and out."

Rayner was already in the room, gloved up and looking for anything that might lead us to the identities of the victims and their killer.

"Well, this party could have gone better," said Rayner. He pointed to a young woman who'd been laid out on the floor and a skinny young man half hanging off the bed. I walked to the bed and looked at him. Shot in the middle of his back and in the side of his head.

"I went through his stuff," said Rayner. "He's French, here in London studying medicine. Perhaps this was a sideline to make some quick cash?"

"According to the hotel receptionist, the woman is a prostitute," said Dark. "She's a regular, very popular. Check out her tattoo. Not sure what it means right now. Maybe it's a coincidence."

We looked at each other. Rayner knows my feelings on things being a coincidence or an accident. I knelt down and looked more closely at the girl. On her shoulder was a wolf tattoo, the same as Delina's.

Then Rayner turned his attention to the third victim, a large man.

"This one is a long-term guest of the hotel. His name is Klaus Seidel. Stays here every six months or so; has the same room every visit. The body outside the door, another male, is Hans Vogt, and we're told, by the receptionist again, that he was Mr Seidel's driver and personal aide. His room is next door."

I nodded and Rayner continued.

"They are both German citizens. They always arrive together and leave together. Same routine for at least the last five years. That's how long the receptionist has worked here, and she remembers them as guests that whole time."

Rayner and I spent the rest of the day at the hotel. I examined both rooms and talked to hotel staff. The CCTV had been shut off during the incident and the hotel manager promised a full investigation into why that had happened.

I told him Detective Sergeant Dark would assist, but I didn't hold out much hope of any great revelation. Whoever had turned off the CCTV was either a member of staff or the shooter, or both. Pursuing that line of enquiry would have meant a lot of work for me, with very little likelihood of a result. Better to look into Klaus Seidel and Hans Vogt.

CHAPTER FORTY-TWO

Monica, Alice and Faith were still staying with my parents, so I decided to make an early start at Scotland Yard.

Klaus Seidel and Hans Vogt were German citizens, so the first thing I did was to check INTERPOL. Both were on the database, and both files had been edited in the last twenty hours. Both files read DECEASED, and neither offered more than basic information. No personal information, no known associates. I was surprised at the lack of detail but put it to the back of my mind.

I put in some calls around Scotland Yard and it was suggested I speak to Perry Wales at the Organised Crime unit. I knew Perry, so I called and left a message.

Robert Olsen was also on my list, and for him I had only a private number. Olsen was MI5, and our paths had crossed on a case a couple of years back when a Member of Parliament and his family were brutally murdered at their country home. I also got Olsen's voice mail, but to my surprise he called me straight back, I think more out of courtesy than out of any sense of duty – and presumably on a more secure line. I gave him the details, and he said he'd look into it. Which meant either he'd look into it or what he knew he couldn't share. I knew it was a long shot; after all, MI5 aren't big on sharing.

I poured some coffee and grabbed a toffee and pecan muffin, then stared at them for a while. My mind began processing the investigations, leads, dead ends, lies, threats, victims, names and priorities in an effort to make sense of everything I was juggling.

The phone rang, making me jump. I grabbed it. It was Perry Wales.

"James Hardy, you handsome bastard," he boomed. "How the devil are you? Still fighting the good fight? When are you going to get a proper job over here with us catching real criminals?" Perry was a joker, as well as an excellent detective.

"I'm doing my best. How's Elaine?" I asked. "You know, Elaine's an angel to have put up with you all these years. Please send her my regards."

Perry went quiet. I could hear him clearing his throat and sniffing. "She left me," he said finally.

"Oh, Perry, I—'

"Didn't you hear? It was about six months ago. She said she couldn't be married to a *real* detective a moment longer. I hear she's with someone in *your* department now."

Perry began laughing so loud at his own joke that I had to hold the phone away from my ear until he calmed down.

"Very good. Very funny," I said. "Everyone knows she married you for your sense of humour, and if that's true she's not going anywhere." Perry laughed despite my poor attempt at a comeback.

"I had you, my friend. Hook, line and sinker," he said. "Now, what do you need?"

I told him about the four bodies at the Carrington

Grande Hotel and that I believed the murders were a professional hit. That I was interested in the two German nationals and their known associates. I held back on giving him too much detail about the rest of the investigation, as I specifically wanted him to focus on Klaus and Hans. Perry listened carefully and asked for forty-eight hours as he was already working on something big for the Flying Squad.

I was drumming my fingers on the desk, considering my next move, when I got a call from Hamilton. She told me she might have some news for me.

CHAPTER FORTY-THREE

I loved how excited Hamilton sounded; it was like she'd just won the lottery.

"The bullets went off for analysis and we got a hit on the NABIS database," she explained. "I still have lots to do on my side of things, but I knew you'd want to hear what was found on the ballistics side right away."

"Definitely. Anything you've got, I'd love to hear it," I said.

The National Ballistics Intelligence Services database was a really big deal, and this was just one more great example of how their work helped investigations move forward and could ultimately lead to convictions. The NABIS team gathers firearms information. They collect, analyse and compare guns, shells and bullets from crime scenes or from seizures. If it's weapon related, it all goes into the database, where UK police forces can run comparisons. It's a bit like the fingerprint database, but for anything firearms related.

"The NABIS team confirmed the handgun used at the Carrington Grande Hotel killings was a twenty-two, almost definitely a Walther twenty-two with a silencer. The same weapon was used to kill a man called Tyrone West eight months ago," said Hamilton.

"That is fantastic news. I owe you big time," I said.

"I won't hold my breath. You say that every time, James Hardy."

"I know. Look, as soon as this is over, I'll buy you a drink, I promise."

"Dinner?"

"Well, okay, dinner and a nice bottle of wine." I laughed.

"It's a date."

"Well, let's just call it dinner and a nice bottle of wine."

"You call it that. I'm calling it a date with James Hardy."

"You never cease to surprise me. You're a very complex woman, Heidi Hamilton."

"You have no idea, Mr Hardy, but I can assure you you'd enjoy finding out how complex I am. Now get back to work, Hardy. The sooner you solve this investigation the sooner you can start paying off some of your debt to me with dinner and wine."

CHAPTER FORTY-FOUR

It felt like I might be getting somewhere at last on Delina's investigation.

I read through the files on the Tyrone West murder and decided to contact the lead detective on the case, a Fraud Squad detective called Laura Chambers. I got put through to her boss, who told me he'd get her to call me. Right now, he told me, she was working surveillance and couldn't be contacted.

It was around nine that night when she called. We arranged to meet at an Indian restaurant called the Old Bengal in Beaconsfield Old Town at ten thirty. She told me I was buying.

The Old Bengal was a modern-looking restaurant inside what had once been a traditional English house. The front steps were lit using pale blue spotlights; inside, the glass and lighting gave the place a contemporary feel. Smartly dressed, attentive waiters ensured I was quickly seated and offered a Cobra beer. A few minutes later the same attention was given to Chambers when she arrived and was shown to our table.

She ordered a glass of red wine and leaned her elbows on the table. Chambers was dressed in a tight-fitting t-shirt, jeans and casual shoes. Her sandy-coloured hair was tied back, and she looked tired.

"James Hardy, I've heard a lot of good things about you. First-class murder detective. The go-to man when it comes to serial killers. Smart, tenacious, tall and good-looking," she finished.

"Not sure about that," I said.

"Don't be modest. I hate that. It's what I heard; some of it must be true," she retorted with a wry smile. Her glass of wine arrived and she took a grateful sip. "I could not do what you do. Psychopaths day after day. Listening to their excuses and witnessing what's going on in their sick and twisted heads. Mutilated bodies. Missing persons. Tortured kids. I don't know how you do it."

Well, she certainly knows how to speak her mind.

"The victims and potential victims," I said. "I do it for them and their families. It's how I am able to do it. It's the only real reason there is to do it. Someone needs to stop the killer. It takes its toll, though, and this work was never my first choice when I joined the Met. But then when does life ever turn out the way we thought it would?"

Chambers looked embarrassed. "I'm sorry. Ignore my mouth. I'm just letting off. I've been stuck in a box doing a surveillance double shift. I'm tired and not thinking. All I really want is a shower and sleep. Can we start over? The chief said I should speak to you. He said it was important."

"Nothing to start over," I said. "I appreciate you giving up your time." I went over the case as quickly as I could. Chambers ate her curry and listened attentively. Eventually I got to Tyrone West and the ballistic evidence linking him to the murders at the Carrington Grande.

"I remember Tyrone West," she said, putting down her

fork. "His friends called him Irish. Never sure why; I always assumed it was an in-joke and something to do with County Tyrone. He certainly wasn't Irish. My feeling was Tyrone got offered an opportunity to make some quick money and soon found himself out of his depth."

"Out of his depth how? And with whom?" It was her turn to talk now, and I was all ears.

"Tyrone Peter West was a smart guy and a hard worker. He started his car-washing business with nothing but a cloth, a bucket and bottle of liquid soap. He started in a supermarket car park. Each time he got himself established the supermarkets would bring in a more professional crowd and throw him out. Eventually he got sick of that and started approaching cinemas. He and a friend were soon clearing four to five thousand pounds a week with the only cost being liquid soap. From there he grew the business to a dozen or so hand car wash stations. He needed more people. He also arranged exclusive deals to have crews washing cars in cinema car parks, supermarket chains and out-of-town car parks.

"Eventually he caught the attention of those who needed what he had in ample supply. Cash."

Chambers put a packet of cigarettes on the table and indicated we should step outside for a while to continue the conversation. We made our way to the front of the restaurant and, having lit her cigarette, she continued. "From what we gathered he was most likely either threatened or blackmailed in some way, but however it started he eventually found he was in over his head with some Albanian mafia types. The Albanians were making a fortune in cash with drugs, prostitution, extortion, illegal goods, etcetera. All that cash needed cleaning, so they wanted an endless supply of cash-rich legitimate businesses to launder their money.

"Tyrone never really had a chance once they heard about his business and how much cash was going through it each week. Once they got their claws into him, it was over for him. However much he generated in cash each day he'd have to add another ten to twenty percent of their dirty money on top. Once it was banked it was clean, it was laundered, and all they had to do then was withdraw their money and spend it on legitimate items like houses and cars. Easy."

"What happened?" I asked. "Why did he wind up dead?"

"That part we don't really know. Perhaps he wanted out. Perhaps the Albanians wanted the business for themselves. Perhaps he just looked at someone the wrong way. All we know is one morning he was found at his desk with one to the head and one to the chest." Chambers ground out her cigarette and lit another.

"Suspects?"

"Plenty of suspects. Suspects aren't the problem. Proving it and making it stick is the problem. For us in Fraud Squad, when there is that much legitimate cash going through a business, proving ten percent of it is illegal is difficult. If I were you, looking at who ordered the murder of Tyrone West, I'd start by looking at a man they call Papa."

"Where would I find him?" I asked.

Chambers laughed. "He's not hard to find. He spends his days in a little restaurant in West London. If you go looking for him, just be careful. To look at him you wouldn't believe he's one of the most powerful crime bosses in London, if not the most powerful. The Albanian mafia has a vice-like grip in London and quite a few major cities in the UK. If you want to know who pulled the trigger, well, that's anyone's guess. If you want to know who ordered it, then right at the top of my list would be Papa."

"Where in West London is the restaurant?"

"The restaurant is in Ealing. It's called Caesar's," she said. She looked at her watch. "I've really got to go. I need some sleep. I'm back on in five hours. If you get stuck, speak to the chief again. He'll arrange a meeting or point you in the right direction. I don't need to tell you to be careful, but be careful. And thanks for dinner." With that, Chambers walked to her car and was gone.

It was now almost midnight and it had been a long day. My head was spinning from all the information I'd gathered. I went back into the restaurant and made some notes. I wasn't sure how much further the case had progressed or whether I had just hit a brick wall. What I did know was that I'd just been handed a big piece of the puzzle, but where it fitted I wasn't yet sure.

CHAPTER FORTY-FIVE

I arrived at the Thameside Catholic School and went straight to the office of the school head, David Alsop. Alsop was a stocky, balding man who was nearly as tall as me. Until he smiled, he looked more like a nightclub bouncer than a head teacher.

"I'm here to see Simon Baker," I told him. "I believe he teaches here."

"He's not in any trouble, I hope?" said Alsop.

"I just need to ask him a few questions. It really is important I speak to him immediately."

I watched Alsop's reaction. I could see he was curious and was weighing up whether to press me for more information.

Unsure what to do, Alsop said, "He's teaching right now."

"I am sorry to have turned up unannounced, but it couldn't be helped. I'm sure neither you nor Mr Baker would want to hinder an investigation."

I could see Alsop was itching to ask what sort of

investigation, but again he held back. "Of course not. Follow me, Inspector."

I followed Alsop through the maze of corridors. All students were in class, and as I passed, I looked into the classrooms. Some rooms were quiet and some were loud and filled with laughter. We climbed two flights of stairs and headed to the end of another long corridor, then took a right and stopped. I discreetly stood back out of sight as Alsop knocked twice and opened the door to the classroom.

"Good morning, children."

"Good morning, Mr Alsop," the children replied in unison.

"Sorry to disturb you, but could we have a quick word please, Mr Baker?"

"Of course," I heard a voice say. "Right, class, I'm stepping out for a moment. While I am out, I'd ask that you take this time to continue your Monet project work, which, can I remind you, is required for the end of term."

The classroom erupted into noise as the children began to open bags and talk excitedly. Baker stepped into the corridor and, without speaking, looked at Alsop and then at me. He looked calm and relaxed. His expression never changed, even when I was introduced.

"Sorry to bother you in the middle of class. I know we like to avoid that," said Alsop, looking at me. "But this is Detective Chief Inspector Hardy, and he tells me he needs your urgent assistance. I thought perhaps the two of you could use the music room. It's empty at the moment. It'll give you a little privacy. If you need me, Inspector, I'll be back in my office."

I followed Baker in silence to the music room. He pulled out a couple of chairs and placed them in the middle of the room. I felt like I was at a parent and teacher meeting. Baker smiled weakly as he saw me notice the small silver cross on his lapel.

"So how can I help you, Inspector?" asked Baker softly.

"I'm sure it's nothing. I almost feel a little embarrassed to be bothering you while you're teaching, but something has come up in the course of my investigation, a part of which is in relation to yourself. As with all investigations, time is a crucial factor, and so I like to avoid delay. I'm sure you understand."

I could sense the elephant in the room, so I just came out with it.

"You may remember me as the original arresting officer, along with Inspector Rayner. I just want to inform you I am here about a separate incident that occurred recently, which, to my knowledge, has nothing to do with your prior conviction."

Baker crossed his thin legs and clasped his spidery hands on his knee. "That's right. I hardly recognised you, but I thought your face was familiar. Isn't it funny how the mind works at blocking out dark memories?"

Baker looked different to how I remembered him. His arrogance was gone. He looked tired. He looked a sad man now. It was as though he'd been broken and beaten but was somehow fighting on. His glasses, beard and cheap clothes threw me off a little, but underneath I saw the man I remembered.

Baker looked at his watch.

"What brings you here today, Inspector? And in case you're wondering, Alsop knows about what happened to me. He and others have helped me understand how my mistakes led me to be thrown to the lions. This is a very nurturing environment. Together with God's guidance, I am now on the right path and, God willing, my mistakes are behind me."

Baker closed his eyes for a long moment and breathed slowly. He appeared to be meditating.

"It turns out I am good at teaching," he went on. "I get to give, and what I receive back is rewarding. When I'm teaching it's hard to believe I am the same person that I was back then. Life is so different now. I feel blessed to have been given a second chance." Baker spread out his long, thin arms. "I'm surrounded by enthusiastic students, and all the staff here have been so supportive. Finding work wasn't easy after what happened. But when I was at my lowest point, I was found. God found me."

Baker slowly shook his head. "It's okay, Detective. I don't expect you to understand."

I couldn't put my finger on it, but I sensed he had been expecting me. He seemed a little too keen to talk and a little too well rehearsed, although perhaps all I was sensing was a man who knew he'd never shake off the past and had accepted that, one day, a police officer would come knocking on his door. Maybe I had become too cynical and was finding it hard to believe this man in front of me had turned his life around. I decided to jump straight in.

"A man fitting your description was seen at the home of Mr Matt Swift."

"I was there," said Baker without hesitation. "The day before yesterday, around nine o'clock Friday evening."

I wasn't expecting that. I sat a little straighter. "You were?"

"Yes. Not for long. You see, I could see it wasn't the right time."

"The right time?"

"Yes. I think Mr Swift had been drinking and . . ." He trailed off.

"And?"

"Well, I don't want to get anyone in trouble."

"I'm investigating a serious assault on Mr Swift, so anything you can offer to help the investigation would be appreciated."

"I see. Well, I think he may have been smoking marijuana. He was slurring his words and I could smell it coming from his apartment door when he opened it."

"And why were you there?"

"Forgiveness."

I purposefully kept my expression blank.

"I've been encouraged to confront my past to ensure a more peaceful future. Part of this outlook involves forgiving those who have wronged me or whom I have wronged. I was there seeking redemption."

"Redemption?" I asked, encouraging Baker to continue.

"To be rescued, I must first atone for my mistakes. I wished to seek forgiveness from Matthew Swift."

"Did you?"

"No. It wasn't the right time. I think he was a little . . . high.' Baker spoke more quietly. "Recreational drugs. Very sad. He was hallucinating. He was talking to me and trying to catch butterflies with his hands."

"Did you enter the apartment?"

"Yes. Only because he was making a bit of a scene and I didn't wish to cause embarrassment for him or his neighbours. I stepped inside, but only briefly. I quickly realised he had company. I never saw who it was, but I assumed it was a girlfriend. She was in another room. Bedroom, perhaps? From what I could gather, his wife was away for the weekend. That sort of adulterous behaviour is not for me to judge. 'Let he who is without sin cast the first stone.' I just felt I had, unfortunately, chosen the wrong time to make amends, and so I quickly and politely suggested I call back another time."

"Did you hear the name of this other person in the apartment?"

"I wish I had. That would help you, wouldn't it, Detective?"

"Can anyone verify any of this?"

"In what way, Inspector? Oh, I see what you mean. Well, I care for my terminally ill mother. I suppose she would be able to confirm the time I went out and the time I returned. But she is very frail. I would prefer it if you didn't burden her, unless it is truly necessary. I'm sure you understand."

The school bell rang. Noisy children poured into the corridors.

"I really should prepare for my next class, Inspector Hardy. I am happy to help you further if I can. Perhaps we should schedule a more appropriate time."

"I'll be in touch."

Baker put a skeletal hand on the door handle to leave. "I will pray for Mr Swift as well as for you, Inspector Hardy."

"Did you seek redemption from Katharine Wells or Toby Fielding?"

Baker turned and tilted his head slightly. "I am sure those names should have some significance but I cannot place them. Do you have something to ask me, Inspector? Perhaps you have something you'd like to accuse me of. You certainly have that look about you. I would suggest you be sure of your facts. Under the circumstances, I have been extremely polite, and fishing the way you are could lead you into trouble. To me, this now feels a lot like harassment. I've paid for my mistakes and am a free man. I really do just want to be left alone to live a peaceful and more meaningful life. Unfortunately, your being here jeopardises all that for me. Rumour, gossip and innuendo are fuel for the wicked."

Baker opened the door, and I watched as he joined the flow of fast-moving children.

I decided to take a few hours off. A little fresh air and perspective could work wonders. I'd probably call Rayner later and talk things over, but right now I fancied a walk, then perhaps an ice-cold beer and something to eat.

CHAPTER FORTY-SIX

Monica and I picked the girls up after school and whisked them away to Brighton for a couple of days by the seaside. I thought it was important to give my parents some space. It would also be beneficial for Alice and Faith, who had been torn away from their family home, to have some excitement. A change of scenery would also be therapeutic for Monica.

The plan was to stay overnight in Brighton on Friday and Saturday before returning to London to spend Sunday together with my parents. With the Gallery Killer on everyone's mind, Mum, in particular, was on edge. She'd called each evening to check we were okay. On Saturday evening she insisted I bring her granddaughters back as early as possible on Sunday; she was in desperate need of a hug from them.

Reading between the lines, it was clear I was in Mum's bad books, as it had been far too long since all three generations of the Hardy family had sat down for a traditional Sunday roast lunch. She informed me that she would be cooking roast beef and Yorkshire puddings and I should be there no later than midday; she wouldn't accept any of my usual excuses. I was not to drop the girls off and disappear back to the office.

When she got like this, I knew better than to protest, and besides, it sounded like a great idea to me. After a couple of days away, all of us sitting down together would round off the weekend perfectly. Apparently, she also needed us to return early Sunday because she required some female advice from Monica about the shoes she'd bought on Friday – it was clear the matter was urgent. Naturally, I could see straight through that and Mum knew it, but she didn't let that stop her.

Mum hugged and kissed us all as we arrived on Sunday. No one was allowed through the front door until she'd embraced each of us, inspected us from head to toe, and commented on how well we looked and how the seaside air had done us good. I also took the flack, this time publicly, for how long it had been since I'd been available to sit down at their house for a proper meal, even though in reality it couldn't have been more than a few weeks.

I said nothing to defend myself, as I could see Mum was giddy with excitement at having us return safely. Dad stood back a few paces with his big smile and watched with raised eyebrows. He shook his head in mock disbelief and winked at me. "For goodness' sake, Sylvia, let them in. Anyone would think they'd just returned from five years in Australia."

"You shush, Thomas Hardy, you grumpy old man. Don't you pretend. I know you better than you know yourself."

"Granddad," called Alice and Faith when they saw him. They rushed over and hugged him.

"Well, look at you two," said Dad. "Now which is which? I know it's only been two days, but you've changed so much. Don't tell me – you're Alice and you're Faith. Right?"

"Noooo," laughed the girls.

"Okay, now let me try again. I used to be a detective like your daddy, you know, so don't tell me. I'll work it out. You're Faith and you're Alice."

"Noooo," shouted the girls again.

"Are you sure? You know, I've got a lie detector around here somewhere. Now, where did I put it?" Dad began hunting around the house, pretending he was trying to find his lie detector, while the girls ran beside him laughing. I could hear him whispering loudly. "You know, I use my lie detector on your grandmother sometimes when she tells me it wasn't her that ate the last chocolate biscuit."

"Soppy old man," said Mum as she watched her husband fooling about like a child. She turned to Monica and me. "You know," she almost whispered, "he was probably more excited about seeing those girls than I was. He was up at the crack of dawn this morning and has been watching that clock ever since."

Dad came back our way carrying Alice and Faith in his arms. Mum held onto my arm and turned to Dad. "Granddad, are you going to show Alice and Faith the surprise for them in the garden? I'm going to try one more time to teach this son of ours how to cook."

"Is it a trampoline, Granddad? Is it a trampoline? You said you might get us one."

"You'd better come this way and take a look. You know, for the life of me I cannot remember what that surprise is. Though I do recall it was *only* suitable for good girls. Have you two been good?" asked Dad jokingly.

"I think I had better go with them," said Monica. "Just to keep an eye on them."

I followed Mum into the kitchen and mouthed,

"Help!" to Monica, who simply laughed and followed Granddad and the girls.

Mum checked the cooking and talked away about this and that. I stood and watched the girls out of the window. They'd thrown off their shoes and were bouncing up and down on the new trampoline. Dad and Monica chatted together while looking on and encouraging them.

"You really should make time to do this more often. The girls are growing up so fast," said Mum.

"I'm doing my best. It's not the sort of job where you can simply clock in and out. We're only a few minutes down the road. You're always welcome to visit *us* more often," I said, regretting the way it sounded as soon as it came out of my mouth.

"I know; it was same for your father. Having the girls here has brought home how important it is to make time. Popping in to see you sounds nice, but you've got your lives and you're all so busy," said Mum. "You know I prefer it when you visit us. I feel we're intruding. And anyway, it's good for the girls to come visit their grandparents. I don't need to say it, but once this craziness is all over, we're here whenever you need us, and your father and I are always available to babysit. For us that would be a treat."

"Why exactly would I need a babysitter?" I knew immediately I'd been set up, and I'd walked right into the real topic she wished to discuss. Mum could see I knew it, but she pressed on regardless; I'd just been hooked like a fish.

"Hear me out," she said. "You're still a young man and you have your father's good looks. Those girls need to feel secure. They need a proper family unit." She looked out of the window. "Helena would want you to move on, and from what I can see you're doing everything but moving on. You're burying your head in the sand, James Hardy."

"So what do you want me to do? Do you want me to join a dating website or start clubbing? Most of the women I meet are either married, prostitutes or in the morgue."

"You're being ridiculous, Jamie. You know exactly what I'm saying. The answer is right under your nose and you know it, so cut that out."

"For God's sake, not that again. She's Helena's best friend. It wouldn't be right. And she's still married. And it would be inappropriate. And we're friends. And if it doesn't work out, it would spoil what we have."

"So you have thought about it?"

"No. You have no idea how I feel, and you know I don't want to talk about it."

"Sounds like you have thought about it and you're making excuses to avoid telling her how you feel."

Monica came into the kitchen then, followed by Alice, Faith and Dad, who was now pretending to be a child-eating monster.

"Raaargh," he groaned hungrily, crooking his fingers at the girls, who screamed giddily and ran behind their grandmother.

I used that as my opportunity to escape and made a beeline for the back garden. I spent the time until dinner watching the girls on the trampoline and chatting to Dad. I could feel Mum's eyes on me through the kitchen window. Dad quickly figured Mum had had one of her talks with me, but he didn't bring it up. I was grateful for that.

CHAPTER FORTY-SEVEN

Sebastian was a treat for her birthday. Nothing more. She was sure of that. She'd been good for twenty-three months and eleven days. But who was counting? And as a birthday treat, Sebastian didn't really count. Putting him to one side, she'd kept the urges at bay.

Those thoughts were always at the back of her mind, and she was always looking at men, and sometimes women, and weighing up their potential. But the fact remained she hadn't acted on any of those impulses, and for that she could be rightly proud.

The newly updated and more secure members' website was interesting her tonight. She was assured that security was now state of the art. No one could get in uninvited – but that's what he'd said last time. She had informed the programmer that should there be another lapse in security and some uninvited visitor did show up, he'd be a programmer who used his nose for typing, while his fingers sat in a jar on his desk.

No members knew of the forum's security breach, and no harm appeared to have been done. Apparently, it was a kid who had hacked the site. He probably hadn't known what he was looking at, and as soon as he realised there was no valuable data to be had he'd moved on. After some time had passed the kid would be visited; no point making it too easy for the police to join the dots. Of course, it wouldn't be her visiting the boy; not her sort of thing at all. She'd review the member profiles and find the right candidate to visit the boy, at once killing two birds with one stone. It might even be worth making it look like an accident, though she always considered that wasteful.

As usual, the members were hopeful that tonight The Mentor might post an update. She was still undecided. Absence makes the heart grow fonder, her mother always said. *Miss you, Mum. I'm going to come visit very soon, I promise.*

Catching up on what members had been up to was both tiresome and informative. Their bragging and petty squabbles were tiresome. Yet, from time to time, a story of a narrow escape or new technique or aberration piqued her interest. At the moment, Simon Baker intrigued her. He was a rising star for what he'd achieved, and the publicity surrounding him was exquisite. He'd certainly caught the public's interest, and as far as she was aware the police still had no clue as to his identity. He wasn't like the rest of the group, however, and the question of whether he would stay quiet about the group, should he be captured, bothered her.

He seemed educated and obviously had a high IQ. He clearly also had family money behind him. He showed some interest in the conquests of others, but he wasn't obsessed like some. And unlike some, he didn't just visit the members' site for kicks. He seemed more interested in technical detail. He asked lots of questions. Maybe she was wrong, but it was as though his need to kill was nothing more than a job of work he felt compelled to do. It seemed that he was genuinely only a member to learn from those with experience. Whether or not he'd continue to kill after his work was completed would depend entirely on whether he acquired a taste for it. Like many skills you work for, once you have acquired them you feel empowered, and then they become very difficult to give up.

"Shut up, Sebastian!" she shouted.

The constant thudding, scraping, banging, clattering and moaning was *really* starting to grate. She'd have to do something about Sebastian sooner rather than later. The only decision was how to end things with him. His neediness had quickly become a turn-off, and so she'd offered to tie him up, knowing he'd jump at the chance of going all *Fifty Shades of Grey*. Now he was completely helpless, gagged, strapped and tied to a chair. He'd been quiet for a while, when he'd thought her leaving him was a tease. Then, after an hour, his muffled calling had turned first angry and insistent and then to pleading.

Sebastian had caught her attention when she'd read of his naughty exploits at King's College University. Several young women had been abducted and their bodies never found. Unlike the police, it hadn't taken her long to track down the perpetrator. After all, his telltale personality traits were obvious to her. Once she'd tracked him down, she'd promised herself she'd have him when the time was right.

Eventually she had decided her birthday was the right time. So here he was, trussed up like a Christmas turkey all ready for the oven, which was on. She'd put the incinerator on a few hours ago in preparation. Now her only decision was how to finish things with poor little Sebastian. Having opened a fresh bottle of wine and poured herself a glass, she began weighing up the pros and cons. After all, these decisions were all part of the pleasure and not to be rushed.

Depending on how it was used, a knife could be quick and it could also be slow. The down side was always the mess, and seeing as how he was in her house, she didn't want mess. *Who wants to be cleaning on their birthday?*

A cord or rope was too masculine and way too much effort and exertion. A tourniquet helped, but always seemed clumsy. *We'll call that a maybe.*

Once again, a gun would create mess, and, really, where was the fun?

A syringe full of something nasty was wimping out, as far as she was concerned, and should really only be used as a way of completing the job in a hurry or when one needed to hide the act.

A bag over the head? "Now that is an interesting option," she said to herself. "Haven't done that in a while. Similar effect to rope or cord or noose but without the exertion. There's the added benefit, once everything is set up, of being able to sit and watch. And with only a little audience participation, the performance could last for hours. And no bloody mess to clean up at the end. Perfect." She raised her glass in a small cheers.

Decision made, she decided she would pop into the other room and give Sebastian an update. It seemed the right thing to do. Yes, she'd break the news to him. After all, it only seemed fair; secrets can lead to all sorts of misunderstandings. She'd explain to him what would happen and why.

Before any of that happened, though, she was going to have a bath so she could feel completely relaxed before his final performance. She doubted he'd take it well, but then again, they never did.

CHAPTER FORTY-EIGHT

I was finishing a salad lunch at Rosie's Tea Shop when two black Mercedes 4x4s pulled up outside. They weren't hiding; they wanted me to know they were there. A suited man in his thirties got out of the lead vehicle. He looked left and right and then directly at me. He was a wiry man with bad teeth. He patted his side to show me he was armed.

The back window of the same Mercedes opened to reveal a man who was probably in his late sixties. He, too, looked at me and, with a warm smile, beckoned me over.

Rosie came and stood beside me. She put a hand on my shoulder and topped up my pot of tea with hot water. "You know they'll get a parking ticket if they stay there too long," she said with a chuckle. Nothing got past Rosie. She could see what was going on but had known me long enough not to ask. Rosie was simply checking I was okay and in her own way asking whether she could be of assistance.

"Thank you, Rosie. Sadly, I don't think they're planning on stopping for tea and, lovely as it is, I'm going to have to leave the rest of my lunch. Would you please call Rayner and let him know I am in a meeting with Papa? He'll know who you mean."

My legs were feeling heavy as I walked towards the Mercedes. I looked back and could see Rosie was already on the phone calling Rayner. I stood on the pavement for a moment and looked left and right. The street was packed with shoppers and was the last place I wanted any sort of firearms incident. I looked up, spotted the CCTV cameras and looked directly into each one.

The wiry man with bad teeth opened the back door of the lead Mercedes and reluctantly I got in and sat beside Papa. Mr Bad Teeth jumped in the front. The Mercedes pulled away, and I looked back at Rosie, who was standing in the doorway of her cafe.

Mr Bad Teeth leaned over from his front seat and frisked me. Once he was satisfied I wasn't armed, he looked at Papa and nodded.

"Forgive me, Detective Hardy. I apologise if this all seems a little theatrical." Papa gestured with his hands as if all this was beyond his control. "My name is Papa Kastrati. It is vital I speak with you," he continued.

"Perhaps we could head over to Scotland Yard and talk there?' I suggested. "I would certainly feel more comfortable."

Mr Bad Teeth in the front passenger seat sniggered. Papa looked at me as though I had made a childish statement. "We will not talk now. I dislike being away from my little restaurant, but I made this trip for you, as it is important."

Papa did not speak again for the remaining journey. He simply looked out of his window and occasionally sighed. The restaurant was called Caesar's, just as Chambers had told me. We pulled up outside and Papa was helped down from his seat by one of his men. He then made his own way to the back of the restaurant. I watched as Papa settled himself. Through the windows at the front of the restaurant, I watched as Mr Bad Teeth and the other men drove away.

I looked around the small and very traditional-looking restaurant. I imagined the menu was much the same, with traditional food made the traditional way. On terracotta floor tiles sat rows of wooden booths with leather seats. A tall, lean, muscular man was attending to the bar area. Behind him I noticed a postcard pinned to the wooden frame of a large mirror. I recognised it to be a black double-headed eagle on a red background, the Albanian flag. Behind Papa at the far end of the restaurant was a door that went through to a white-tiled kitchen. The door closed behind me, and I was alone in the restaurant with Papa and the tall man behind the bar.

Papa lit a cigar and beckoned me over. "Come, come. Please take a seat. We have lots to discuss. I am having a coffee. Would you like something? Actually, no. I insist you *must* have something. After all, you are my guest."

"A coffee, thank you," I said. I could feel my phone vibrating in my jacket, and the buzzing was loud in the empty restaurant.

"Please answer your phone while Orel brings us our coffee," said Papa.

I took out my phone. The large display showed it was Rayner. Papa held out his hand to take the phone. I figured I felt safer knowing Papa was happy to speak to Rayner, so I handed it over.

"Detective Rayner, this is Papa. You may not remember, but we briefly spoke many years ago. I am here with your friend and colleague Detective Hardy."

Papa raised his eyebrows and smiled as Rayner spelled

out, in ways only Rayner could, what would happen should I be in any way harmed. Eventually Papa spoke again. "I understand your concerns. I assure you no harm will come to your friend. He is here with me at my restaurant, and I would appreciate it if we were given some time to talk."

Papa handed me the phone and I put it up to my ear. "I'll see you later," I told Rayner. "No point driving all the way over here. So far Papa has been a polite and generous host. If perhaps a little unconventional with his invitation."

I put the phone on the table and Orel placed a strong black coffee in front of me. Papa closed his eyes and sipped his coffee.

"Good," said Papa. He looked at the bar man beside us. "Orel here is a good friend. He will make sure we are not disturbed while we talk."

Orel looked at Papa and then at me and returned to the bar. My gut told me Orel was a little more than just the restaurant's barman.

CHAPTER FORTY-NINE

He seemed so ordinary as he told me of his life growing up in Albania and the struggles of day-to-day life. He was a man in later life telling me a version of his life story.

I could see the pain in his eyes as he told me of how he had married young and quickly lost his beautiful young wife and only child, a son, in a fire at a rented flat. That pain, he told me, had changed the course of his life. I listened and for a time forgot just how dangerous this man was.

He never mentioned his crimes; he wasn't looking for forgiveness. Perhaps he didn't see what he had done to survive, or what he continued to do to acquire so much power, wealth and influence, as something in need of forgiveness. I got the feeling he believed he had simply followed the predetermined path of his life one step at a time. He believed he had no more control over his direction, he told me, than a feather would have if caught in a hurricane.

"But we have the ability to make choices," I said finally. "A feather does not."

Papa stroked his fine grey hair with his cigar hand and leaned forward. "So, we come to choices," he said thoughtfully. "I often considered life to be the hurricane and the feather to be our choices. Do you believe we are truly able to make choices without the hurricane of life influencing their direction?"

"Every day we make choices. Some big, some small," I said. "Some days we make one important choice and some days we make lots of small choices. All those choices accumulate. Day after day. Month after month. Year after year. At the end of a life, we are the sum of those choices."

Papa narrowed his eyes and glanced over my shoulder at Orel. "They told me you were clever, a thinker. That you make the tough choices most men will not make," said Papa.

"I don't need a philosophy lesson. Just tell me why I am here," I said. I knew now Papa was learning as much about me as I thought I was learning about him. For all I knew, the saga of his growing up was a figment of his imagination, a story he'd created to simply give him time to observe me, to read me. I felt a little like I was sitting before him because that was his choice. I was ashamed to admit it to myself, but at that moment I felt like the feather and he was the hurricane. I knew he saw that realisation in my eyes. He didn't need to say anything; he could see in my face he had made his point.

"Why am I here?" I repeated.

After a long silence Papa said, "There are men who can be bought. There are those who can be coerced. Some men need only to be threatened. And some men, well, let's just say they are obstacles that have to be removed. You, I fear, are an obstacle. Your need to find answers and your need for justice make you one of those I cannot buy or coerce."

"Are you threatening me?" I asked. I looked over my shoulder and saw Orel at the bar checking stock levels. I was now feeling a little jumpy and wanted to keep one eye on the barman.

"Goodness me, no. I am merely stating a fact. I want you to understand my situation before we discuss our predicament."

"And what is our predicament exactly?"

"I have become aware of a case you are working on. From what I hear, there have sadly been several untimely deaths. Young women. Some of these women may in the past have had some association with one of my businesses."

I said nothing and Papa continued.

"We are looking into the circumstances surrounding these incidents. I assure you it will be dealt with. And when it comes to justice, it will be swift and final. I simply need you to give my organisation a little time to deal with the matter."

"What about Klaus Seidel?" I decided to take a chance and see whether the cases were connected.

"Klaus? We're looking into that too."

He was lying. He knew Klaus but didn't know he was dead. He had also just admitted that he wasn't surprised someone in his organisation would have likely killed Klaus. I pressed him further. "Someone in your organisation is out of control. He's killed several young women plus Klaus and his bodyguard, and you're asking me to look the other way?" I asked in disbelief.

"I am asking you to be smart. The women will have justice, and so will Klaus. These matters need to be dealt with internally."

"Are you admitting your involvement?"

Papa looked at me as though I was becoming tiresome.

"I am merely suggesting that, through a little mutual understanding, the perpetrator of these crimes will be punished. They will not be punished by Scotland Yard or sentenced at the Old Bailey, but nevertheless they will be punished."

I jumped to my feet and leaned over Papa. "There is only one rule of law in this country. I think it's time I left," I said furiously.

I felt a hand on my shoulder. I turned to see Orel standing beside me, and then I looked down as I felt a small blade pressed against my ribs.

"Please, sit down. Papa hasn't finished." said Orel.

"It is time I was going," I said. "This meeting is over."

Papa nodded to Orel. "Life is harder than it needs to be for the stubborn man," he said as a parting blow.

I walked out of Papa's restaurant without looking back. Mr Bad Teeth was back outside waiting for me. He drove me to my car, which was parked in the street outside Rosie's Tea Shop. Lunch at Rosie's seemed like an age away. Mr Bad Teeth was all smiles when we reached my car. He reached out, grabbed my hand and shook it vigorously.

"No hard feelings. Sorry for any inconvenience. Enjoy the rest of your day," he said repeatedly. "No hard feelings. Goodbye for now."

I climbed into my car and dialled Rayner's number. As Rayner answered I noticed a bright yellow plastic supermarket bag on my front passenger seat.

"Rayner, it's me. I'm okay. I'm going to call you back in a few minutes," I said absent-mindedly. I leaned over and grabbed the bag. It was heavy, and I lifted it onto my lap. I opened it and looked inside. I couldn't believe what I was seeing. I pulled out bundles of fifty-pound notes. The bag contained cash, thousands of pounds. I picked up my phone and called Rayner back.

"You had me worried there for a minute, mate," said Rayner.

"No, I'm okay. I have a problem, though," I said.

"What sort of problem?"

Across the street, a young freelance photographer was capturing the images that he had been assured would fast-track his career.

CHAPTER FIFTY

I'd stayed at my parents' home to see Monica and the girls. Although Monica was feeling stronger, she was having trouble sleeping due to repeated nightmares.

It was six forty-five and we were sitting at the breakfast bar drinking hot tea and talking. I had the feeling Monica was needing to talk as part of her recovery, so I sat quietly and listened. Her injuries, though minor on the outside, went far deeper psychologically, and I knew from experience they shouldn't be underestimated. I decided I'd speak to my psychologist at Scotland Yard and get some advice, perhaps try to get a referral for her. We talked for a couple of hours before Monica took a shower.

I was washing cups in the kitchen when I got a call. A report had come in that a homeless man, Tom Ryan, had seen two men throwing something bulky into the Thames river. He'd told the attending officer he might be homeless but he wasn't stupid. He'd served in Iraq and Afghanistan and knew what a body looked like and how you handle that sort of weight. He'd heard about the murdered women found in the river and was sure these guys were disposing of a body. He was also able to give a description of the car, a dark-blue Mercedes, most likely C-Class or E-Class, probably C-Class. The two men were white. It had been dark and he'd been quite some distance away, but he was certain of what he'd seen. He was apologetic he couldn't give us more, but by the time he'd got to the bridge the men were gone.

A team with divers from Thames River Police were called and they did sweeps along the river. It didn't take them long to find the body. It was a woman. Like the others, she was wrapped in plastic sheeting and had been strangled and stabbed multiple times.

Rayner came straight over when I arrived at the scene. "How's Monica?"

"Getting there," I said. "The swelling is going down, a few minor bruises and cuts, but physically she's fine."

"That can only be good news. Send her my love. I'll pop 'round and see her before starting my surveillance shift," said Rayner.

"She'd like that. So, what have we got here? Are we certain this is related?"

Hamilton looked up from the body. "Definitely. Same MO. Same knife. Same plastic sheeting. The only difference is this girl has no wolf tattoo. Another thing I can tell you is this girl hasn't been dead long; perhaps six hours. I need to test it, but I wonder also whether her makeup is theatre makeup. Perhaps our girl here was an actress or worked on the stage."

The woman had been pretty just like the others, although she was perhaps a little older. I looked at her and wondered what her story was. How had she ended up in the hands of the monster that had done this to her? I got to my feet and grabbed Rayner's arm.

"I've been considering going to see Vladimir Kastrati. I

got a tip, although it might be nothing. If I do it, I could do with some backup if you're up for it."

Rayner looked at me doubtfully. "What have you got on him? What have you got that ties him to any of these women?"

"Nothing concrete. His name has come up. I'm just curious. Let's pay him a visit. Let's shake him up and see if anything falls. Who knows – we might get lucky."

"So, you think he might be so racked with guilt he'll confess?"

"I am not sure we'll get that lucky. If I get nothing better in the next few days, do you want in?"

"I definitely want in. Don't think I'm letting you go see that scumbag without me."

CHAPTER FIFTY-ONE

I arrived at my desk around ten after walking Alice and Faith to school. Walking gave the three of us time to talk, and the girls would open up and tell me what was on their mind. Those were precious moments.

I could sense something was going on the moment I arrived at Scotland Yard. Before I even reached my seat the phone on my desk was ringing. I had been informed Chief Superintendent Webster would like to see me. I was pretty sure I knew what it was about.

"Come in, Hardy. Take a seat," said Webster.

"Good morning, sir," I said while trying to gauge his tone.

Webster looked miserable. He pushed a newspaper article across his desk. It showed pictures of me with the money and of me shaking hands with Mr Bad Teeth; the pictures looked as damning as they were meant to. I started reading.

Scotland Yard Super Cop Shock

Scotland Yard appear to have distanced themselves from one of their most talented lead murder detectives after a series of sensational revelations. After weeks of painstaking investigation by photojournalist Kevin Charles, we reveal exclusive evidence that the Met's most high-profile and celebrated serving officer, Detective Chief Inspector James Hardy, has been photographed accepting money from London's notorious criminal underworld.

This newspaper's undercover work brings into question the integrity of the so-called "Super Detective," who ended the reign of terror by several of Britain's most terrifying serial killers. Initial photographs appear to expose DCI James Hardy holding private alcohol-fuelled meetings in a top London restaurant with suspected members of London's mafia underworld.

Later photos then show the once-trusted London detective agreeing to deals and shamelessly shaking hands with gangsters in broad daylight on the very streets he swore to protect. Further pictures show him brazenly counting bags of cash in his forty-thousand-pound BMW 5 Series.

Highly decorated DCI Hardy famously lost his wife when she bled to death in the street close to the family home after a knife attack by Tony Horn.

Horn was found guilty and sentenced at the Old Bailey to 27 years for the murder of Helena Hardy. Numerous reports suggest DCI Hardy blames himself for his wife's untimely death and has been unable to cope with the loss.

At the time of the attack, the workaholic detective was investigating a series of brutal attacks by serial killer Edward Richter, who is currently serving five life sentences.

The slaying of DCI Hardy's wife left the widower to care for their two young daughters alone. Now in a torrid relationship with a married woman, there are many stories suggesting that, in his grief-stricken state, DCI Hardy went *on gambling and drinking binges which sources tell us left him close to financial and personal ruin.*

So far, the Metropolitan Police Service have declined to comment, leaving us to wonder what other nefarious activities are yet to be uncovered.

"The newspaper editor wants to know whether we have any response before they go to print," said Webster. "Well, anything you want to add?"

"I drive a Toyota, sir."

"For Christ's sake, Hardy, this is serious. I give you space to do what you do because – well, because you do what you do better without interference from me."

"It's all fabricated; you know it is. As for the money, well, it was handed into evidence last night. I was about to write it all up this morning when you requested a meeting. I knew I'd been set up, and I expected we'd be having this conversation. I perhaps should have called you at home last night and given you the heads-up. Sorry."

"Legal are looking at getting an injunction to get the article suppressed while we investigate. I am not going to ask what happened yesterday; that will come later. It will mean a formal investigation, of course, which means more time and more bloody paperwork for both of us. I just want to know how you could have been so stupid."

"I guess I just had a bad day," I said.

"Well, today isn't going to be much better. You're going to have speak to Legal Services, the IPCC and the Director of Media Communications, and that's just for starters." Webster was lifting papers on his desk, presumably looking for a list of whom he wanted me to talk to. I got up to leave before he found it.

"Sit down. There is something else," he said.

"Yes, sir."

"Rayner told me what happened yesterday. How you got picked up. Are you okay?"

"Yes, sir."

"And your daughters?"

"They're fine, sir. Thank you."

"How's Monica?"

"Better, sir."

"And what about your workload? Are you coping?"

"I'm on top of it, sir."

"You look like hell."

"Thank you, sir."

Webster sighed and sat back in his black leather chair. I could see he had something on his mind. I hoped he didn't give me his 5P talk about how we deliver a Product and about Public Perception and how so much of Policing is about Performance both in the sense of results and in the sense of visibility. How the show of blue lights, uniform, stripes, medals, visibility, bravery and awards are all a part of the performance. How, as serving police officers, we should accept so much of what we do is unrecognised work, work that happens in the background, away from the public eye, and how it is vital we are also seen to be serving. I'd heard his speech many times before and really didn't need to hear it again this morning.

Instead, Webster opened a desk drawer and pulled out a form. He looked at the form and then at me and then at the form. He picked up a pen, signed it, then handed it to me.

"You have been chosen to be part of a trial. You and a few select detectives. You are one of those who meet certain criteria, one of which is your service record and another of which is the type of cases you appear to specialise in. That, and London's very real threat from terrorism and an overall rise in gun crime year on year. It has been decided certain senior detectives are to carry firearms."

"This isn't for me," I said without hesitation. "There are plenty of detectives this is more suited to, but not me."

"Just yesterday, in broad daylight, you were taken off the street by the Albanian mafia. During your last investigation, you got thrown out of a second-floor window. You have been stabbed and shot more times than I care to remember. Your job investigating serial killers, kidnappers and rapists makes you and those you love a target every time you walk out the front door. Your girlfriend – or female friend, as you like to refer to her – was beaten during an abduction, which I would strongly suggest is likely to be related to a case you're working. Most of this occurred in just the past few months – shall I go on? I'd say you more than qualify, and if carrying a firearm as a precautionary measure isn't for you, then who in God's name is it for?"

"Do I have a choice?"

"Yes, you have a choice. Nothing's changed. All British police officers have to volunteer to carry a firearm, and you are volunteering."

"I see."

"For pity's sake, carry the bloody gun. Set an example for younger detectives. They look up to you; you're a bloody legend in your own lifetime. You know better than anyone the streets have become more dangerous. We both knew this day would come. I guess we both just hoped we'd be long retired before it got to this point. Ultimately, this comes from Downing Street. It's political. So do me a favour and sign the paperwork, then pick up your firearm."

"Yes, sir."

"Look, the way things are going you may just be

grateful for it. You can get lucky only so many times. Protect yourself; protect your family."

I got up to leave and felt like an entirely different detective to the one who had walked in. I had never anticipated becoming an armed officer. The British police force I'd joined didn't routinely carry firearms; those officers who did were trained specialists. I was qualified, but I had very mixed feelings about carrying a weapon day to day.

"Hardy," said Webster, "send in Rayner. He's also been selected, so I may as well get it over and done with. I am sure he'll be as reluctant as you. He's going to give me hell I suppose – what a bloody day."

CHAPTER FIFTY-TWO

Vlad watched the parade of small vessels pass through the narrow stretch of sea between his new beach-fronted house and the small island of Brownsea. His newly built home was on one of the most sought-after stretches of coastline in Great Britain. He was pleased with his investment. It was the perfect place to hold a meeting with his new European contact. Klaus's departure from this world had left a vacancy, but his loss was someone else's gain. That someone was an Englishman living in Geneva.

Anya came across the balcony and stood beside Vlad. Her hair had grown long and was up. She wore an Indian-inspired summer dress from her new designer wardrobe. The cut was perfect, and so was she.

"Can I get you anything?" asked Anya with a smile.

"A coffee would be good, but no rush. With this view across the bay and you beside me, I have all I need. I feel so different these days – calm." Vlad looked at her. "You look stunning. You have changed me, Anya. With you next to me I feel like a man who can build something, something substantial, a legacy. You have done that.

Building this new home and finding you – that is not coincidence. That's fate. It's destiny."

Anya smiled reticently. She put out her hand and touched Vlad's face. Vlad pulled her to him and kissed her. "You're so beautiful, Anya. If we had time . . ." he said, running his hands down her back and over her hips.

"But we don't," said Anya, pushing away his hands playfully. "Your guest has arrived and he's a part of the new future. Our future," she said.

Shaun Foster was tall, slim, tanned and handsome. He wore a pale-blue suit with matching waistcoat. His white shirt was open at the collar, and he wore navy crocodile-skin shoes. He looked relaxed as he walked onto the balcony with an outstretched hand.

"Pleasure to meet you, Mr Kastrati."

The two men shook hands and Shaun looked at Anya. He saw no ring and was unsure how to address her, so he waited for an introduction.

"This is Anya, who I hope one day soon will become my wife."

"Call me Annie," said Anya. "How was your journey? Was your flight from Geneva comfortable? I trust our driver collected you at the airport without incident and made you welcome?"

"A pleasure to meet you, Annie," said Shaun. "And thank you. It was a short, comfortable flight and a mercifully short drive. A two-hour flight from Geneva is a welcome change to the many long-haul flights of recent weeks. I wake up some mornings trying to recall which country I am in."

Anya smiled. "You're clearly a man in demand. Would you like a drink, Mr Foster? I was just about to make coffee for Vlad and green tea for myself."

"Call me Shaun. Yes, a green tea would be wonderful. Thank you."

Vlad watched as Anya headed back across the balcony and into the house. He admired how quickly she had transformed herself from a frightened young girl to an elegant and sophisticated woman who commanded the room. He had nurtured that. He had seen the potential in her and taken her as a rough diamond and made her sparkle. Now every man who met her wanted her, but she belonged to him.

CHAPTER FIFTY-THREE

She watched Simon Baker from the far side of the busy
Costa Coffee shop. It felt exhilarating, the two of them in
the same room. Two wolves in a room full of lambs. The
coffee shop was crammed with mothers, their dribbling
infants either asleep in a designer buggy or being
comforted or fed.

The mothers spoke a language she could neither
understand nor comprehend. To her they were aliens,
much like every other person she came into contact with.
The only person in the room of any significance was
Baker. He was someone she understood. Like her, he was
an apex predator. Intellectually he might be of interest,
although looking at his thin, wiry frame she was not sure
he could be her type in any physical way. *What was her
type?*

Baker wouldn't be the life companion she sought, but
he could be a welcome distraction for a while. She'd
observe him, study him and follow his accomplishments.

A drooling baby stared at her from the table next to
her, its eyes fixed on her face. A gummy smile crept across

its pudgy cheeks. The mother looked at the baby and then at her.

"He likes you. He's such a good judge of character. You like the ladies, don't you? Don't you? My little baby boy. Buh, buh, buh, buh," said the mother.

She began lifting the baby in the air, to the delight of the other mothers and the drooling infant.

The Mentor didn't smile and said nothing. Instead she thought, "With any luck, he'll grow up to murder you in your bed, you stupid bitch. Invade my space again and I'll do it for him, today."

Today she was a redhead, a homeless woman carrying a plastic bag full of scrunched-up clothes. She loved her transformations. Quality wigs and hours spent mastering the skill of makeup artistry meant she could be unrecognisable from one day to the next. She'd even invested in an accent and dialect coach for a while. He claimed to have worked with Nicole Kidman, Jeremy Irons, Kate Winslet and Guy Pearce, amongst others. He had been very good. Naturally, he was gone now. She remembered his gold ring, encrusted with a ruby. She'd kept it as a souvenir.

She wondered what Baker was thinking. He looked so ordinary; she saw no concern at all on his thin bearded face. Unlike her, he hadn't been born with what they had in common. At least she didn't think he had been born with that thing that set them apart from the rest of society. A predator with the desire, the need, to kill for no reason other than the satisfaction it brought. No, she felt sure he had been created by society, and yet he wore it comfortably. No angst, no troubled eyes or furrowed brow. Baker looked at ease as he read the newspaper and sipped a cappuccino. His only concern appeared to be the flakes of almond croissant on his tweed blazer.

Time to play a little game, she thought. The Mentor put on her threadbare, stained coat and weaved her way unsteadily through the mothers and buggies towards Baker. She was close now. She could hear him breathe, see the pores on his face, the hairs on the back of his hands. She bent down beside him and pretended to pick up an envelope from beneath his table. She passed it to him with a shaky hand.

"I think you must have dropped this, my love. Here you go." The Mentor gave a big yellow-toothed smile then wiped her nose on her coat sleeve and held out a gloved hand. She watched as Baker looked at the envelope and recognised his name on it. She smiled inwardly. He looked at her and then at her stained red-gloved hand.

"That was very kind of you," he said as he looked around the room for who might have left the mysterious envelope. He reached into his jacket pocket and handed her a five-pound note from his wallet.

"Thank ya, love. You're a very 'andsome young man. You kinda remind me of me late husband. He was tall and fit too. You've got 'is eyes – warm and tender." She could see the discomfort in his eyes as she leaned in closer and then closer still. She gave him a good smell of her dirty clothes and watched how he leaned back, repelled. *What a rush.*

Out of the corner of her eye she could see a young barista eyeing her. He was weighing up whether he needed to intervene and move her along. They only tolerated someone of her sort for so long, she knew. Homeless coffee drinkers were bad for business. They made other patrons feel uncomfortable and that just wouldn't do, wouldn't do at all. *Well, tough luck. I haven't finished yet. You come near me, barista boy, and I'll butcher your pretty face.*

In her own time, The Mentor picked up her bags and

headed out the door onto the street, first heading one way and then heading back the other, quietly muttering and humming to herself for effect.

She pictured Simon Baker opening the envelope. A note, a genuine note, handwritten on a fine cream wove paper, from The Mentor. A message direct from the very person who, only moments before, he'd been unaware had stood right beside him. Within touching distance. She couldn't hold that against him; nobody would have suspected. Nobody actually knew what The Mentor looked like; that was all part of her game. That was why she was The Mentor and he the student. She pictured his hand trembling in excitement as he read and savoured every word:

Congratulations on achieving so much so soon,
   With preparation and purpose, you've left not a clue.
   Keep your distance (this is your party),
   From Scotland Yard's finest, an inspector named Hardy.
   Take careful steps. We're enjoying the show.
   Keep us informed; we would hate you to go.
   Stay sure-footed and one step ahead for me,
   And do what you can to fool Hardy.
   – Carpe Diem, The Mentor

She continued her bag-lady performance until she reached her car, which was in a quiet car park some distance from the town centre. She removed her coat and wig and threw the bags in the trunk.

"Quite a performance," she said to herself. With her gloved hand she dropped Baker's teaspoon into a clear plastic evidence bag then carefully put the bag away. "You can never have enough fingerprint evidence or insurance. It could even be a wonderful device to send police inspectors in the wrong direction for one of my students. For a price, of course. There's always a price."

The Mentor started the car. The radio came on and the next song was introduced: "Time Is Running Out" by Muse. She hadn't heard it before. It was certainly not her usual choice, but on this occasion its regimented rhythm and lyrics caught her ear. She hummed along and felt wonderfully uplifted.

CHAPTER FIFTY-FOUR

Guy Lyons pushed against the wall and stretched out his hamstrings. At fifty-eight he could feel he wasn't getting any younger, and stretching was now vital before a run.

He'd just recovered from a painful calf-strain injury, and where in the past he'd felt invincible, today it was a case of prevention being better than cure. He swapped legs and stretched again.

He pictured his route in his head and then headed off at a slow warm-up pace. Summer was his favourite time of year for his morning run, and the earlier the better. He pretty much had the route to himself. Little pausing for traffic, few cyclists and rarely other runners. It sometimes felt he was all alone in the world. The still and quiet were what he cherished most and a real incentive for getting up at such an ungodly hour.

Passing through town, he shifted gear as he reached the bridleway. It had rained a little in the night and the path was nice and soft underfoot. The air felt fresh, and he looked out across the fields to where he often saw hares sitting like boulders. He settled into a comfortable pace and let his mind drift off. The run became a meditation as his breathing fell into a steady, regular rhythm.

Not a soul in sight. All he could see ahead was the bridge that led to the small beech wood, which, in turn, led on to the open wetland and the nature reserve. The estuary was the noisy part of his run. Birds would be making all sorts of calls, but that sort of noise was welcome. He picked up the pace a little as he crossed the wooden bridge and passed his favourite oak tree. *How old must a tree like that tree be? Two hundred, three hundred years? It must have seen so much. So many people must have passed by, so many generations come and gone.*

The path curved left, and now the sun was on his back. He could feel its warmth. He felt good, he felt strong, so he lengthened his stride. He passed tall, willowy reeds and headed along the narrow path that would take him back to the bridle path. Here the path curved right. He rounded the bend and almost tripped over the back wheel of a bike. Sitting up and leaning against a tree was the cyclist. His helmet was cast aside, and he was holding his head. His legs looked bloodied, and there was blood pouring from an apparent head wound. He looked up as Lyons approached.

"Good morning," he said. He raised his eyebrows in a way that said, "This is a great start to the day!"

Lyons stopped. "What happened? Are you okay?"

"I'm not sure. I think the front wheel caught a root or a rock or something. I went straight over the handlebars. I must have blacked out for a while, but I'll be fine. A little dizzy, a little nauseous, but I'm sure it's nothing. I just wish I could get this bleeding to stop."

"I can't leave you like this. Let me call an ambulance."

"I don't want to be any trouble. Besides, they'd never get an ambulance way out here." The cyclist closed his eyes and began retching as though he were going to throw up.

"You might have a serious head injury. I need to call an ambulance."

"Perhaps you're right. Perhaps it's more serious than I first thought. I keep dabbing it but the blood just won't stop. Damn, I feel such a fool." The cyclist lifted his hand and looked at the blood-soaked tissues. "If it's not too much trouble, perhaps you could call my wife. My phone is here in this pocket." He indicated the right side of his jacket.

Lyons knelt beside the cyclist and unzipped the pocket. He reached inside but felt no phone. At the same time, he felt a sharp stabbing pain in his stomach. Confused, he looked at the cyclist, whose face was now covered with a wide and knowing smile.

"Hello, Guy. It's me, Simon Baker."

Lyons stared at the cyclist, first in surprise, then recognition, then disbelief. Another sharp stabbing pain. Another. Another. Lyons stumbled and slumped to the ground. He watched helplessly as the cyclist got to his feet and towered over him. Guy saw a knife in his hand.

"Guy, you're going to bleed to death now. You were part of the conspiracy to bring me down. The lies you printed bled me of the life I should have had, so I think it's only fitting I return the favour. I picked a beautiful spot for your death, and what a glorious morning for it. What did you think of my acting skills? I even rehearsed it, you know, just for you. I wanted to make sure I got everything just right for when you and I finally met. And here we are. Perfect. Please don't try to get up. You'll simply bleed out faster. Gosh, lots of blood, isn't there?"

Lyons could only watch as the cyclist bent over and stabbed him again several more times. He felt no pain, only a *thump, thump, thump* as the knife was thrust again and again and again.

Behind him, Lyons could hear a bird singing. He wished he had the strength to turn and look at it. He thought of his family and wished he'd stayed in bed this morning, stayed at home with them.

Lyons turned his head towards the path he'd come along, hoping for a saviour to rescue him. Instead, he caught sight of his beautiful oak tree. He felt an overwhelming urge to touch it but no longer had strength to move. He lifted his eyes and could see the very top of the great oak pointing up to the heavens, its ancient canopy rising high above everything around it. *Magnificent.*

If that great oak could speak, how would she judge us? he wondered. *What would she say of what she saw here today?*

CHAPTER FIFTY-FIVE

As soon as the murders of Toby Fielding and Katharine Wells and the attempted murder of Matt Swift had been confirmed as the work of one man, a milestone had been reached. Interest in the investigation escalated, and the story was now hot news not only in the UK but around the world.

The press conference was the busiest I'd attended in a long time. Serial-killer cases have a way of capturing the public imagination, and the news networks know that. As sad as it sounds, a serial-killer story sells. All the networks were poised to latch on to any new angle they could get hold of. I peered out from backstage and recognised faces from the BBC, Channels 4 and 5, Sky News, CNN, ABC and Fox. Journalists from the broadsheets and the tabloids were either talking, typing or making calls. The place was packed, and I wasn't looking forward to this one bit.

I'd been under pressure for several days to make a statement, and with Matt Swift's close shave I was unable to delay it any longer. I'd received my orders from above.

I always felt press conferences were like walking a

tightrope. I didn't want to release certain facts, yet I needed to use the press to my advantage. At times like this I remembered advice given to me by a senior detective, now long retired, when I was preparing for my first press conference: "They don't expect you to have all the answers. They've got a job to do, just like you. Plan what you want to tell them and tell them no more. They need words on a page and you need answers. Go out there and give a little to get a little."

I knew the victims' families would likely be watching, and there was also a very good chance the killer himself would be interested. The aim of the press conference was to make a public appeal for witnesses and information leading to an arrest; it had to be more than just answering the news media's questions and dismissing rumours and speculation. What I didn't want to do was in any way boost the killer's ego by implying we had no leads or lines of investigation, as that might embolden him and put others at risk. While detectives tracked down Simon Baker, I also didn't want it going public that Matt Swift had identified who he believed the killer to be.

I reluctantly walked to my seat, accompanied by the chief superintendent, a lawyer, a public relations officer and a couple of other suits. We'd gone over what we would and would not disclose, and I felt well prepared. Although I'd still rather have been doing almost anything else.

I started by introducing myself and confirming a few details about the case we had decided to release and one or two I hoped would benefit the investigation. After what felt like thirty to forty minutes, I opened the floor to questions. I answered a few from faces I recognised and whom I knew to be professional and reliable.

At the back of the room I could hear rumblings, which I ignored. Then an inaudible question from a journalist I didn't recognise came from the back. I could see the face of the journalist calling out, but I didn't recognise it. I assumed he was a big mouth, a new guy, trying to make a name for himself.

There are plenty out there like that; often they're on the fringe, and sometimes they're after nothing more than a conspiracy theory. The discontent grew louder, and I watched as an officer moved to the back to help contain whatever was happening. Then the journalist broke through and moved forward so I could see him. I was sure I didn't recognise him. He had a shock of red hair and a goatee beard. I caught an accent, perhaps Australian, perhaps South African or Irish or Scottish; over the disquiet I couldn't make it out.

Then a hush came over the room and the man repeated his question. Australian accent. His voice suddenly became clear, and in an instant all eyes were on me for the answer to an impossible question.

"Paddy Coben, Coben's News Desk. What hope is there of catching this 'Gallery Killer' *before* he kills again, when Inspector Hardy, one of Scotland Yard's leading murder squad investigators, has no clue whatsoever to the killer's identity? How safe are the streets of London right now, Inspector?"

I said nothing. My press officer was shaking her head at me in a way that said, "Don't you say a bloody word. Not one bloody word."

Coben started pushing his way to the front. Cameras and microphones were swinging from him to me, back and forth, to and fro, as he launched question after question.

"Okay, try answering this one. This one's a bit easier: What would you like to say right now to the family of the next Gallery Killer victim, Inspector, the next victim who will be tortured and then murdered because you're not as smart as the Gallery Killer? I think, mate, that everyone here and everyone watching would like an answer to that one."

I was on my feet in an instant, which I knew looked bad. The chief superintendent grabbed my arm, which made the situation look worse still. It looked like I was ready to go toe to toe with this idiot, which under different circumstances I might well have done. The room erupted. Cameras and microphones turned from me to him and back again. He was taunting me. I knew it. Baiting me for a response. Here was someone out to create headlines of his own, out to make a name for himself at the expense of the victims and the progress of the investigation. This guy was more interested in creating a story where there wasn't one.

"That's all for today," I said. "As soon as we have more, we'll let you know. Thank you for your time today and for the professionalism from the rest of the room."

I turned and left the meeting. Behind me I could hear general protestations as Paddy Coben was escorted out of the building. I, too, felt the frustration of the journalists at having the press conference cut short. I was angry; at this point I couldn't work out how much of a disaster the press conference had been or how it was going to look in the morning. I assumed I'd find out soon enough. Nothing I could say now would change tomorrow's news and how it would be perceived. The press conference had been hijacked by an egotistical idiot.

I took off my tie and thrust it into my jacket pocket. I'd made Scotland Yard look bad, which hurt, and I was worried that the perception of the families might be that the whole investigation had become a circus. What hurt more was that they might feel we were no closer to bringing anyone to justice.

I had to put this behind me and focus. My overwhelming desire now was to get out of the building as quickly as possible and get on with the job – go visit a crime scene again or interview a witness or speak to some neighbours. Anything that meant solid progress.

CHAPTER FIFTY-SIX

I needed space to calm my overloaded brain, and so I drove to Mum and Dad's to see everyone and soak up some love. It was time to recharge my soul by getting some family time. Alice and Faith were sitting cross-legged on the living room floor watching *Hetty Feather* on TV. They both looked up and waved.

"Hi Daddy. Nana's in the kitchen with Monica. I think they've been waiting for you. We don't think it's anything you've done, this time."

That sounded both good and bad. Alice and Faith must have been discussing what was going on with Monica and Mum. From what they'd heard and what they'd seen, they'd drawn their conclusions. They truly were the daughters of a detective.

I stopped off and gave my girls a hug. "Can I stay here with you?" I tried to sit down between them.

"No, you can't. Go face it like a man," said Faith, and the two girls began pushing me away. I gave them both a kiss then headed to the kitchen to discover what fate was in store for me this evening.

Mum and Monica were at the kitchen table studying a letter. I liked that Monica felt she could turn to Mum for advice. For a moment they were silent, and then finally Mum spoke.

"Monica's had a letter from Scott's solicitor," said Mum. "It's about the divorce."

I looked from Mum to Monica and back to Mum. I had assumed this would be a good thing; I'd assumed wrong. *I must be missing something.* Neither said anything, so I stuck my neck out.

"That's good news, right?" I felt like I was being forcibly blindfolded and pushed into oncoming traffic.

"He's changing the agreement we had. He's filing on grounds of adultery. He's claiming it was all my fault and that I had an affair," said Monica.

I opened the fridge and took out a beer. I took a long sip while I waited for the punchline. None came.

"That's ridiculous," I agreed. "But so long as you get shot of him, and the sooner the better. He's bad news, and the more distance you can put between you and him the better."

They looked at me silently.

"Have a seat, sweetheart," said Mum. I stayed standing; I looked at Mum and then at Monica. *What was I missing?* Then the penny dropped. I didn't need to ask, but I played along.

"Who is the affair with?"

I could see in their eyes what was coming next. I knew Scott and the way a mind like his worked. He'd turned bitter and spiteful and wanted to lash out and hurt as many people as possible, my family included.

Monica was visibly shaken. "I'm so sorry, James . . ."

Mum put her arm around Monica. "Don't you apologise for that rat of a man," she said. She gave me one of her looks that got me to stand taller and focus on what was being said.

"Scott is claiming you had an affair with Monica. Scott is also claiming that it started just before Helena's funeral. That you were having an affair with Monica while your wife lay dying. We all know this is . . ." She bit back a word. "I won't swear, not even under these circumstances. But you know what I'm saying." She gave me a look that said, "You idiot. Say something to show you understand it's not Monica's fault."

Inside I was reeling. I knew Scott was angry about losing Monica, but I really had had no idea he could sink this low. He knew what he was doing. He knew how this would strike a blow.

This felt like a knife to the heart, which was just what Scott had intended. I left the bottle of beer on the worktop and sat down next to Mum. She put one hand on mine and the other on Monica's. I was feeling torn between what was best and what was easy. *Should we simply accept the grounds for the divorce so we could be rid of Scott and all move on?* I was worried what effect accepting this might have on Alice and Faith if they ever found out. Never mind the fact that I was willing to allow Scott to denigrate the memory of my marriage and their mother for the sake of ease and less conflict. Monica could protest; there were no children involved. She and Scott had no children.

The only real winners in prolonging the divorce would be Scott and the solicitors. *How could I do this to Helena? Would she want me to accept the lies and rise above them for the sake of the girls? Or would she want me to fight for the truth, again for the sake of our daughters and for the memory of our marriage?* I could see we were all angry and upset, and of course that was just what Scott wanted. If *he* couldn't be happy, then why should anyone else?

216

It was Mum who spoke. "This family," she said as she squeezed our hands, "has had more pain than it should, but what that pain has done is bring us closer. It's made us stronger in a way many families will never understand. Now you two need to talk, and together you need to decide what should be done. And I want you to know that whatever you decide, we in this family – well, we know the truth, and that is all that matters. We around this table know the truth. Those girls in there are what matter, and so long as I have breath in my body, I will do all I can to protect them and all those I call family. Now what that – please excuse my language – shit of a husband of yours is doing is not right and is not decent, but you both need to look to the future and not to the past."

I opened my mouth to speak, but Mum stopped me with one of her looks. She was going to speak her mind, and I knew better than to interrupt her, especially in her own home.

"Now, I am not going to try to figure you two out and it's not my place, and even if it was this isn't the time. But what I do know is that Scott has a temper, and, unfortunately, he's been poisoned with hatred. We've all seen it," continued Mum as she pressed a finger on the letter in front of us all.

"This is one of those times when the Hardy family unites, and Monica, you know in my eyes you're family. I've known you your whole life. And don't you ever, ever apologise for what that obnoxious man has done. We know the truth. Helena, God rest her beautiful soul, knows the truth. We all know there are battles worth fighting and battles that are not. That man is poison. He was poison when you left him and he's poison today. What is important right now is that we permanently extract his poison from our family and we do it quick." Mum stood up and squeezed us and kissed each of us in turn.

"Now I'm going to see my granddaughters and you two are going to think about what I said. And Jamie, this is one of those times you put aside that stubborn streak of yours and you listen to your mother."

I knew she was right. I hadn't given Scott's frame of mind much thought with everything going on, but he was hurting, and people have a strange way of behaving when they are in pain. I had no idea what he might do if we put up resistance, and I for one didn't want to risk finding out.

I could also see Monica was hurting. She was staring glumly at her hands, blinking back tears. Inside I was hurting too, but, largely due to my anger at the false accusation, my male pride was smarting even more. I always like to win, and that was pretty pathetic under the circumstances.

Mum could see this from the expression on my face and gave me another of her looks as she left the room. *Do what's right for your family. They come first.*

"You know what, Monica?" I said brightly. "This calls for a celebration. You're getting a divorce. A year from now you won't care about what the bloody grounds for it were."

I got to my feet and began to sing and did one of my crazy Irish jigs on the spot. Alice and Faith, hearing the commotion, came running into the room, followed by Mum. When the girls saw me dancing, they grabbed hold of me and I danced them around the kitchen. I grabbed Monica and Mum by the hand and pulled them up onto their feet, and we all went a bit crazy for a while with dancing and laughing and singing. Alice and Faith squealed with delight, and the whole atmosphere quickly turned into a celebration. Dad appeared from wherever he'd been hiding and looked on in amusement.

"Who's hungry?" I said at last, putting my hands on my knees and panting. "Time for a celebratory meal. Who wants to eat out?"

"Me, me, me!" Alice and Faith ran to the front door to put on their shoes and Mum went to help them.

I took Monica to one side and hugged her and kissed her on the forehead.

"Thank you, James," she said softly. "You don't deserve this. The last thing you need is me adding my problems to your life. If I had known . . ."

"Together, we'll get past this. We've been through worse over the last couple of years. You and I make a good team. Let's just take each day as it comes. Together we'll get our lives back on track. All that happened today was we got knocked sideways, so now we need to work to get back on track. And one way to do that is with pepperoni pizza and a good bottle of red wine."

CHAPTER FIFTY-SEVEN

Orel sat on his bed reading. Beside him sat the case. He glanced at it from time to time. It had been several years since he'd been asked to open it. It called to him occasionally, but he'd ignored it. He'd hoped those days were behind him. Perhaps after his next job he could retire for good.

Orel poured another single malt, sipped it and continued to read for a while. *The Old Man and the Sea*, his favourite Hemingway. After a time, he put down the book and carried the case to a small white coffee table, where he sat for a moment and stared at it. Finally, he opened it.

Seeing the gun in its foam surround, he first felt a flicker of excitement and then sadness and finally grief. He knew he would do what needed to be done, and he would do it with ease. Without a second thought. That was what filled him with sadness. Then, when he saw what he had done, again, he would be filled with grief. Not grief for the dead but grief that he had become again the man he thought he'd left behind. The man who could so easily take a life.

Orel closed the case. He sat on the bed again and drank the remains of the whisky in his glass. He looked at his books on the shelf beside the window. He knew he could have been a better man. The older he got, the more he resented his life and the choices he'd made. No matter how hard he tried he somehow seemed unable to shake off who he had become and escape his past.

Reluctantly, Orel returned to the chair and opened the case once more. This time he took the gun out and began cleaning it and checking it. He couldn't bring himself to look at his books as he cleaned the gun. Dickens, Steinbeck, Hemingway, Twain, Faulkner, Fitzgerald and Shakespeare all stared down at him. This would be the last time; he would make sure of it. He loved Papa, and so he had to leave. To find peace, he would need to disappear. It would be easy to suggest to Papa it was a good idea to leave after this, to lie low somewhere for a while. He knew how to do that; he'd done it before. It would then just be a case of not returning. He hoped in time Papa would understand.

CHAPTER FIFTY-EIGHT

The helicopter touched down at Bournemouth Airport. The Flying Squad had received a tip that a man by the name of Shaun Foster had arrived in the UK, and they really wanted to grab him while he was there.

I was met at the airport by Flying Squad officer Aiden Osborne. Osborne looked more like a surfer dude than a Scotland Yard FS detective. Tanned skin, shoulder-length sun-bleached hair, piercing blue eyes, loud open-necked short-sleeved shirt, cargo shorts and flip-flops.

Osborne was wired and talkative as we drove from the airport to the reconnaissance location. He thrust a file into my hand. "I've been tracking Foster for nine years on and off."

I began reading the file as Osborne gave me a potted history.

"Shaun Peter Foster is wanted in at least five countries for offences ranging from tax evasion to murder. Foster is a man for hire, and although he dabbles in arms dealing and contract killing, his true expertise is the movement of goods. He has a reputation for being able to move anything; if it's illegal to move it and you have the money, he'll make it happen."

"How do you know this is your man? It says here he uses disguises and false identities."

Osborne stared at me like I was the worst kind of idiot. "Intelligence," he spat. He was on edge and under pressure. My guess was he'd been undercover a long time and was finally hoping for some payoff. Under normal circumstances he was probably a pretty decent man, but today he was like a pressure cooker.

"In your arena you're some sort of success," he said. "I get that. I respect that. Right now, you're in my back garden. I don't want you here but I was overruled, which is fine. It happens. You obviously have friends up top and your own agenda. Just don't get in my way and don't screw this up for me or my team. If you understand that, we'll be firm friends. Right now, we have zero time before Foster vanishes again. I don't want to be babysitting some paint-by-numbers murder detective, but we're going to make the best of it. Keep your mouth shut and your eyes open, and don't get yourself killed – I hate the paperwork."

"I won't get in your way. I'm here only because Foster is meeting Vlad Kastrati," I said.

"Right," said Osborne. "I read your case reports, as I like to know who I'm working with. I'm sorry about your murdered friend. And your girlfriend – she okay?"

"She's good, thanks. Still shaken but getting better."

After thirty minutes or so we pulled up outside a small bungalow in a quiet suburb. Inside was hot, stuffy and a hive of activity. Tables had been pulled together and maps and paperwork and photos were laid out. A female officer sat in the hallway talking on her phone. She looked up momentarily, nodded, and carried on talking. Two men were preparing to leave and putting on Kevlar vests and checking weapons. I automatically placed a hand on my own brand-new Glock.

"Listen up," said Osborne to the room. "This is DCI James Hardy. Some of you may know him. Most of you will have heard about him or read about him. If you don't know him, then all you need to know is he's one of our very own Scotland Yard murder detectives. Extend to him our kind of professional courtesy."

A joker in the hallway called out, "I hear you're tight with the Albanians. Any chance of a loan? I'm a bit short this month."

Everyone laughed, and another officer high-fived the joker. Osborne patted me on the back. "I guess news travels fast, and bad news fastest of all." He walked over to a table full of printouts where four men stood. "How are we doing?" asked Osborne.

"We're ready to go," said one of the men who was chewing gum at a hundred miles an hour. "We've got two boats, another on standby. Coast Guard's ready. Plus a helicopter if we want it. Local police are briefed as much as they can be. They seem switched on and pumped up, ready for action if they're needed. We're about ready to head out and get this done."

"Well done, guys. Don't forget – Foster is international, so if we screw this up, we look like dicks not only back at the Yard but also in France, Germany, Russia, China and stateside – you get my meaning?"

"We've got this. Foster's not going anywhere."

"Stay safe," said Osborne.

Two men grabbed bags and headed out the door. The woman from the hallway got up and left with them. Osborne blew her a kiss and winked. She mouthed back an expletive and gave him the finger.

"So, what have we heard from our contact?" asked a short, stocky man.

I looked at the photos on the desk. Aerial photos of the house and gardens. Roads in and out. The stretch of beach behind the house. There were faces. I recognised Foster from the file. Vlad was there. Mr Bad Teeth was there and a couple of his friends. A few faces I didn't recognise.

Then I saw Anya's face. She looked different, but it was definitely her. I picked up the photo. Osborne looked at me then at the men around the table.

"Hardy, let's talk," he said.

We headed through to a kitchen area and Osborne shut the door. He opened the fridge and pulled out two cold cans of Coke. He handed me one and paused before filling me in on a little extra-operational detail.

CHAPTER FIFTY-NINE

Osborne sipped his Coke while he considered how much to tell me and where to start. I decided to help him out.

"How long have you known? I'd assumed she was dead." I was angry and I was loud and I didn't care who knew it.

"Listen, it's complicated. Anya isn't dead. She's alive and kicking and has been helping the Drug Squad. They've been trying to get evidence on Vlad for years. She agreed to assist them.

"A few days ago, the Drug Squad passed along intel about a possible meeting between Foster and Vlad. That was when Flying Squad got involved, and I flew in from Miami. Anya's been a real asset. She's passed along times and dates, and today, thanks to her, we're going to nail Foster and your man Vlad the Wolf."

"And that sounds okay with you?" I said.

"It's not ideal, but yeah. It works for me."

"Anya should be in protective custody. She's not trained for any of this; she should be receiving counselling. She's a victim; she's vulnerable; she's a possible witness to murder.

You have deliberately put her in harm's way. Vlad is an animal – he will not think twice about killing her."

"She's not a child," said Osborne. He sipped his Coke and watched me.

"What?"

"She volunteered. Seriously, man, she volunteered. Remember the woman detective in the hallway? The one we nearly tripped over when we arrived? The sexy one who gave me the finger as she left? Well, she's Drug Squad. Her name is Kerry Barnes. She tried to pull Anya out, and your Anya wouldn't hear of it. I think Anya's exact words were 'I am staying. I am close to Vlad. I'm going to cut his balls off and shove them down his throat while he sleeps. I'll do it for Delina and the other girls.'"

I was angry and confused.

"Yeah. Your little princess Anya is one tough cookie. I guess in the end Drug Squad and Anya came up with a better plan than simply cutting off his balls. Though that would have worked for the Drug Squad, I'm sure. For them that would still be a result, but laws being the way they are these days . . ." Osborne laughed at his own joke.

"That's unacceptable. You've put an innocent woman in harm's way. If anything happens to her it's on your head, and I will make sure you answer for it."

"Perhaps in your world everything is neat and tidy. You simply follow the breadcrumbs left by some psycho. Out here, things are dirty. Neat and tidy doesn't exist. Every choice is a bad choice. But we are still expected to get results. If you really can't stomach that, then catch a train back to London. Sounds to me like your girl Anya has more balls than you."

A knock at the door prevented any further discussion. A head peered round the door.

"It's time. We're ready to go. It's now or never."

Osborne looked at me almost sympathetically. "Hardy, this is bad business all around. Put on a vest, check your weapon, and let's get this done."

We drove the mile or so to Vlad's beachfront house. My primary goal now was to ensure Anya was kept out of harm's way. And if Vlad got taken down in the process, that would be a bonus.

CHAPTER SIXTY

There was an eerie sense of calm as we waited for word. Everyone was in position outside Vlad's house.

"Remember, quickly and quietly. We want surprise and zero casualties," said Osborne. He looked at me and continued. "All units, quickly and quietly. Go, go, go." A team of two moved in and worked on opening the huge ornate gates.

Everyone moved quickly once the gates were open. Suddenly it felt like there was movement everywhere. At the same time as we approached from the driveway, a boat landed on the beach to the rear of the house. Halfway up the long driveway we split into three groups. One team continued straight on. One team split off and went right. I was part of a team that went left.

We met little resistance. It seemed none of Vlad's men fancied their chances against such a show of force. Weapon drawn, I ascended a staircase on the outside of the building. It led up to a decked area at the rear of the building. As I got higher, I saw Foster and Anya. They were at a table talking. At first, they were oblivious to our presence. I saw no sign of Vlad.

From inside the house and to my right, Osborne and two officers approached through open patio doors. As they moved onto the decked area, I completed the stairs and moved onto the decked patio to join Osborne. Foster had no way out.

Seeing us, Foster jumped to his feet and in one fluid movement was behind Anya. He smashed the stem of a glass and held it to her throat. I looked into Anya's wide eyes and tried to reassure her through my own. Foster knew he had nowhere to go and was buying time to think. He dragged Anya to her feet and together they moved to the edge of balcony. He looked over the side and down to the garden and beach below. Moored below was Vlad's boat, *Wave Goodbye*. I followed his line of sight and could see what Foster was thinking. I also realised if he got to that boat with Anya, she was dead for sure.

"You're a smart man, Foster," I said. "You can see there is no way out on this occasion. The house is surrounded. There are men on the boat down there." I nodded towards *Wave Goodbye*. Foster looked back down at the boat. "Plus, the Coast Guard are waiting further out to sea."

Despite his hopeless situation, Foster remained calm. It was as if he believed he was in control.

My weapon raised, I took several steps closer. "Where's Vlad?" I asked. "Where is he now?"

Whatever went through Foster's mind at that moment I'll never know. Maybe he thought Vlad had set him up. Maybe he thought Vlad was an undercover informant. Maybe he just thought Vlad had saved his own skin. Whatever it was, it ended the standoff. From behind her,

Foster whispered into Anya's ear. Her eyes widened and she looked left, towards Foster, as he spoke to her.

Foster then turned Anya to face him. I stepped forward and raised my weapon.

"Let her go, now!' I shouted. But Foster ignored me. Instead, he raised the hand holding the broken glass above his head and with his other hand he pulled Anya close. Then, to everyone's surprise, he kissed her.

"Thank you. I've wanted to do that all day," he said to Anya. "I now have something to cherish during the long years ahead." Using her as a shield, Foster calmly got down on the floor behind her, first to his knees and then to his stomach. He spread his arms and legs on the hot wooden decking, then smiled and watched Anya as officers ran over and cuffed him.

Osborne had his man. I, on the other hand, did not. Vlad was gone. At that moment, though, my only care was that Anya was safe. I holstered my weapon, ran to her, then walked her to safety.

CHAPTER SIXTY-ONE

There had been no sightings of Vlad since just before we entered the house. Foster wasn't talking. Anya told us Vlad had received a call and excused himself sometime before we arrived. Osborne assumed Vlad had been tipped off. Osborne's priority had always been to get Foster, so he was happy with the result; in fact, he was almost giddy. He was shaking hands with everyone and patting them on the back. "Great job" and "Job well done," he kept saying.

I, on the other hand, wondered what had gone wrong. This wasn't how I had expected the day to go. However, it was a good day in the sense that Anya was safe. She was now under the protection of the Drug Squad; I had talked to her briefly before she left and introduced myself and reassured her Monica was fine. I told her Monica and I would check in on her in a few days, once I was back in London.

By late evening, I was alone in Vlad's house except for a couple of local police officers posted out front to keep the house secure. For some reason, I couldn't bring myself to leave. I had come here to face Vlad, to stop him and to bring him in for what he'd done. Where along the way had everything gotten so mixed up?

I walked through the house, and as I went through the kitchen I picked up a packet of cigarettes from the worktop. I hadn't smoked in almost ten years and I knew I'd regret the decision tomorrow, but right now I didn't care.

I walked down to the beach and as I walked, I smoked. It was getting late and the sun had pretty much gone down. It had been a hot day, and although it was a clear evening there was a chill in the air, so I buttoned up my jacket and lifted my collar. I could hear birds along the shoreline arguing and preparing to roost; the tweeting, piping and cawing was an easy distraction. I tried to block out the noise so I could think, but my mind was refusing to focus. I considered phoning Alice and Faith and Monica but decided to do it later. I was missing them, but I knew I was feeling low and didn't want to pass on that vibe.

I needed time to clear my head and put together a strategy for what to do next. There was so much going on. The day shouldn't have ended this way; Vlad should have been in custody. Was he tipped off, or did he really just get lucky? Who would have tipped him off? Had it been one of our own? Was he gone for good, or would he come for Anya? If it was one of our own, what did this person know of Anya's involvement?

I ground out the cigarette and lit another. I stood staring at Vlad's boat then looked back at the house. So much money, I thought. It always seemed to me that the wealth these people accumulated must be directly proportional to the misery they caused others.

It was getting dark and I was getting cold. I realised I was hungry and remembered I hadn't yet made arrangements for sleeping. I'd need to find a hotel. I turned and began the walk back up the narrow path to the house.

Partway along the path I stopped and took out my phone to send Mum and Monica a text message, letting them know I was safe and I'd see them tomorrow. I asked that they let Alice and Faith know I loved them and missed them. I finished my message and pressed send. As I looked up, I felt the full force of a fist in my face. I went down hard. Blood poured from my broken nose and my eyes filled with tears. A kick to the stomach and a stamp to the ribs quickly followed. Through the low light and tears, I recognised the figure of Vlad. The Wolf had left his den and was on the hunt.

"Hardy, the only reason you are not dead is because I need information. Once I have it, I will kill you. If you lie to me, I will also kill your family," he said.

I struggled to my feet and leaned against the fence lining the path. "You left?" I said. "Why would you come back?"

"I didn't leave. But you knew that, didn't you? That's why you're here. When I built this house, I had some private rooms fitted. Those rooms are not on any plans. I don't know why, but from time to time I have to be alone with someone special, and during those moments I cannot be interrupted. I understand you knew Delina. Just like the others, she cried and begged when I took her to my private room and showed her the blade – they all cry and beg. But, in that moment, right before I slip the blade between their ribs, I can't hear them. I'm lost in a moment of pure ecstasy. I only see their mouths opening and shutting, like little fishes." Vlad was in my face now, opening and shutting his mouth like a fish.

"The need comes and goes, Mr Policeman Hardy. It comes and goes. They come and go. Life comes and goes."

"What do you want?"

"Good question. You know what? Before we get down to that, let's go somewhere more comfortable. Let's go back to the house, where you and I can be all alone. We'll be cosy. Maybe I can have a drink. You can have a bleed. What do you say? Does that sound like fun?"

Vlad pressed a gun to my head and motioned me forward. I thought about the gun under my buttoned jacket. I had an advantage in that British police don't routinely carry a firearm, so why would he look? I prayed he wouldn't.

CHAPTER SIXTY-TWO

Vlad pushed, shoved and prodded me up to the house. He insisted on telling me about his day and how, having been holed up in a single room for almost seven hours, there were certain oversights that he could now see would need to be rectified in future room designs.

We reached the top of the garden, turned right and climbed the same staircase I'd climbed earlier that day – under very different circumstances.

"I watched everything on CCTV, of course," said Vlad. "I've got cameras all over the house and garden." I pictured Vlad behind me with a Cheshire cat grin on his face.

We climbed the last few steps and reached the terrace, where I stopped and wiped my bloody nose with my sleeve. I took the chance to look down for the two officers on duty below.

"They can't help you, Hardy. They're off duty, permanently," said Vlad. A shadow below caught my eye and caused Vlad to turn his head and look. That was the chance I needed. I twisted around and brought my fist down on his face at the same time I raised my leg. I launched him down the staircase with my foot. Vlad fell backwards, and as he toppled his head and body collided with the handrail. In an effort to break his fall he dropped his gun and made a grab for the railings. He rolled and smashed his way down the steps.

I took a few steps back and, pulling open my jacket, took out my Glock for the second time that day. I hesitated for a moment to take stock. *Should I run? Should I fire? Should I arrest?* I stepped forward and pointed my weapon. Vlad was already back on his feet at the top of the stairs. I stepped back and allowed him onto the terrace.

"You're under arrest," I said. "Get face down on the floor."

"Really? I don't think so, Hardy. I've tried prison. I didn't like it. It's the poor food, mainly; it doesn't agree with me." Vlad took a step forward.

"Get face down," I demanded. Again, Vlad moved forward, his hands out and to his sides. He was unarmed. He just kept walking towards me.

"If you were going to shoot me you would have done it already. How about instead we make a deal? We'll call it even, and I'll just jump into my boat down there and we can pretend like none of this ever happened."

Out of the corner of my eye I again caught sight of a moving shadow. *Was it real or a symptom of the blow to the head? Was my mind playing tricks on me?*

In the darkness, a voice came from the shadows to my left.

"Never hesitate."

I stepped back and glanced from side to side, trying to locate the voice.

"Never, ever hesitate," came the voice again, but this

time from behind me. In the darkness, I could see nothing. I kept the gun trained on Vlad.

Vlad recognised the voice and saw him first. "Orel, my friend," he said. "I'm happy to see you. What are doing here? Now, Hardy, you have a very serious problem."

"I came here to find you, Vlad," said Orel, who was passing through a patch of light.

"I have this under control, though perhaps while you're here you could cover poor Detective Hardy while I take his gun," said Vlad. He stepped forward to grab the Glock, and I stepped back to prevent that happening.

Out of the darkness Orel came up close behind me. He pressed his gun against my head. "Put the gun on the table," he whispered.

Slowly I placed the gun on the table and Orel picked it up. Vlad rushed up and for a second time punched me in the face. As I fell, he punched me once more, this time to the side of the head, causing everything to go dark.

When I came to, I was in a chair in the kitchen. My hands were fastened to the back of the chair with zip ties. I looked around. My right eye was swollen shut, forcing me to look as best I could through my one good eye. The house was quiet, strangely peaceful. The double doors to the terrace were closed. My mouth tasted of blood. My nose and ears throbbed. I could see Orel leaning against the breakfast bar, watching me. Vlad was close by, pouring himself a whisky. He was behaving oddly; he seemed almost manic. I wondered if he'd taken something and was high.

"Why did you hesitate?" said Orel, snapping his fingers to get my attention. He was talking to me. I looked at him blankly. "When Vlad fell down the stairs earlier. You hesitated. You stopped to think instead of just shooting him. Why?"

"I didn't hesitate. I need to arrest him, not kill him," I said.

Orel stood up from the breakfast bar and walked towards me, waving my gun from side to side as he spoke. "You hesitated. You know as well as I do that Vlad here is a rapist, a coward who tortures and murders innocent women. Unlike you and me, Vlad here has given up trying to understand and nurture his humanity. He is not interested in what it is that makes him human. He has no concept of order. He does not see the beauty of life but instead is controlled by his own selfish desires. He is an untrustworthy dog. Yet you hesitated to put him down when you had the chance, and now look at you. So I ask again, why did you hesitate?"

Vlad downed his whisky and poured another. "If it's all the same to you, Orel," he said, "and because I am in the room, can we perhaps not have this conversation right now?" He pulled a knife from a block and flashed it at me. "How about instead we find out from your new friend who gave up my location today and who gave up the fact I was meeting Mr Foster. Then let's get the hell out of here."

I pushed back in my seat, shifting my gaze from Orel to Vlad.

"Vlad, you enjoy your drink. I wish to have a conversation," said Orel. He began admiring my gun and then continued. "I have decided to retire after tonight. I'm going to vanish. So I think it's important, then, that my last kill should make a difference. I'd like it to mean something and to be significant."

Orel raised the Glock and pointed it at me, first at my chest then at my head. He looked me in the eye and then turned and pointed the gun at Vlad. Vlad never saw it coming, and I watched in amazement as Orel put a bullet in his head. Vlad sank to his knees, disappearing out of sight behind the bar. Orel walked around it and fired twice more, then looked over at me.

"Today is your lucky day, Hardy." Orel removed the magazine from the gun and racked it empty. Checked the chamber. Then placed it on the breakfast bar in front of me. "Never hesitate again." Orel cut the ties and released my hands. "Papa told you he would take care of the situation, and he has. This ends tonight. You're free to go." Orel handed me a handkerchief for my nose. "Leave through the front. There are things I need to do here."

I picked up my Glock and walked slowly out of the house.

From the roadside, I watched as flames and smoke began to engulf the building. I felt a sense of closure as I watched them rise up against the night sky. I sat and rested on a low wall across the street from the beach house. I winced as I touched my nose and felt my eye. I ached all over and felt exhausted. I took out my phone and called Monica and the girls. I needed to hear the familiar voices of those I loved.

As soon as I heard the excited squeals of my little girls, a wave of comfort and reassurance hit me, and I was unable to prevent tears from rolling down my face.

CHAPTER SIXTY-THREE

Monica and I visited Anya several times over the next few weeks. Monica went with her to counselling; it was good for both of them. She also helped Anya find a shared flat with some college students. I was relieved to see that Anya was quickly putting the recent events behind her and getting her life back into some sort of order. It was reassuring to see her coping so well. As the weeks passed, I visited less frequently, and although I didn't lose touch exactly, when I did call by Anya was usually either out or busy. It all seemed natural enough, and I was pleased she was moving on.

It was around four months after the events at the beach house that I was called by Detective Kerry Barnes.

"Remember me?" she said. "I was with you and Osborne at Vlad's beach house."

"Of course I remember you, Detective Barnes. How are things in Drug Squad?"

"Busy, busy. You know how it is. We congratulate ourselves on making one huge seizure when we know another five got through," said Barnes. "How's your nose? I hear it got busted pretty badly."

"Good as new. You'd never know it happened."

"Great news; that's great news," she said.

"Anyway, you didn't call me to talk about my devilishly good looks. How can I help?" I was a little apprehensive asking, as the investigation into the shooting of Vlad was finally being wrapped up.

"You're right. I do have something on my mind. The thing is, I might be able to help you. Meet me out front as quickly as you can. I'm across the street in a silver BMW."

I grabbed my coat and headed out. When I had seen her last, Barnes had been kitted out in Kevlar, ready for action. Today her hair was down and she was wearing a hint of makeup and looking relaxed in casual clothes; she looked very different.

"Glad you could make it," she said as I climbed into the passenger seat. "Let's go for a little drive."

"What's this all about?"

"It's better I show you," she said, pulling away from the kerb. "But let's just say, after I interviewed her and took her statement, your girl Anya and I got chatting. At the time I couldn't put my finger on it, but something just didn't sit right with me. Since then, the whole thing has been nagging away at me. Something just didn't feel right. Whether it was the way she too easily agreed to help – I don't know. At the time, I wanted Foster so badly I just happy she volunteered. But after the raid, I couldn't stop thinking about all the pieces. You know how it is; it's what makes a detective a detective, I suppose. We just never know when to let go."

"Osborne told me she volunteered," I said. "To be honest, I didn't believe him. The Anya I was told about was scared and on the run."

"She did volunteer, and she came through, effortlessly. She delivered Foster. You nailed Vlad. It was all so neat and tidy, it almost had a silk bow on top."

I looked at her and thought how neat and tidy wouldn't exactly be the way I would describe the events that day.

"What are you getting at?"

"I did some follow-up work," said Barnes.

"Really? What sort of follow-up work?" I asked.

"I know you've been helping her get settled, and I can only assume you have questions, even if you're not sure what they are. I'm pretty sure you don't stay in touch with every witness on a case. I also know you're too decent to be hanging around her because she's hot."

I ignored the last part. "How about you get to the point. What are you suggesting? Do you have a question? If you do, just come right out and ask it." I wasn't sure where Barnes was going with this and now felt I was being scrutinised.

"I'm not suggesting anything, and I didn't mean to deflate your male ego." She paused, indicated, and pulled over. "Here we are. We'll park here and walk the rest of the way."

We got out of the car and headed to Knightsbridge, where we crossed the street and stood opposite Harrods. Barnes's phone rang. She talked loudly. "Yep. Okay. Okay. We're right across the street. We'll head around the side."

She turned to me and nodded towards the side street. "Perfect timing. They're on their way out," she said.

"What are we supposed to be looking at?" I demanded impatiently. Barnes looked at me and smiled playfully. I wasn't happy about being kept in the dark but played along. We crossed the road and stood alongside a row of luxury cars, all parked and waiting for the millionaire shoppers to return.

Barnes nudged me. "Keep watching." After a few minutes of people coming and going, the doors opened and Barnes indicated this was what we had been waiting for. Out stepped a finely dressed young woman who was smiling and laughing. She was arm in arm with a much older man who was carrying several Harrods bags. I recognised him instantly: it was Papa. He wore a tailored suit and looked ten years younger. He turned his head and the couple kissed; Papa then opened the door to a shiny white Range Rover and the young woman started to get in. As she did so, she looked left and right. Looking my way, she paused and then looked again. She lowered her sunglasses and then took them off to get a better look at me.

"Anya?" I said to Barnes. I watched in disbelief as she got into the Range Rover and then leaned over and gave Papa another kiss.

"Yep," I heard Barnes say beside me. "We can't prove it, but I guess she struck a deal with Papa. Papa clearly had a plan to use us to remove Foster and Vlad. Anya was his way of making sure he had the right information to make that happen. Smart, huh?"

I took a step forward and felt Barnes's hand on my shoulder. "Your girl Anya is doing just fine. She's landed well and truly on her feet. From what I understand, she is now living the millionaire lifestyle. This is just a little shopping trip before she and Papa, who's like a new man I might add, jet off for a few weeks on his yacht in the Mediterranean."

I watched as the Range Rover approached, but I couldn't see past the tinted windows. I wondered whether Anya was watching me as the vehicle passed us.

"Sometimes," said Barnes, "we get the result we want,

but not in the way we want it. In my book, it's still a good result."

CHAPTER SIXTY-FOUR

I was owed some leave, and Chief Superintendent Webster had insisted I take some now that Vlad's investigation was wrapped up.

"I don't care what you do so long as it's not working on any investigations. Now get out of here. I don't want to see you for at least a week, preferably two," said Webster with the best of intentions.

With no contact from the Gallery Killer for months now and no firm evidence implicating Simon Baker, now seemed the right time to move my little family back into our home. Mum and Dad had been amazing, as always, but I felt like we all needed some day-to-day normality back in our lives. Whatever that was.

I was spending precious time with Alice and Faith, and I was loving it. I didn't see how it could be done, but it got me wondering whether I could find a way to have a better work–life balance.

A few days into my leave, we were returning from Windsor and a day at Legoland. Monica was going out with girlfriends that evening, so I called home to let her know I hadn't forgotten and I was on my way. I then called Rayner, and he decided he'd come over around nine, after the girls were in bed, for a beer and to keep me in the loop about ongoing investigations. There was a lot happening and things were moving fast, so he was happy to keep me up to date with the direction the investigations were taking, so long as I was recuperating.

The girls were in their pyjamas and were excitedly telling Monica about their busy day at Legoland. I herded them upstairs to read stories and talk, giving Monica space to bathe and get ready for her night out. The girls couldn't resist running back and forth between rooms to see what Monica was wearing, offer advice and makeup tips, and try on a little makeup themselves. Eventually the girls settled down and after some prayers for Mummy, we turned out the lights and I went downstairs.

Monica was in the kitchen. She was all dressed up for the evening and checking her phone for messages. She looked beautiful. Heels, a tight-fitting black dress, hair up and just a little makeup.

"Wow, you look great. Are you sure you're not going on a date? Come on, who's the lucky guy?" I said.

"Now that, Detective, would be telling."

"Well, enjoy yourself. Relax. Have fun. Be good. Don't drink too much. Stay safe."

"You sound like my dad."

I thought I might as well lay it on thick. "To be on the safe side, I'd like the names of everyone you're going out with tonight. I'd like their mobile numbers, their home addresses and home telephone numbers. Who is the designated driver? Is your phone fully charged? Do you have your pepper spray? You know, I may even have a spare taser in the back of my car. Shall I get it?"

I guess Monica could see I was exhausted, despite my

effort to stay upbeat and my teasing. "Are you sure you're okay with me going out tonight? I don't need to go. I can go another time. It really doesn't matter."

"You're kidding, right? I'm fine. You're not to worry about me. You have your own life, and the last thing I want to do is get in the way of you rebuilding it. Anyway, Rayner's coming over for a beer. I'll be fine."

There was a knock at the front door. "I guess that's my ride," said Monica.

"You have a great time. It's not too late for me to find that taser."

"You really are a bundle of fun," said Monica, laughing.

"I'm just saying you can never have enough self-defence tools when you look as good as you do."

I opened the front door to two of Monica's girlfriends. Another two were in the car waving to me. I waved back. They were all laughing and already having a good time.

"Good evening, Detective Inspector," said the two women on the doorstep. They were giggling, and clearly I was missing a joke. I recognised them as Sam and Ali. I was pretty sure they'd already had a glass of wine (or two or three) and their girls' night had started some time earlier.

"Good evening, Samantha. Good evening, Alison."

"We were wondering," said Samantha, trying hard to suppress her laughter, "is it only the constables, or are detectives like yourself also equipped with a big truncheon?" Beside her, Ali let out a snort and covered her mouth with her hands.

Monica gathered her two friends and whisked them off the doorstep, giving me a backwards wave as she herded them down the walk. I watched the three of them laugh and giggle like teenagers down to the car and then I waved as they drove off.

I closed the door behind me, and the house felt quiet and empty. I could still hear the laughter of the women ringing in my ears and it felt good. It brought back memories. Happy memories. I grabbed a cold bottle of beer from the fridge and checked my watch. Rayner would be here soon. I took the opportunity to check on the girls before he arrived. They were fine. Fast asleep. They'd crawled into bed together, as they often did. How there was enough room in the bed for the two of them with all Faith's soft toys piled in as well I wasn't sure, but they managed it.

I went back downstairs in time to come face to face with Rayner, who was at the back door holding up a case of beer and an arm full of reports.

Here's my date for the night, I thought, and ushered him in.

CHAPTER SIXTY-FIVE

I groped about in the darkness and found my phone.

"Hullo?" I said, trying to sound awake.

"Is that you, Hardy?" asked a voice that sounded way too perky for this time of day.

"Who is this?" I asked. I must have sounded angry.

"Sorry to call you so early, but this just couldn't wait. Not one moment longer. I'm so pleased you and your family are back. I've been waiting very patiently."

My head was still foggy as I sat up and turned on the bedside light. "Who is this?"

"Very kind of you to ask. It's me. I thought perhaps we might pray together. In light of recent events."

"Baker?" My eyes widened. I was fully awake now.

"Just like that. You are as sharp as they say. I feel so blessed; of all the detectives at Scotland Yard, I got you. The Yard's brightest. Now, enough of that. I am going to keep this short and sweet, because we are both busy, busy boys with so many commitments to keep."

I interrupted in an effort to avoid Baker taking control of the situation. "How about you and I meet. There's a lot we can talk about. You can share what's on your mind, and I can give you my full attention."

"Well, that's rather rude. I'm hoping you'll give me your full attention right now."

I pressed back. "Why not give me some time to wake up, and we'll meet somewhere with great coffee."

"That is rather clumsy of you, Detective. But I am in a very forgiving mood, as I have been working through my list and I'm feeling rather chipper. There's a word that isn't used often enough these days: chip-perrr! Redemption is so rewarding. It does take a little work, mind you. You definitely get out what you put in. Now, I really would rather you didn't interrupt me, as this is an important day and there is lots we have to get done. Both of us. There are people who will be relying on you being the superhero 'Hardyman' today. I've decided to head to a favourite retreat for a while, but don't worry. I'll be back once I've had a little R and R."

It was a risk, but I needed to try to get this conversation back on my terms. "Why?" I asked.

There was silence from Baker.

"Why?" I repeated. "Why are you murdering innocent people like some mindless psychopath?"

More silence. I could hear his breathing become heavier and more rapid. "I am not insane, you know. You can't force me to feel remorseful with your petty insults. Please don't pretend you don't understand why I am punishing them. And you certainly aren't going to spoil our little game today."

"Perhaps you think you're some sort of god-made flesh who can hand down his own form of justice. You're nothing but a pathetic little man who murders, in a cowardly way, unsuspecting and innocent people." I hung up the phone before he could reply. I felt confident he'd call back. He'd called me for a reason, and I hadn't given him a chance yet to give me that reason. His ego meant he had to call back. Baker needed an audience; he needed me to be a part of his game. He would call back. He needed recognition and maybe some understanding of what he wanted to achieve. In his fantasies, I'm sure he imagined I understood his reasoning and felt sympathy for his cause.

I grabbed my clothes and put them on, all the time looking at the phone. I suspected he was really confused now: this turn of events wasn't what he had imagined. He would have prepared this conversation in his head. Gone over it, time and time again. Probably imagined me a little in awe of his ruthlessness and the way he meted out justice.

I slipped on my shoes. The phone rang as I began to tie the laces. I finished the second bow and answered the phone.

"You interrupted me again," Baker said stiffly. "That is very, very rude. Do that again and I will ensure the next on my list suffers more than all the others combined. And I will tell them and their family why. Then I will come after your little princesses. See, now you've turned me into a monster on our special day. Let's begin again, shall we?"

Baker loved the sound of his own voice, and I was wondering whether this was all an act or whether he really was this delusional. Without waiting for my reply, Baker continued.

"Now that little charade is over, I want us to be honest with each other. I'll start.

"At first, this was about payback. As time has gone on, I've realised that this role I have is so much more than that. There are so many nuances to what I am a part of. It took me a while to understand but once I took the time to stand back, I could see the big picture. I realised then just how remarkable the whole thing is. It's almost like there is an industry relying on murder. You know what I mean, right? There's you, me, the press, the whole legal system, prisons and parole boards. So many people rely on what we do. There's the research, the tools needed to fulfil our roles, and on and on. So many people are relying on me and you.

"Eventually, of course, Simon Baker will become a brand name. Like Ted Bundy, Jack the Ripper, etcetera. So I've decided that once I have completed my current list, I will write a new one. And I wanted you to be the first to know. It's true I stumbled on this path. I'll admit, I can't take credit for that. But we never know the intended path of our lives. It finds us."

I let Baker talk. All this was being recorded on my phone, and although I wouldn't be able to necessarily locate him, the information would be valuable for psychological analysis. And while he was talking, he wasn't killing. Perhaps I could also build some trust and get something out of him to help me track him down.

"You know those men you mentioned – Ted Bundy, Jack the Ripper?" I said. "They couldn't stop. But as you said, you're not insane. You can stop. How remarkable would that be? That would be really something. You could be unique in the way that you chose to stop. That would truly be a story – the story of how serial killer Simon Baker handed himself in. Imagine the press coverage that would generate."

Baker sniffed. "Enough. I thought you'd be a better listener. I thought you'd hear me. I thought you'd understand. You're supposed to be something special. They told me I was lucky I had you. They were wrong. You're not special: you're clumsy. The Mentor told me I had to watch out for you; she said you had a unique understanding. But you don't. Enough. I've had enough."

Baker went quiet again. I could hear his rapid breathing, hear him seething, his anger and exasperation. I was getting to him.

"The Mentor?" I asked. He'd said more than he wanted to. "Who's that? And who did you mean by *they*? Are there others like you? Where? Who?"

The line went dead. Baker was gone. This was still Baker's game we were playing, but at least I now had a better understanding of his rules. He wasn't fulfilling his sick fantasies alone.

A few seconds later a text message came through on my phone. Baker hadn't finished with me just yet.

CHAPTER SIXTY-SIX

The text message from Baker made me go cold. It was short and sinister:

GO C MY MOTHER. LEFT U A GIFT – WIFE'S BITCH LAWYER. HURRY. EXPIRES SOON. BYE 4 NOW XXX

Was this a trap? I wondered. Had Baker become more sophisticated? Perhaps he'd developed a taste for traps, encouraged and emboldened by his psycho friends or The Mentor, whoever that might be. I felt sure he was angry. The coolness he'd displayed during our meeting at the school had quickly evaporated once he felt off balance. On the phone he'd made mistakes, given me too much. He'd betrayed The Mentor and the others he'd spoken of just by mentioning them. He'd broken their trust. That would have set off all sort of emotions for him.

I knew from experience that his sense of superiority would temporarily feel diminished, thanks to his having made mistakes. I'd seen it before in other cases, and I knew it wouldn't last long. He'd adapt and learn, just like with anything we are driven to do. And Baker was driven. He now had a taste for what he was doing; he'd said as much by admitting he was writing a new list of targets. I also knew he wouldn't stop unless I stopped him.

Today he wanted to play a new game, one that had probably been planned for weeks, maybe even months, and his phone call this morning had been to make sure I was on board.

I called the Yard and spoke to Rayner, who arrived at Baker's home a few minutes after me. We both chose to wear Kevlar as we headed to the front of 232 Crescent Drive. We checked our weapons in silence. The chief had been right: under these circumstances I certainly felt more comfortable carrying a firearm. Only Baker knew what was waiting for us inside, and that filled me with dread. My firearm meant the odds were a little more evenly balanced.

"You need to make some new friends," said Rayner as we approached the front door. "Serial killers will never want to simply hang out with you, drink beer and watch the Cup Final, you know."

His wisecracking meant he was on edge. We both were. His eyes told me he knew as well as I did we could be walking into a trap. His body language also told me I wouldn't have a cat in hell's chance of stopping him going into the house with me. If there was any chance at all of saving a life, Rayner was going in. Rayner knew the same went for me.

I checked the front window but couldn't see inside.

"I'll go 'round back," said Rayner. "Give me the count of twenty."

I nodded and watched him disappear down the side of the house.

". . .Seven, eight, nine, ten," I counted to myself. When I got to twenty, I knocked on the front door and called out: "Police. This is the police." I knocked again, louder.

Nothing. I hammered my fist and rang the doorbell and called out again. Nothing. Then the door chain rattled and the lock clicked. I stepped back. The door opened. It was Rayner.

"The back of the house is all open," he said.

Neither of us knew whether that was a good thing or a bad thing. Rayner headed back through the house to the kitchen. I stood in the hallway for a moment and simply listened. The house was quiet. Rayner and I made eye contact and I indicated I was headed to the front room on my right. I pushed open the door and caught the strong smell of cigarette smoke. I stepped into the 1970s-style front room. Beside the bay window was an old woman in a chair. Cigarette packets were piled high on the table beside her and boxes were scattered at her feet. Her head was back, covered in a plastic bag. I removed the bag, but the old lady was ice cold and had no pulse.

His own mother was now another name on Baker's list. What was going through his head? What did he want? I listened numbly as Rayner called for an ambulance.

Upstairs I heard scratching, a rapid, repetitive scratching. We made our way up the stairs to the second floor. Rayner went first and I covered him. The scratching was getting louder; it would last a few seconds then stop. Then start again. At the top of the stairs were five doors. The scratching was coming from the second door on the right. Rayner and I raised our guns and approached with caution.

There was silence, and then the scratching started again. My heart was pounding. I raised my weapon, ready to fire if necessary. Rayner grabbed the door handle and in one quick, smooth motion swung open the door. There in the dark stood a small dog, a pug. He looked at the two of us for a moment with huge, glossy black eyes, gave a short, sharp bark, then ran between us and disappeared down the stairs.

"We'll question him later," said Rayner, trying to relieve the tension. Right now, I was in no mood for wisecracks; I felt sure this wasn't over. Baker was sending me a message; my fear was that it would be grotesque and bloody. Baker was upping his game and he wanted me to know it.

We moved to the next room, which was the bathroom. It was empty; I felt a mixture of anxiety and relief. The next room was a small bedroom. Again nothing. The next room was smaller and appeared to have been used as an office but was now almost empty. There was no computer, and only bare shelves and an empty filing cabinet.

The final room was locked. The key was missing. I knew from the sick feeling in my stomach that the gift promised by Simon Baker was behind this door. Rayner took position to cover me. I took a step back and threw my shoulder at the door.

The room burst into view in all its horrifying glory.

CHAPTER SIXTY-SEVEN

In all honesty, I wasn't prepared for what we encountered next. No furniture, no decoration, just bare walls and floorboards. The room was empty. Empty except for the woman hanging by her arms and neck. Suspended in mid-air, she looked like she had been crucified on an invisible cross. Instead of a crucifix to hold her, however, a noose came down from the ceiling and was biting into her neck. Ropes fastened to each wall held her arms outstretched. Her ankles were bound and her feet were resting on a box. Her head was flopped forward and her long hair covered her face. There were streaks of blood on her chest, stomach and legs.

I holstered my gun and ran forward. Outside, sirens wailed. Officers and paramedics were arriving, yet my world at that moment had shrunk to what was right in front of me. I grabbed the woman and held her while Rayner cut the ropes. We laid her on the floor and I gently swept aside her hair and checked for a pulse. I didn't need to; she opened her eyes and began coughing and shaking violently, pushing me away and making an awful animal-like moan. Her mouth, chin and neck were caked in dried blood. Her scared eyes stared at me.

"She's alive," I called over my shoulder to Rayner. "She's alive. Get a paramedic, now!"

The woman went quiet and calm.

"You're going to be fine," I told her. "You're safe. I'm a police officer – we're police officers. Paramedics are on their way. It's over now. You've been so brave. It's all over; you're safe. I promise. You're going to be okay. Can you tell me your name?"

She didn't speak. Her calm evaporated and she put a hand to her mouth and sobbed hysterically. Rayner returned with a duvet and we covered her. She felt so small in my arms and I continued to hold her trembling body.

"Paramedics are coming," I said soothingly. "They're coming up the stairs. They'll be here any second."

Rayner was agitated and angry. He paced the room, looking at the small ornate box the woman had been standing on. He walked around it, knelt down beside it, got back up and began pacing again.

I knew what was inside long before Rayner told me.

I looked sympathetically into the woman's eyes. Her body was spasming, and periodically she rocked from side to side in my arms. Her howls of anguish and sorrow went right through me, but I held her and did my best to comfort her.

Paramedics came into the room now and moved quickly to stabilise the woman. Her belongings had now been found and identified her as Lucy-Ann Chandler, age fifty-seven, a popular and outspoken radio and television arts critic. She, like the other victims, had been shocked and outraged when she'd heard of Simon Baker's deception and treatment of his talented wife and had publicly denounced him, as had the others.

I watched as the paramedics lifted Lucy-Ann into the back of the ambulance, then looked across the street to the house where Rayner was briefing the forensics team. He and I have known each other for a long time and he knew what I was thinking. Neither of us needed to say anything.

Rayner took charge of the crime scene and I watched as he co-ordinated the teams. Everyone was keen to do their part in an effort to put an end to Baker's madness. I needed to escape; Baker was getting to my head. I needed space to take stock. In a split-second decision, I climbed into the back of the ambulance. In that moment, I needed to feel like I was being of help, and if that meant nothing more than comforting this terrified woman, then so be it.

I sat with Lucy-Ann until early evening. She had been sedated to help with the shock and her pain. She had drifted in and out of consciousness throughout the day. Her stillness gave me time to think, and seeing her injuries gave me further impetus, if any were needed, to stop Baker once and for all.

Throughout the day faces from the forensic and fingerprint team came and went; they needed samples for comparison. Her husband and grown-up sons were on their way and would arrive around midnight; they were driving the four hundred-plus miles from Edinburgh. They'd want answers, and I'd have questions, but not right away. First, they'd need time as a family to cry and to comfort one another.

Lucy-Ann was sleeping and I doubt she heard me, but I whispered to her I was leaving for a while and that I'd be back soon. I was of the opinion that Baker's plan had been to inflict pain and humiliation on Lucy-Ann; if he'd wanted her dead, he'd have done it. So even though I didn't anticipate any further threat from Baker, I decided to station an officer outside her hospital room.

I sat in my car in the hospital car park and called Rayner. He hadn't calmed down that much, if at all.

"He cut out her tongue," he said through gritted teeth. "He cut out her tongue and put it in the box, and then made her stand on it. What sort of monster does that? I have never wanted anyone so bad. We have to catch this prick, whatever it takes. Whatever it takes."

"What did the note say?" I asked.

"How did you know there was a note?"

I ignored the question and Rayner repeated the note's message: *Your mother should have told you to watch your tongue. Well, now you can.*

We talked for an hour or so and then he told me to get home and get some rest. He insisted there was nothing that couldn't wait until after a good night's sleep. I drove out of the car park but I couldn't go home. Something was eating away at me; I was missing something. So instead of turning left out of the car park, I turned right and headed back to Scotland Yard.

Fuelled by coffee, I spent the night re-examining the case notes, re-reading reports, listening to recordings, comparing photographs and going over Baker's family history. I listened over and over to his call to me. I needed to understand Baker better than I did. I needed to understand who he really was, why he was doing what he was doing.

Baker had been one step ahead of me at every stage. If I wanted to catch this man, I needed to know his next move, and that meant knowing more about how he thought. I had come to the decision over the course of the last few days that the fraud case and the imprisonment of his wife were only a small part of a bigger picture. I was now convinced that if I began to dig deep enough, I'd discover what was really driving Baker to act out his horrific fantasies. Why take the risk of punishing the victims so dramatically?

These crimes had to be more than simple revenge. They had all been elaborate and unnecessarily staged: he was making statements. I needed to figure out why he took the time and risk. If I wanted to figure out where he was going next, I needed to figure out where he'd been and who the real Simon Baker was.

CHAPTER SIXTY-EIGHT

At 10.35 a.m. I walked into Rayner's office and put a photograph down in front of him. He stopped eating his breakfast sandwich and looked up at me.

"You look terrible. You've been here all night, haven't you?"

I ignored the question. "He's here," I said, and pointed to a small cottage in the picture. It was on a hilltop overlooking a Cornish beach. In front of the cottage stood two adults and a child about nine years of age. "This is where it started," I said. "That's Simon Baker, and those are his parents."

Rayner took another bite of his sandwich and looked at me and then again at the picture. "Okay," he said. "Okay, so they went on holiday to the Cornish coast. What am I missing?"

I grabbed the remaining half of Rayner's sandwich and sat down. "As a child, Simon Baker's family stayed at his grandparents' cottage in Saint Ives, Cornwall. They were well-known local artists and ran creative workshops. When his grandmother and grandfather passed away, the property passed to Baker's mother. I checked, and it's still in her name. The property will most likely pass to him, but that isn't relevant right now. What is relevant is that Baker still visits the property from time to time for purposes of maintenance."

Rayner looked unconvinced. "You're thinking he's hiding out there?"

"There's more. This isn't the first time Baker has experienced what he would consider rough justice. It turns out his grandfather was accused of raping an eleven-year-old local schoolgirl when Baker was just nine. Baker saw the whole sorry story play out in all the local and national newspapers. It was a real scandal at the time. The grandfather protested his innocence, but locally he received death threats and suffered violent abuse, and one of the barns he used as a workshop was burned to the ground.

"Eventually it was proved another man had raped the girl, a man from out of the area with a string of sex offences to his name. By that time, it was too late. The damage to Baker's grandfather's reputation was done. Baker senior became more and more depressed. Rumours continued unabated, and he realised he'd never completely clear his name, that there would always be those who talked behind his back, that the slander would continue.

"One morning Baker's grandfather walked out to the nearest cliff edge, just a minute or so from the cottage, and blew his brains out with a shotgun.

"Young Simon was staying with them at the time and it was he who found the body. His grandmother never recovered from the shock. Heartbroken, she passed away within a few months."

Rayner sat silent for a few moments. "But Simon Baker

actually did commit his crime. He was actually found guilty. He served his time," he said doubtfully.

"Yes, I know, I know, but in his own warped mind he still feels some miscarriage of justice took place. Unlike his grandfather, Baker has gone on a rampage, taking vengeance on those who spread rumours or reported on his crime."

Rayner scratched his head furiously. "Where does that actually get us?"

"Guess what date Baker's grandfather took his life."

Rayner shook his head. "I don't know. Yesterday?"

"Very close," I said. "In just three days' time, it will be the anniversary of his grandfather's suicide. If this is all about Baker seeking some sort of mixed-up recompense, not only for himself but his grandparents, he's going to go back to the cottage. He may eventually be going somewhere safe, maybe out of the country, but I can almost guarantee he'll visit the cottage first. He may even already be there."

"What about his wife? What about Mrs Baker? Surely he'd go after her next. Surely she's unfinished business."

I paused for a moment. Was this more about his wife than his childhood? I doubted it. My gut told me he was going back to where this had all started. But what if I was wrong? Was tiredness playing tricks on me?

"I'm going to the cottage in Cornwall," I told Rayner. "You look after Mrs Baker. Speak to her and guard her around the clock if you have to. Let's not take any chances."

CHAPTER SIXTY-NINE

Entering the sleepy house through the back door had proved to be no challenge at all. His excitement now surged to another level, and he tried to remain cool and collected, but his whole body was tingling with anticipation. He ran a gloved hand along the kitchen worktop and opened the fridge. The open door lit up the dark kitchen. He pulled out a couple of grapes and popped them into his mouth. Juicy. He wanted to linger, take his time, extend the pleasure.

He stayed as long as he could downstairs, taking in the feel of the home, going through newly washed and folded clothes, clothes ready for ironing. Silently moving through the rooms, he looked at framed photos, smelled scented candles, picked up and replaced ornaments. He smelled the soaps in the downstairs shower room. Jasmine. He went back to the kitchen and sifted through the dirty clothes waiting in the washing machine. Holding them close. Smelling them.

Finally, he reached sensory overload and headed for the

hall stairs. He touched his back pocket, took out the rope and wound it twice then three times around his left hand.

He climbed the stairs, listening. *I'm here for you, honey. I'm here at last.* His whole body was buzzing now. This was taking him to a whole new level of euphoria. The only downside was he had to make the fun look like someone else had done it. He'd thought about that long and hard and decided the payoff was worth it. The look of astonishment on her face would be worth it. When she realised that his would be the last face she ever saw, the sacrifice would be worth it. The last face in her lifetime. He'd take a souvenir. No, two: one for him, one for a friend.

He gently pushed at the bedroom door. For a moment his whole body trembled, then calm washed over him. Purpose and focus took over. The curtains were open and moonlight streamed into the room. The silvery moonlight created a magical scene. Mrs Baker was on her side with her back to him. *She wants me to surprise her.* He felt breathless. There in front of him was her perfectly peaceful contoured shape. Her hair like silk on the pillow. The curves of her body. He gazed at the satin sheet, which rested on her legs then flowed up over her hips, down to her waist, smoothly back up to her soft shoulders, and finally down again to rest on her delicate neck.

He gripped the rope tighter and held himself back a moment longer to savour and capture this image of perfection. Exquisite.

With lightning speed, he bounded across the room and in one movement lifted her head, wrapped the cord around her neck, and pulled it tight. *Gotcha!* Not too tight but just enough. He needed her to turn, to see his face. He needed her to look into his eyes, to see recognition. She must know.

Immediately he knew something was wrong. He'd done this enough times to know it didn't feel right. There was no real weight to the body. Then all hell broke loose. Shouting. Lights. Guns. Police. He froze, then sat back on the bed. He turned his head and looked down at Mrs Baker. She was a dummy, a fake. Her grotesque synthetic face looked at him, taunted him. *Who's the dummy now?*

Rayner took out his phone and called the Yard. They'd made an arrest, but it wasn't Simon Baker.

CHAPTER SEVENTY

I was driving with my foot to the floor, on my way to Cornwall. I felt strong, but I knew in reality I was exhausted. Like so many times before, I was running on strong coffee and adrenaline. My head and body were a swirling ball of anticipation and fear.

I was driving the four hours to Cornwall on nothing more than a hunch. If I was wrong, I'd have lost a day and Simon Baker could be long gone. I pushed those thoughts to the back of my mind. I needed to stay positive; my hunches and my instincts were good, I told myself. Detective work is the process of elimination; I'd eliminated the alternatives and was making the only logical next step. I kept telling myself, "If I have this right, I can end this now." But the long drive and tiredness introduced time, time to think and time to doubt my instincts. Knowing it was only mind tricks didn't make stopping the worry any easier. I pressed on at full speed, using my lights when necessary. The sooner I got there, the sooner I could put Baker down.

. . .

Just after midday I parked a safe distance away and began walking towards the single hilltop cottage. It was a long walk; I hadn't parked close, as any sound from an approaching vehicle would be carried on the wind, even over the sound of seagulls and crashing waves.

I hunkered down behind a dry-stone wall some two hundred metres from the cottage. Through my field binoculars I would be able to make out the faces of anyone arriving or leaving. I watched the house for close to an hour and saw nothing. I felt sick to my stomach. What if I was wrong? I tried to get comfortable. If I was to approach the house, I wanted to be sure Baker was in there. This was my best chance of cornering him, and if he saw me before I saw him, he'd be gone in a flash. Despite my eagerness, it was patience and surprise I needed now. As soon as I had a positive ID, I'd call for backup. Right now, this was all on me.

It was a long and gruelling wait. The sun had been beating down on me all day, and I could feel my neck and face were burnt. My back and knees were aching, and my tongue and throat were parched.

Nothing happened at the cottage all day, and then around 9 p.m. a silver E-Class Mercedes slowly made its way to the house and parked up outside.

I watched as a couple got out of the car. The summer evening light was fading fast and I was having difficulty picking out their features. The woman got out first and immediately pulled a light scarf over her head. She looked elegant and wore a two-piece suit and heels that didn't suit walking on the uneven ground outside a Cornish cottage. A tall thin man got out, opened the car's back door and pulled out a travel bag and a bottle of wine from the back seat. As he lifted them out and began to stand, I focused the binoculars on where his face was going to be when he straightened. I needed a positive ID. No mistakes: I needed to be certain it was Baker before I moved in. As he lifted his head and straightened his body, the woman came around the side of the car and blocked my view. Doubt began to creep through me, mocking me.

The tall man opened up the cottage and the couple entered. The lights went on inside, but I was no better off. The cottage windows were small, and I knew I'd never make a positive ID from here. For all I knew they were holiday makers renting the cottage for a romantic few days away.

"Okay, get off your arse and go take a look," I muttered. Great; now I was talking to myself.

I checked my weapon and thought about what I needed to take. If all hell broke loose, it was best I be able to move quickly. I left everything except my Glock, which I checked a second time. Nerves.

I waited a few minutes until it was a little darker and then followed the dry-stone wall. I stayed low and followed it straight for a few minutes and then turned left and followed it up the hillside until I eventually came to a gap for the driveway to the cottage. I passed over the driveway and followed the wall until I was up close. Then I climbed over and, staying low, headed to the rear of the cottage. I stopped and crouched behind a log pile. My heart was racing. All my senses told me Baker was in that building and he had another victim with him. But if I was wrong and burst in, the repercussions didn't bear thinking about. At the very least it would be a serious internal investigation, as well as a dream come true for the press. I couldn't allow someone to die, but I had to be sure it was him.

I edged along the side of the building and made my way to the first window. I peered in and could see no movement. My heart was hammering and felt ready to explode out of my chest. I listened and could hear the woman. She sounded distressed. I moved fast to the next window. I could hear voices. The woman was calling. Was I too late? I unclipped the Glock and peered in through the window. The woman was drinking red wine and singing along to music.

All at once, she stopped and fixed her eyes on mine. She paused for a moment, then screamed. Simon Baker came rushing in from another room. My heart pounded. It was him. *I've got you.*

He looked at her, then followed her eyes to the window.

CHAPTER SEVENTY-ONE

I moved quickly to the front of the cottage and kicked open the front door. "Scotland Yard Police, Inspector Hardy," I said as I held out my warrant card. "Simon Baker, do not move. Stay right there."

The woman dropped her glass of wine and ran for cover behind a small green sofa. I pointed at her. "I'm a plain-clothes police officer. For your own safety please stay right there. Do not move."

Baker took his chance. He turned on his heels and ran back through to the next room. I raised my weapon and followed him. I paused at the entrance to the room. Cautiously, I took the couple of steps up and entered it. Set against the wall at the back of this room was a narrow staircase leading to what I assumed was an attic room. I began to cross towards the staircase when, through the posts, the barrel of a shotgun appeared. I threw myself forward to the foot of the staircase, turned and fired. I missed, and a post beside Baker splintered.

Baker couldn't turn the shotgun fast enough. He

turned to run. I fired again, deliberately wide. The bullet grazed his shoulder; he stumbled and began reeling in pain.

"Christ – you shot me," screamed Baker in disbelief. "You really shot me?" He dropped the shotgun and focused his attention on the wound. He slumped back on the stairs. "How could you shoot me, James?"

"Simon Baker, you're under arrest for multiple murder."

Baker smiled at me and began to laugh, which caused him to wince in pain. "We had fun though, right? And we'll still spend time together? Hours and hours and hours discussing my case and the investigation, right?" he asked.

I said nothing. I cuffed him and dragged him through to the front room. I called for local police assistance and an ambulance, and then I called Rayner. The woman was sitting outside, leaning against the front wall of the house. I passed her a blanket from off the sofa.

"Kelly," she said. "My name is Kelly Lyle."

"Detective Chief Inspector James Hardy. James."

"Is he really that serial killer I read about, James?"

"Yes."

"Would he have killed me?"

"I don't know." I wanted to give her a better answer but I really didn't know.

"Why didn't you kill him?"

I looked at her, not sure what she was asking me.

"Nobody would have known," she continued. "You should have killed him, James. He's killed so many people. Yet he gets to live. Hardly seems like justice."

Unsure what to say, I said nothing, and instead watched as she lit a cigarette. It was dark now and the tip of the cigarette glowed.

"He's losing a lot of blood," I told her. "I had better go and check on him. The ambulance is going to be some time yet."

Then Kelly Lyle surprised me. "I can help. I was a doctor, a long time ago. I worked in the United States. Saw my fair share of gunshot wounds. I'll take a look." She got up and went inside to attend to Baker.

Kelly cleaned and dressed the wound while I paced and called again for the ambulance. I could hear Baker mumbling in the background, a lot of nonsense and egotistical crap.

"We had fun, didn't we, Hardy? The Mentor said it would be fun, once things really got going. I think The Mentor will be proud. Look how far we've come." He began to laugh and wince from the pain.

Kelly finished up and followed me as I stepped back outside the cottage. The reception was better outside and I was keen to hear how far away the ambulance was. I dialled the number again and walked about trying to get a better signal.

A piercing scream from inside the house stopped me in my tracks. I spun around and looked for Kelly. She wasn't outside with me. I was sure she had followed me out of the cottage. I ran inside and saw her on the floor with Baker on top of her. They were both covered in blood. Whose blood? I looked and looked again. The blood was Baker's. With his hands still cuffed behind his back, he was fighting with Kelly. Blood pumped from wounds to his neck. There was blood everywhere.

Kelly raised her arm and stabbed Baker again. In her hand, I saw the stem of a broken wine glass. The glass she dropped earlier, I thought. I dragged Baker off her and watched as he took his last gasping breath.

"He tripped me with his foot and threw himself at

me," said Kelly, panting. "He was trying to bite my face. I pushed him and scratched him. I stabbed him with the glass – I had no choice. I couldn't get him off. Where were you? You left me!"

"You're okay. You did the right thing. I'm sorry – I saw you following me out of the house."

Kelly began sobbing. "Is he dead? Did I kill him?"

"Yes. He can't harm you now. He can't hurt anyone."

Any urgency I felt before had gone. I stepped outside and looked at the stars and watched as the distant flashing blue lights of the emergency services moved closer. Kelly got herself cleaned up as best she could and joined me outside again. The blanket was wrapped around her shoulders. She crushed out a cigarette and lit another.

"So much for giving up," she said, showing me the cigarette. "Perhaps today isn't the day."

We laughed uneasily.

"Perhaps you're right," I conceded.

"He said his mentor was going to kill me and then kill you and your family. Did he hear voices in his head? Or did he have an accomplice?"

I looked back at the cottage where, inside, lay the bloody, lifeless body of Baker. "No, he worked alone," I said confidently, even though, somehow, I wasn't entirely convinced.

Kelly pulled the blanket tighter over her shoulders. "Am I safe?"

I thought about Alice, Faith and Monica at home and how I wished I could be there with them right that second. "You're safe. We're all safer. For whatever reason, he thought all this was a game. The game is over."

Kelly leaned in and put her head against me, and instinctively I put my arm around her. We watched the first police cars approaching up the long, uneven driveway to the cottage.

"Thank you, James," said Kelly.

We looked out at the night as a million stars shone down.

CHAPTER SEVENTY-TWO

Kelly Lyle was back from Cornwall and for now the police had completed their questioning. She dropped her travel bag in the hallway and picked up the post. She slipped off her heels and walked silently to the kitchen. She poured herself a large, cold white wine. The house was dark and quiet, which she welcomed after her recent experience. She had always felt at ease in the dark and was comfortable with solitude.

She walked to her office and placed the bottle of wine and the envelopes on her oak desk. Having switched on a reading light, she settled into her chair and drank deeply from her wine glass. Unable to resist any longer, she turned in her chair to face the cabinet and slid open the door to reveal the safe. Spinning the dial, she hoped she wouldn't be disappointed.

The safe door opened to reveal the batch of envelopes she'd been saving. Kelly smiled to herself. She took the jiffy bag from the small pile and, with a knife from her drawer, sliced it open. She emptied the contents onto the desk and read out the two accompanying notes, one of which read,

To our Mentor,

I have achieved so much thanks to your guidance and wisdom and the help of the group.

The investment has been worth every penny.

Find enclosed a souvenir as requested.

Carpe Diem, SB

Kelly opened the back cover of *The Great Gatsby* and removed the USB stick. She picked up the silver Saint Christopher necklace. She held it up and then turned it over to read the inscription: "To Our Darling Katharine. Happy 18th Birthday. Love You Always, Mum and Dad."

Kelly lit a cigarette. She then set light to the note, placed the burning paper in a silver ashtray and watched as it burned out. She admired the necklace, enjoying the significance of what it meant and imagining what had taken place for it to have become a part of her collection.

She finished her cigarette and her glass of wine and then walked over to a narrow floor-to-ceiling bookcase. She slid it to one side, revealing a second large safe set back into the wall. Originally designed for a bank, the safe had been modified to Kelly's specifications. It was around two metres high and two metres wide. She opened it to reveal shelves, hooks and drawers, which had been installed along with power and spotlights.

Kelly opened one of the display drawers and placed the Saint Christopher necklace on the black velvet surface.

"Perfect. Thank you, Mr Baker." She stood back to take in the vastness of her collection. The safe was full of rings, bracelets, watches, earrings, necklaces, and even a gold tooth, souvenirs all sent to her by appreciative clients, students and admirers from all around the world.

"I'm going to need a bigger vault," she mused. "Perhaps a walk-in vault. This is almost as much fun as collecting my own souvenirs. Almost."

Smiling reflectively, Kelly 'The Mentor' Lyle decided it would soon be time for a new game of cat and mouse.

Detective James Hardy would perhaps fare better than her previous adversaries.

CHAPTER SEVENTY-THREE

I felt I had come up for air and was finally able to breathe again. Once more, I could focus on what mattered most to me – my family.

Being surrounded by so much love, I had to ask myself how I was able to get so lost in the nightmares that crept into my life. I could only assume that it was precisely because I had this lifeline that I could descend to the depths I often had to. Monsters live in dark places, and to catch them you can't be afraid of the dark.

It was Sunday, and my home was filled with music, conversation, laughter and the smell of great British home cooking. Monica and Mum were working together on preparing roast lamb with garlic and herbs, minted new potatoes and an impressive array of summer vegetables. Having offered to help, I didn't need to be a detective to work out my woeful culinary skills weren't required. Instead, I was informed the meal was almost ready and I should go make myself useful by helping Dad wrangle Alice and Faith to the table – with washed hands.

I watched as Dad chased the girls from room to room.

In his usual comic manner, he was more interested in making them squeal with delight, repeatedly hiding and jumping out on them, than actually getting them to the table. Eventually he ran out of puff, and when the girls approached to check he was okay, he grabbed them and carried them off for hand washing.

The house phone began to ring. Mum looked at me in a way that said, "I know you're going to answer it and we both know you shouldn't." I hesitated for a moment and then picked up the receiver.

"James Hardy," I said.

"Detective Hardy. Sorry to intrude. I know how precious family time is to you," a woman's voice said.

"Who is this?"

"Forgotten me already, James?" the voiced teased. "Even after our romantic evening under the stars? You remember our time together outside the little Cornish cottage, don't you? You and I sat huddled together waiting for the emergency services while Simon Baker's lifeless and bloody corpse grew cold. You know, I could so easily have ended you there, and to all the world it would have looked as though you were just one more casualty of Mr Baker."

"Kelly Lyle?" I asked. My mind raced trying to fit the pieces together. "I don't understand."

"Does Kelly 'The Mentor' Lyle help you? Goodness me, I hope you're going to be smarter than this when we start our games. I was worried Simon Baker had given the game away, but it appears you're still clueless."

"What do you want?" My mouth felt dry.

"So glad you asked. Though you could sound a little more excited. I mean, just for you, I have decided to play again sooner than I had anticipated. You should be flattered. Before we start, however, it is important you understand the rules."

"Rules?"

"Jamie, I am so glad you asked. The rules are simple – there are no rules. There are no limits to which I will not go. Nothing and nobody is beyond my reach, and I don't play fair. You must understand I expect you to fail at stopping me. During the course of our adventure together, innocent people will get hurt and consequentially die. We'll embark on our journey very soon, but right now I don't want to give too much away and spoil any surprises. I know you have a full house, so I'll let you get back to your family. Give Monica and the girls a kiss from me. I'll be thinking of you." With a click, the phone went dead.

Alice and Faith ran past me and hid behind the sofa. Dad was pretending he couldn't see them.

"Everything all right, son?" He could see from my expression things were far from all right. I stared at the phone for a moment, blew out a breath and smiled gamely. "How about you help me get those two little rascals to the dinner table before we're all in trouble with your mother?" Dad said. "They must be hiding around here somewhere."

With a loud, playful roar, I turned and reached out to grab Alice. Dad rounded the sofa and approached from the other end to snare Faith. It wasn't long before Dad and I had the girls cornered.

"It's ready! Dinner is on the table," called Monica.

And just like that, family life resumed. For the time being, at least.

* * *

Walk in the Park, *the second book in the series is out now.*
Continue DCI Hardy's journey today:
Available on Amazon

WALK IN THE PARK

Chapter 1

Regent's Park, London

He stood and watched as the final moments of her life slipped away.

She was very pretty; much prettier than the last one. He stared at her smooth white legs. He considered covering her naked lower half but decided he no longer wanted to touch her.

You can be like that when they find you, he thought.

The hammer would need to be cleaned again, he thought. He'd need to burn his sweater and jeans. His trainers he could put in the washing machine. They were too expensive to simply throw away. And anyway, he hated new trainers; they were ridiculously bright white when you first got them.

She was still now. No more gasping for breath. The spasms, jolts and twitches had stopped. He stared at her lifelessness for a few seconds. Fascinated.

He wondered where she might have been going. Had she been on her way home? Going to work? Or simply enjoying a walk in the park?

He stopped himself. Don't think about it. The bitch is dead. It's over. Move on.

Over his shoulder he could hear ducks, their wings violently flapping and pounding the water. They were fighting and making a godawful row. Eventually one of them gave up and flew away in noisy protest.

Time to go, he thought.

He walked across the grass to his bike, which lay next to the path where he'd dumped it. Lifting the bike, he leaned it against himself. He opened the pannier and dropped the hammer inside.

Without looking back, he set off for home. The challenge of getting to his room without being stopped by Mum lay ahead. She always had questions. Where have you been? Do anything nice today? Do you need any laundry doing? What would you like for dinner?

He'd stay in for the rest of the day. Sit with Mum, eat snacks and watch the quiz shows —she loved quiz shows. He might be on the news later.

The warm breeze felt good on his face as he picked up speed. The smell of summer filled his nostrils. The park was his favourite place; it felt like freedom.

The woman flashed across his mind. He tried to remember whether she'd said anything. With each woman it was the same: he heard their noise, but never precisely their words. He could guess what they were saying but it was strange how the words became nothing more than background noise. In some ways he felt it was fortunate; he didn't need their words rattling around in his head. He only wanted to remember how each accomplishment felt.

He felt good, and he knew for a few days he'd walk

with a bit of a swagger. He hoped the good feelings would last longer than last time. He wouldn't do this again. He definitely wouldn't do this again.

With a smile, he pressed on. He was feeling so energised that the pedalling was easy. Life felt good again.

He turned his face away and looked at the trees as he approached an old man walking his small copper-coloured dog.

"Come on, Sheeran, my friend," said the old man. "Forget the squirrel. Do your business and let's get home, I don't want to be out here all day; your mother will begin to worry about us."

The dog ignored him and continued to pull on his lead towards his furry nemesis.

The old man tugged the little dog and they continued along the path they walked every day.

ALSO BY JAY GILL

Walk in the Park
Short Thriller

When a close friend of DCI James Hardy is murdered, the detective questions whether taking the law into his own hands could ever be justified.

Detective James Hardy is enjoying a rare day out with his two young daughters when he makes the mistake of answering his phone. It's his boss.

A young mother, out walking her baby, has been murdered in broad daylight. The attack is followed quickly by a second terrifying, vicious assault on a young woman who is a dear friend of Hardy and his daughters.

Shaken and heartbroken, Hardy agrees to assist the team leading the investigation into a ruthless murderer dubbed *The Regent's Park Ripper.*

Knowing that in all likelihood the killer will soon strike again, the investigating team must put aside their differences, and work day and night to prevent more senseless deaths.

Over the course of the harrowing investigation, Hardy must constantly challenge his own very personal need for revenge. But all of that may change when he unexpectedly finds himself face-to-face with the suspect in a deadly confrontation that may change Hardy's life, and those of his loved ones, forever.

Angels

After the brutal murder of his wife by a crazed drug-seeker, Detective Inspector James Hardy walks away from his career as a Scotland Yard homicide detective. He has found love again, and, together with his two young daughters, he's making a fresh start in a small seaside town.

With his new career as a consultant taking off and the demons of the past behind him, Hardy's life couldn't be better.

But the peace is about to be shattered.

When a series of shocking murders take place in the seaside town, Hardy is contacted by local detective inspector Emma Cotton for advice. As Cotton investigates the killings, Hardy learns the disturbing crimes have all the hallmarks of a serial killer linked to his past.

The notorious Kelly Lyle, known as The Mentor, has surfaced again, and has Hardy and his family in her sights. As she embarks on her latest bloody campaign of murder and revenge, she rips apart the detective's new life – and reveals a dark secret that shatters everything Hardy believed to be true about his wife's death.

Hardy balks at being forced out of early retirement, but whether he likes it or not, the killer appears determined to draw him back into a world he wants to leave behind.

Knowing it will take something monumental to catch his attention, the killer raises the stakes and abducts someone Hardy loves more than life itself.

Is Hardy about to lose everything he's fought so hard to keep?

Hardy's only choice is to work with DI Emma Cotton

to discover the hard truth behind the killer's motives. If they play the killer's game, they might be in time to stop a tragedy beyond comprehension.

Hard Truth

DCI James Hardy's new-found peace is rocked when Kelly Lyle 'the Mentor' returns.

During her bloody campaign of murder, she rips apart the detective's new life and reveals a secret that shatters everything Hardy believed to be true about his wife's death.

James Hardy has walked away from his career as a Scotland Yard homicide detective. He has found love again, and, together with his two young daughters, he's making a fresh start in a small seaside town.

With his new career as a consultant taking off and the demons of the past behind him, Hardy's life couldn't be better.

But the peace is about to be shattered.

When a series of shocking murders take place in the seaside town, Hardy is contacted by local detective inspector Emma Cotton for advice. Hardy learns the disturbing crimes have all the hallmarks of a serial killer linked to his past.

Hardy balks at being forced out of early retirement, but whether he likes it or not, the killer appears determined to draw him back into a world he wants to leave behind.

Knowing it will take something monumental to catch his attention, the killer raises the stakes and abducts someone Hardy loves more than life itself.

Is Hardy about to lose everything he's fought so hard to keep?

Hardy's only choice is to work with DI Emma Cotton to discover the hard truth behind the killer's motives. If they play the killer's game, they might be in time to stop a tragedy beyond comprehension.

All Jay's books are available on Amazon.

Inferno

Searching for the truth, means coming under fire.

DCI James Hardy was hoping for a quiet life. He stepped away from his career at New Scotland Yard and moved his family to the south coast to start over. For a short while, life was good. But now the past is catching up with him.

Hardy recently learned that Edward Fischer, the man he arrested for a string of killings, is also the man who orchestrated his wife's murder. And now, Fischer has escaped from prison and is on the run.

Fischer is a free man, and before he leaves the country and disappears for good, he's looking for compensation from Hardy. The sort of compensation money can't buy. The kind that will cause Hardy pain and suffering.

And when Hardy's new home becomes a target and his family come under threat, he finds he has no choice but to step up and do what he's best at... catching killers.

All Jay's books are available on Amazon.

ABOUT THE AUTHOR

Born in Dorset, southern England, Jay Gill moved to Buckinghamshire where he worked in the printing industry, primarily producing leaflets and packaging for the pharmaceutical industry. After several years of the London commute, and with his first child about to start school, he realised it was high time for a change and moved back to the south coast of England. This change freed up time for him to write the detective stories he dreamed of one day publishing.

Safe to say, he's caught the writing bug in earnest now. With three Hardy novels and a novella under his belt, a growing "family" of characters both good and heinous, and a host of exciting new ideas bouncing around in his head, Jay busily juggles his writing and family life and is hard at work on the next instalment in the DCI James Hardy series of thrillers.

Want to hear what he's working on, and enjoy DCI Hardy bonus material?

I *occasionally* send newsletters, usually once a quarter. I talk about what I'm working on, new releases and other bits of news relating to the DCI James Hardy series.

It's easy to join my mailing list, and you won't get spammed (I promise):

1. Receive news, announcements and updates on new releases before anyone else.
2. Read a profile of DCI James Hardy called: Who is James Hardy? *(Exclusive to my mailing list, you can't get this anywhere else.)*
3. Access to bonus scenes from *every* book in the Hardy series: For example, you'll find out what happens to the nasty piece of work, Melvin Barclay - featured in Hard Truth - when Kelly Lyle catches up with him again. *It isn't pretty!* There is also a scene from INFERNO which has been described as taut and nerve-shredding. *(Exclusive to my mailing list, you can't get it anywhere else.)*

Sign up for updates at www.jaygill.net/newsletter

Made in the USA
Las Vegas, NV
12 June 2021